LOST HARBOR

What Reviewers Say About
Kimberly Cooper Griffin's Work

Tides of Love

"This was such a sweet story about coming to terms with change, assessing wants and desires over morals, and putting yourself first. ...Just a lovely story with lots of heart and sentiment. Great to explore reflecting and resetting everything while being true to yourself."—*LESBIreviewed*

No Experience Required

"*No Experience Required* is full of realistic, multidimensional characters. ...I liked the honest and straightforward way that bipolar disorder was discussed, and I feel like I understand how those with the disorder feel a little bit more than I had before. I think that so much of this book is relatable to readers in different ways, and can help us all stop and think about others and the bigger picture a bit more. Even if readers do not know anyone with bipolar disorder, or are not in a same sex relationship, the matters at the heart of the story are universal. ...*No Experience Required* is a well written and engaging book. I thought the issues of dating advice and mental health were very well handled, and I honestly would love to see more from all the characters in the book. I will be reading more from the author."—*Sharon the Librarian*

"The author does a thorough job of explaining Izzy's condition, her internal workings, hopes and fears. ...This book straddles a space between a being a romcom and something more serious (given that the protagonists are dealing with a mental disorder and paternal homophobic physical violence). One of the best things about the book is that at the end we feel that this couple will really be happy together because they seem to have got their shot together and have learnt how to be a couple that communicates and cares for each other."—*Best Lesfic Reviews*

Can't Leave Love

"Sometimes you just need a romance that will melt your heart, bring a tear to your eyes at least once or twice, and leave you with a warm, happy feeling at the end. Add a couple of the cutest dogs, and you have a wonderful story. That is exactly what I found in *Can't Leave Love* by Kimberly Cooper Griffin. Besides being a beautiful love story, this book deals with some serious issues which is where the occasional teary eyes may happen. ...This is a well-written romance with well-developed characters (both human and canine), set in a lovely small town, with just the right amount of angst to make the story interesting. It is exactly the type of romantic tale that I love to read. In fact, I think I've found a new author to add to my list of favorite romance writers. I will definitely be looking for more from this author."—*Rainbow Reflections*

In the Cards

"Both main characters are very well developed and easy to connect with. The secondary characters are also well-written, especially Marnie, Daria's younger sister who is autistic. As the mother of an autistic son, I can tell you that Marnie is realistically written. The romance is fairly lighthearted and uplifting though the two mains do have several hurdles to overcome. They get a bit of a paranormal/magical push to help them find and fall in love with each other. ...I truly enjoyed this book."—*Rainbow Reflections*

Visit us at www.boldstrokesbooks.com

By the Author

No Experience Required

In the Cards

Can't Leave Love

Sol Cycle

Oceana Series Romances

Tides of Love

Sweet Spot

Lost Harbor

LOST HARBOR

by

Kimberly Cooper Griffin

2024

LOST HARBOR

ISBN 13: 978-1-63679-463-1

This Trade Paperback Original Is Published By
Bold Strokes Books, Inc.
P.O. Box 249
Valley Falls, NY 12185

First Edition: February 2024

CREDITS
EDITOR: BARBARA ANN WRIGHT
PRODUCTION DESIGN: SUSAN RAMUNDO
COVER DESIGN BY JEANINE HENNING

Acknowledgments

Thank you to Sandy Lowe and Radclyffe. I'm proud to be a part of the Bold Strokes team.

Barbara Ann Wright aka Barbara Scissorhands. Or is that just when you're working on my manuscripts? I'm grateful that you know which words to cut and which ones to let shine.

Every author should have a support system and I am forever grateful to mine: Finnian Burnett, Ona Marae, Nicole Disney, Millie Ireland, Avery Brooks, Cindy Rizzo, Jaycee Morrison, and Renee Young.

Michelle Dunkley just gets me and my writing, and I love her for it.

Finally, nothing is more meaningful to a writer than their readers. Thank you all for reading my stories, writing the reviews, and getting lost in the worlds that would have been trapped in my head without your support.

Dedication

To Summer, my everything.

CHAPTER ONE

Topeka, Kansas, early spring 1994

On a gray day in early spring, eighteen-year-old Alice Johns fingered her dead grandmother's rosary as she sat on the battered wooden bench in the small Greyhound station on Quincy Street in Topeka, Kansas.

The place had been as quiet as a rectory until about an hour earlier but was now bustling with the dozen or so passengers waiting for the westbound bus to arrive. Alice's new shoes had mud caked along the soles from the family driveway that was more potholes than gravel. Part of her wished she'd taken one last look at the worn clapboard house she'd lived in all her life, but there wasn't much to see in the inky dark of predawn. Not even the porch light was on after her father had switched it off as they left. Everyone else was still asleep.

She'd packed her small suitcase the night before and had lay awake in the pose of a corpse all night atop the old Chanel bedspread. She'd worn her traveling clothes, hadn't wanted to wake the others when she'd gotten up to leave. There'd been no need since the good-byes had been said the night before over her favorite chicken supper. It had just been her father and her on the long drive down dirt roads into town, and he'd dropped her off on his way to his shift at the mill. Her bus didn't leave until nearly noon.

He'd left the truck running at the curb under the single dim parking lot light, and she'd slid down from the seat as he'd jumped out his side, grabbed her suitcase from the bed of the truck, and walked around to the sidewalk with it. His cowboy boots had *scritched* in the grit of plow sand left over from the last snowstorm.

He'd rested his hand on the top of her head as he'd placed her suitcase at her feet. "Now, don't give no trouble to the sisters, you hear me?"

She'd looked into his brown eyes, the same fawn color as hers. "Yes, Daddy."

"Get yourself on that bus, and write your mama and me to let us know you got there okay." His eyes had scanned the front of the bus station and never returned to hers after that.

"Yes, Daddy."

"Off you go." He'd flicked his hand toward the station doors as he'd turned to leave. She'd picked up her suitcase. Butterflies had filled her stomach, getting wilder with every step she'd taken up the old granite stairs. His pickup was already halfway down the street when she'd turned at the doors to wave good-bye. She had no idea when, or even if, she'd see her family again, but she was making them proud by going off to California to be a nun.

In the station, waiting, she'd prayed, read her bible, and watched the sun rise. The terminal had gotten busy before slowing again in the hours she waited for her eleven thirty-five bus to Oceanside, California, where Sister Mary Helen would pick her up after the nearly twenty-four-hour ride.

Used to country folk, having lived all her life on a soy farm several miles outside of the city, she drank in the variety of humanity that wandered through the building. She had to get up and move because a young man in jeans barely hanging on to his bony little fanny stretched out on the bench she'd been sitting on. He was far enough away but smelled like he hadn't showered in a month.

Moving was hardly any trouble since she only had her small suitcase, a sack of food, and her rosary. She didn't need much. The convent would provide most everything while God provided the rest. When her bus arrived, she left her food next to the sleeping young man and prayed that his belt would keep his pants from falling all the way down.

CHAPTER TWO

Oceanside, California, early spring 1999

On a bright blue, cloudless day in early spring, twenty-three-year-old Alice Johns fingered her dead grandmother's rosary as she sat on the battered wooden bench in the seedy Greyhound bus terminal on Tremont Street in Oceanside, California.

A marine in combat uniform slept sitting up on the other end of the bench, leaning against a duffle bag. His arms crossed his chest, and his outstretched legs were stacked at his boot-clad ankles, his camouflage hat pulled over his eyes. Snoring quietly, he looked unbothered by the noises around them.

Changed out of the habit she'd worn for the last five years, Alice felt just the opposite: jittery, unprotected, and skittish. She had a one-way ticket to Topeka tucked into her Bible, and she'd lost the ability to interact with the world after nearly five years of Catholic study, the first four years attending Santo Benedictine College, and the last several months serving at the Blood of the Crucifix Convent, both of which were on the same campus where she'd lived and worshipped during her failed journey as a nun.

As of that morning, she was just a layperson, stripped of her calling. Tears coursing down her cheeks, she pulled the ticket out of her Bible and studied it for the twentieth time. Her bus had already come and gone. Yet, she'd sat and waited. For what, she did not know. She hadn't heard from her family in over two years. She'd continued to send letters once a month for a while, but even she had stopped writing after no response to the last twelve letters. Last year, communication had been reduced to an impersonal exchange of Christmas cards.

As the oldest of seventeen siblings, and the oldest girl, family tradition meant for her to become a nun. The other girls would get married right after high school to young men from their church and raise families. The boys would marry girls from their church and work the soy farm with their father. As far as she knew, six of them had left home by now, including herself. With eleven siblings still at home in their five-bedroom farmhouse, she couldn't go back. There was no room and no money. Furthermore, she had no desire to go back. Especially not as a failed nun.

Everything she loved was back at the Blood of the Crucifix Convent. At least, it had been. She sat in the bus terminal wondering how she still had tears left to cry and prayed for God to show her options.

"Excuse me."

Alice looked up to see a beautiful woman holding a young girl's hand. She smiled, not bothering to try to dry her tears. "Hello."

"You've been sitting here for six hours. Do you need help with something?"

Alice didn't know what to say. "I...I don't know."

The woman sat next to her, the little girl still holding her hand. "Do you need a safe place to stay?"

Alice stared at her hands. "I suppose I do."

"My name is Lupe. This is my daughter, Gem. My husband is over there." She pointed to a tall man standing near the ticket window talking to the man Sister Caroline had purchased Alice's ticket from. "We have a place you can stay."

Maybe she should have been afraid. But she wasn't. She'd prayed for God to send her guidance, and here it was. She felt nothing but goodwill from Lupe and her family. So she stood and followed them out of the bus terminal.

CHAPTER THREE

Present day

Angelica once did something stupid, and the price she paid for it was her heart, Alice wrote after chewing on the end of her pen for a few moments.

It wasn't awesome, but it didn't suck. It told the story, beginning to end. She could call it a bit of flash fiction, and Taylor would be pleased.

She laid her pen down and folded her hands over her stomach, the crucifix pendant under her blouse a comfort beneath her palms. Why had she agreed to join a writing group, anyway? What did she know about writing stories?

Taylor was the reason. Sweet young Taylor with the clear soprano, dark eyeliner, and tendency to wear all black. Taylor was exactly half Alice's age at twenty-three and three quarters and was in the same church choir. Unlikely friends, they'd gotten to know each other at rehearsals, and Alice had found that Taylor had moved to Oceanside almost a year before to take a job in graphic arts for an app creator, and she hadn't yet made any friends.

It was hard to fathom why such a smart, pretty young woman didn't have friends, so Alice had asked her to go for coffee, and they'd quickly forged a friendship. Alice had eventually pieced together the reason for Taylor's lack of friends: she tended to bury herself in work, play online games, hide beneath her dark wardrobe, and hang back in social situations. All of which was a shame because Taylor was a fascinating young woman.

Thus began Alice's not-so-secret goal to find Taylor some friends, preferably people her own age, such as her neighbor Shia and her girlfriend, Rose. She hadn't introduced them yet, but she would.

In the meantime, Alice spent time with her, trying to find fun things for them to do, and they discovered a mutual love of reading. They both loved fantasy novels, and for the first time ever, Alice shared her secret addiction to romance novels. When Taylor hadn't made fun of it, Alice had agreed to join an online book group with her that had allowed Alice to openly embrace her favorite genre.

Now, a few months later, after attending other meetups Taylor had suggested, Alice was at her desk working on her weekly writing prompt: the price of a heart. Romance was her favorite genre to read, but it was the hardest for her to write. She couldn't relate to it. However, she'd read an article in her church's New Year's missalette that had put her on a path toward "getting out of her comfort zone." The idea had been that growth could only come from venturing into unknown places.

The concept had hit her hard. She'd become a creature of habit. Although she was going to meetups with Taylor, she still tended to keep to routines. She'd been trying to help Taylor all that time, but she was basically in the same boat. Sure, she had friends, but with most of her friends in relationships now, she was left with work and church as her only activities.

Studying the missalette, she'd tried to envision what getting out of her comfort zone meant. While the church flyer had been general, it had probably meant things related to religion. Alice was already as devout as a person could be, so she'd decided to focus on getting out of her comfort zone as it related to everything *but* religion.

So far, she'd joined the book club and the writing group, she'd picked up Pilates in addition to the yoga and power walking she'd been doing for years, and had added lemon bars to her cookie baking routine. She'd also started volunteering at the humane society on North River Road. Having lived on a farm for her first eighteen years, she'd cared for a variety of animals as a kid, but none of them had been real pets. And she hadn't had a pet since, except for her jellyfish tank that she'd taken from Brandi when Brandi had started breeding seahorses.

Joe the English bulldog was to thank for her volunteering at the shelter. She'd loved him ever since she'd crossed paths with him and his humans while out on her power walks. She'd soon started carrying dog biscuits in case she ran into them. Until then, she'd been happy with her jellyfish. Lately, she'd been thinking about maybe getting her own dog. The problem was, despite growing up on a farm, she couldn't stomach the work that came with a pet. Namely, the poop. And the vomit. And the butt-scooching thing dogs did when their anus itched.

Just thinking about all those made her gag. Wondering if she might get over it with a little immersion therapy, a tactic she'd learned by researching ways to get out of her comfort zone, she'd visited the Humane Society. A sign that said they were seeking volunteers told her she'd made the right decision. Now she spent almost as much time at the shelter as she did at her full-time job at the mission as the assistant to the director of historical preservation.

As for her job, she loved it. She really did. Working onsite at the San Luis Rey Mission was something she felt lucky to get to do. Not only did it keep her connected to the religion she'd loved so much—but couldn't remain a part of due to the unfortunate events that had happened twenty-five years earlier—it gave her a sense of purpose in preserving a part of history that might otherwise have been lost to time. The California mission system had a rich and interesting history, albeit from a perspective told by the surviving cultures. It was Alice's passion to make sure that the full history didn't fade away in the shadow of a church that tended to take the main stage in the world's history and not give credit to the people who helped make it happen. In the case of the missions, it was the indigenous people.

Alice wasn't a ground shaker or a rabble-rouser. She preferred to work behind the scenes helping people, educating them. She slipped history nuggets into the tours she gave at the San Luis Rey Mission about how the local tribes had taught the visiting Spaniards how to make flour from acorns and adobe bricks from the native soils. She also told them how the Spaniards paid them back by enslaving them, stripping them of their culture, and wiping them out with disease.

It brought her satisfaction to make sure the indigenous people were not forgotten. Sometimes, she daydreamed about joining protests, shaking signs, and joining her voice with others to fight for injustice. Sometimes, she berated herself for not doing it twenty-five years ago when Mother Superior had escorted her away from the convent, telling her that they couldn't allow their nuns to succumb to sins of the flesh, especially when it was with another nun. But advocating for herself was harder than doing so for others. Which brought her around full circle to getting out of her comfort zone.

Angelica's heart needed her attention now, followed by a visit to the Humane Society where a sweet pit bull-Great Dane mix named Dolly awaited an afternoon walk.

CHAPTER FOUR

There was only one more box to unpack, and Bridget Moore sprawled on her couch sipping a beer. She stared at the battered white cardboard box sitting in the middle of her custom-made coffee table, one of three pieces of furniture she owned—including her king-sized bed and the suede sofa she was now sitting on—all of which she'd bought when she'd lived in Denver ten years ago.

Moving as often as she did, averaging a new city every two years, she'd learned to travel light. Still, she was exhausted. Not one to do things half-assed, she considered unpacking the one box that had moved from place to place with her for twenty-five years. But she hadn't looked through it since the day she'd left with it at the Blood of the Crucifix Convent. No sense opening it now. What did she need with a Bible, a rosary, a wall crucifix, and a folded habit?

Nothing, that's what. Yet, she'd carried that box from city to city since she'd left, and she'd probably carry it to the city after this one and the one after that. Once, when an old girlfriend had asked her what was in it, she'd said it was penance.

She'd forgotten about that until just now.

Grinning, she put her beer down and picked up the big Sharpie sitting on the table next to the box. PENANCE, she wrote across one side before she lifted the box and put it on the top shelf in the hall closet.

There. She was moved in.

Her phone rang from the table in the living room. She picked it up along with her beer and went onto the balcony of her sixth-floor apartment overlooking the beach. The balcony was the reason she'd bought the place. The views were beautiful. The breeze was perfect coming off the water, bringing the smell of happiness with it. She leaned against the rail, taking in the quiet evening.

"Bridge here," she said after seeing it was LeeAnne, the department coordinator for her sales team.

"Hi, Bridge. How's it going down in SoCal?"

"So far, so good. Just settled into my new place. How are you and the family?" Bridge was glad she was adept at the how-are-yous and other inane pleasantries in life. Being in sales, they came easily to her. Especially when her mind was wandering back to the most difficult time of her life, and she wasn't really up for having her intuitive friend asking her questions she didn't want to think about right now—or ever, really. A twinge of...something made her grimace. Maybe someday, she'd tell LeeAnne. That was what friends did, right? And LeeAnne was the closest thing to a best friend she'd ever had. It was hard to nurture friendships when a person moved as much as she did. She had to fight her instinct to keep people at a distance.

"We enjoyed a nice boat trip around Lake Washington this afternoon. Larone rented a pontoon with a couple of friends. The Seattle sun blessed us, all the sailboats were out, and Jory was in hog heaven." Larone was LeeAnne's husband, and Jory was their three-year-old son. Another reason Bridge was happy to have LeeAnne in her work life. Bridge usually had no patience for kids, but she stopped everything when Jory was around. She loved that little guy.

"Give him a big old kiss from Auntie Bridge, okay?"

Aside from Jory, Larone, and LeeAnne, Bridge was happy to have moved out of Seattle. She'd enjoyed the proximity to the ocean, but the dreary weather really got to her. If she didn't travel three weeks out of every month, she probably wouldn't have lasted the two years she'd lived there. Oceanside was a huge improvement in that category. It was worth the reminders of her ancient past to be back in the dependable weather, beautiful views, and away from the constant dampness of the Pacific Northwest.

Besides, it was time to think about slowing down now. LeeAnne had casually commented that Bridge had been working like she was running from the devil for too long. She'd said it over old-fashioneds one Friday evening in the bar down the street from the office in Seattle. That had been six months ago, and it had sat within her for a couple of months before she'd gone to her boss, Sage, to discuss a deceleration plan for her career trajectory at their company, AthletaHealth.

Sage had been surprised but had said that she'd do whatever it took to keep the best sales executive she'd ever known happy. Bridge was employee number one, aside from the two robotics engineers and one bioengineer who'd founded AthletaHealth nearly twenty years earlier. She wasn't one of the founders, but the three nerd doctors considered her a partner of sorts, and she was the fourth largest stockholder in the company.

While Sage was her boss, it was only because Bridge didn't want to be. Plus, Sage was good at her job, having gone to school specifically for business. Bridge knew her theology degree would have gotten her only so far up the ladder. She had a healthy amount of respect for Sage, so she wanted to give her some time to get used to the idea of her slowing her roll at the company.

Bridge loved her job, but LeeAnne was right. She'd been working so hard for so long, she'd lost touch with how to relax. With ideas of finally using the sailboat her parents had given her a few years earlier, she started dreaming of moving back to San Diego to begin planning her retirement, however many years away that was. She wasn't sure San Diego would be her last landing spot, but it was a good place to begin the deceleration.

"I will when he wakes up. He's been out for almost two hours, and I've needed it." LeeAnne's response pulled her from her brief foray into how she'd ended up so far away from one of her best friends.

Bridge laughed, remembering how nice it was to be able to hand the kid off at the end of the day. "What's up? Why are you calling during mommy free time?"

"Your meetings with SoCal Orthopedics have been pushed out to next week, and I've adjusted your entire calendar past that."

Bridge dropped her head between her shoulders, leaning against the railing of her balcony. "You're kidding, right? The meetings that *had* to happen this week or not at all. The meetings I had to work everything in my life around, including paying double for movers and closing fees just so I could choreograph every move in my life around SoCal Fucking Orthopedics? You mean those meetings?"

LeeAnne's chuckle across the line caused her to laugh, too, and she couldn't keep up the false indignity. "I'm not gonna say I told you so, but I did tell you so. Robert is a huge flake, but you're a phenomenal sales machine, and this deal will happen. And when it does, everyone will be happy. Including you and your bank account."

Bridge flapped her hand, knowing LeeAnne couldn't see it. She often felt guilty about her embarrassingly large bank account, and it made her uncomfortable to complain or gloat about big deals. Her joy came from the people whom her efforts got the prosthetics to. Giving them back the mobility they'd lost was everything to her. Sometimes she wondered if the satisfaction it brought was connected to what she'd once hoped would have been the impact she'd have had on people as a nun. She might not be ministering to their souls, but helping to make their bodies closer to whole was a rush she never got tired of. She tried not to think too hard about that. Because when she did, she wondered if she had a bit of a God complex. Which would be gross. Especially with her agnostic relationship with God. The Church. Her failure.

Stop. The past was the past.

Her work benefitted everyone involved, not just her. Not just her bank account. Success wasn't only about the money. She blew out a silent breath. The move was making her think too much.

She'd have to deal with all of it someday. But today was not that day.

"What does this week look like for me, then? Did you pull some future stuff up to fill in the dead air?"

"Let's see...Robert promised next week will happen. That means..." LeeAnne paused as if she was looking at something, and Bridge prepared herself to be sent to some state in the Midwest. She'd changed her home base to San Diego, but as a regional sales executive, she still had to travel. Not to mention, the special clients she still handled around the globe.

At least for now. The plan was to start paring down her client base. In addition to employee number one, Bridge was both the most successful sales executive, and the longest employed. She'd been working at the company for fifteen years. And she was a little tired. As part of her deceleration plan, she was about to start transitioning some of her clients to other sales execs. Getting some of them off her hands was going to be a relief. She loved them, but they were so much work, and Robert was probably the most work of them all.

She sighed as LeeAnne reviewed her schedule. She'd known there was a big chance that Robert would flake, but she'd still hoped to spend the week in her new home, even if she had to work. "You have the entire week off."

Hope had her hearing things. "I'm sorry. Did I hear you say—"

"You have the entire week off? Yes. That's what I said. Sage told me to block this week for you. Just because the biggest deal you have on the books is rescheduling for next week doesn't mean you have to fill it in with other deals. She wants you to take the week off and relax. You've been working hard. She said, and I quote, 'tell her to go out and find some women to have fun with.'"

"I'm sure you told her HR might have a problem with that, right?"

"To which she replied, and I quote: 'HR can go fuck itself. I meant women to play bingo with. If HR thinks otherwise, they have dirty minds.'"

"I'm not sure that's any better, but I get what she's saying, and I appreciate the time off."

"All righty, then." LeeAnne paused. "I hear the spawn waking from his nap. I'll pay for this time of quiet by him staying awake until midnight. Pray for me when you're playing bingo with all those women, okay?"

"I will. Don't forget to kiss that little angel for me."

"I won't. And Bridge?"

"Uh-huh?"

"I miss you like crazy."

"Hey. We'll just have to plan trips to visit each other. I'll teach Jory how to surf."

"I didn't know you could surf."

"I can't, but I plan to learn."

"That's the spirit."

They hung up, and Bridge walked back into the apartment, stopping in front of the floor to ceiling windows in her living room facing the ocean. In the late afternoon sunlight, the water was a shimmering expanse until it hit the cloudless blue sky on the horizon. She couldn't wait to take her boat out there. Other than that, she wondered what she was going to do with her life when she wasn't selling prosthetic hands anymore. For the second time, she was facing a future with no plans. This time, however, she had a feeling of being anchored in a safe harbor instead of being cast into an unknown and tumultuous sea.

Chapter Five

The air-conditioning in the San Luis Rey Panadería was a blessing as Alice entered the old adobe house that had been converted into a restaurant over a century ago. Shaded by huge eucalyptus trees, it was one of the scattering of buildings around the old mission that was not part of the mission property but still under the San Luis Rey Mission Historical Society's purview.

The same family had owned the building since it was built and had once owned all the buildings in the cluster, but the panadería was the only one that had remained in constant use. This also meant that it had been altered the most over the years. In recent years, the historical society had helped restore the outside to its original look, but the inside was still very much vintage 1970s. One half of the inside was dedicated to a Mexican bakery that did very brisk business catering to people who loved authentic breads and bakery goods. The other half of the shop was a Mexican restaurant attached to a large outdoor patio. It did most of its business on the weekends when it had live music and dancing. During the week, it was more sedate, mostly serving tourists from the mission.

Alice found Taylor sitting at a table on the patio next to the water fountain. It looked like she was the only customer, which wasn't unusual during the midafternoon. Alice slid into the seat across from her friend and pulled a carafe of ice water over, pouring some into the empty glass sitting next to the silverware wrapped tightly in a paper napkin.

"You didn't take one of those electric scooter things all the way out here, did you?" Alice asked.

Taylor lowered her menu. "You're like a ninja. When did you get here?"

"Just now. Don't worry. I won't ever let you miss a fascinating moment with me by not letting you know I'm in the vicinity."

Taylor squinted at her. "You're so weird."

"I prefer unique. Less stigma." Alice dipped a chip in the salsa.

"Okay, you're so weirdly unique."

"Thank you. Now, tell me. Did you ride one of those scooter things down here?" She nibbled on the chip.

"I took the bus. I only use the public scooters around town. Why do you ask?"

"I saw one parked outside. I get so worried seeing all the young people zipping around. None of them wear helmets."

"It was parked outside when I got here. This is too far on busy roads. They're fun, though. I'll take you out on one sometime. We can stay in Oceana where there's less traffic."

Alice pursed her lips and wrinkled her nose. She'd made a promise to herself to push her comfort level. "Okay. But I'll wear my bike helmet."

"Cool. It'll be fun. How about tomorrow? It's Saturday. We can pick a couple up at the Seaside Café. There are usually a few parked out there."

"I'll have to check my social calendar," Alice said. It was her usual response to being invited to do anything. It was funny because she wasn't all that social, but it also gave her an out if she wanted to ignore the offer. "Why aren't you at work?"

"Monday's Labor Day, and the owner gave us the day off for a four-day weekend. I so needed this. I'm a little burned out."

"Is that why you were so distracted that you didn't notice my grand entrance? How does one get burned out at twenty-three?"

"I suppose in the same way one gets burned out at thirty-three, forty-three, fifty-three, or sixty-three. Spending more time working than relaxing. Taking on more than you can get done. Making work more important than your health. Working with people who stress you out. Doing a job that doesn't fill your soul. Having a boss who questions your work ethic just because you actually take your fifteen-minute break a couple of times a week. Sitting next to Randy, who eats corn nuts like they're popcorn and having to listen to that hellish crunching all freaking day long." Her words came out quicker and more forceful with each new indignity.

She paused and breathed out as if trying to calm herself. "There's more, but I just grossed myself out talking about Randy and his corn nuts perversion." Her hands were buried to her scalp, clasping handfuls of shiny, straight, black hair. Alice would have laughed if Taylor wasn't really stressed out. And whoever Randy was, he needed a fire hose taken to him.

"I can't tell if you have a problem with corn nuts or Randy."

"Both. Have you heard of misophonia?"

Alice tapped her temple. "Phonia has to do with sound. Miso is either soup or a derivative of not liking something. Contextually, I don't think you were referring to soup, therefore I'll hazard a guess that it might mean not liking a sound? You hate hearing him eat those corn nuts?"

"More than hate it. I can't stand to hear people eat anything, but Randy is a gross pig of a human being. He wears food-stained graphic tees, jeans that could probably stand up by themselves, and has this big bushy beard that always has crumbs in it." Taylor grimaced. "And his feet stink."

Alice reached over and laid her hand on Taylor's. "It sounds like you need this day off."

Taylor grinned. "You think?"

They both laughed, and Alice decided on the carne asada. After the server finished taking their order, Alice took two pennies from her purse and handed one to Taylor. "For making a wish from the fountain."

Taylor took her penny and held it, squeezing her eyes shut. Her lips moved as she made her secret wish, and she tossed it in the water. Alice made the same wish she always made: blessing her family in Kansas and asking for a bumper soybean crop.

"I'm glad you asked me to lunch," Alice said after taking a sip of water. "I have the opposite problem from burnout with my job. I'm bored. I fear the ship is sailing itself too well these days."

"What do you do at the mission? Are you a priest or something?"

Alice placed a hand flat on her chest. "Heavens no. Women can't be priests in the Catholic church. I work for the San Luis Rey Historical Society. We oversee the operations of the mission and the property as a historical site in parallel with the Roman Catholic Diocese of San Diego. The priests live here, run the seminary, and use the church, but the historical society isn't part of the church." Alice took note of Taylor's confused expression. "I consider myself a religious catholic with the little 'c.'"

Taylor shook her head. "Yeah. I don't get it."

"With the little 'c' catholic just means 'universal,' whereas, with the big 'C,' it refers to the Catholic church. I used to be a Catholic, but I'm not anymore. I'm a universal or inclusive Christian. Religion is very important to me, and I like what it represents and how it gives people a safe guide in a scary world. But I think people should be allowed to celebrate their beliefs, no matter what they are, as long as they're respectful of others. That's why I go to the Unitarian Universalist Church. They welcome all religions."

"Can I tell you something?"

"Sure."

"I have no idea how all the different churches are related or are not related to each other. Religion just wasn't a thing in our house. I know people get all bent about which religion is the 'right' one," she said, using air quotes. "But they all sound the same to me. I honestly don't get it. But I like our church. If nothing else, it introduced me to you."

"What brought you to our church, then?" Alice asked, deeply interested in Taylor's views on church and religion. She'd never met anyone who didn't have an opinion, good or bad. She liked to think she was good with either, but it made her sad when people couldn't overlook the bad when there was so much good. At least in her opinion.

"The sign."

Alice smiled. She was the one who came up with the messages displayed each week on the digital billboard in front of the church, along with service hours, special events, and other things, depending on what was going on that week.

"Was it the message? Or an event?"

"It said, 'Your family is just inside these doors.' I wasn't doing so great that week. I missed my family. Work kind of sucked. I was in a really bad place. So I went inside. There was nothing specific going on, but there were a few people sitting on the couches in the big room," Taylor said, referring to the open area outside of the room where services were held.

"I try to alternate heartfelt messages with witty ones."

"I like the witty ones better, to be honest. But it drew me in." Taylor sipped her water and watched her over the rim of her glass. Alice felt like she was being sized up. Taylor's eyes told her it was in a good way. "You're a cool person, Alice," Taylor finally said as she set her glass down. "You're so sure of who you are, and you accept people as they are no matter who they are. I've never met anyone like you."

The comment meant everything. "Thank you, Taylor. Every person is a miracle."

"That's why I wanted to have lunch with you today. I wanted to talk to you about something."

"What is it?" She rested her hand over Taylor's, sensing she was nervous.

Taylor rubbed her free hand up and down her thigh. "You know how I moved here from Detroit for a job?" Alice nodded. "That wasn't really the reason. I needed to get away."

Alice wanted to ask why but just squeezed her hand and listened.

"I needed space to figure out who I was, who I wanted to be. I couldn't while my family kept telling me who they expected me to be. It sounds stupid, I know, but I spent my entire life just sort of going with the flow. I'm the youngest of five. My sisters and brothers all knew exactly who they were. For a while, I believed I did, too." Her eyes grew unfocused as she stared over Alice's shoulder. "Until I didn't."

Alice patted her hand. "I can feel how nervous you are. All feelings are valid, but I want you to know that you don't need to feel nervous with me. I doubt there's anything you can tell me that will change how I feel. You're a kind person. That's all that matters. Everything else is just flavoring."

Taylor smiled and took a deep breath. "I'm a trans woman. A trans lesbian woman. I only started expressing my true gender after I moved here. The first thing I did was go out and buy new clothes. I know it's not all about the clothes, but it felt good to pick them out with the real me in mind. Does that make sense?"

Alice wondered how Taylor would react if she said it made perfect sense to her as a person who'd given up so much of her identity when she'd entered the convent. Her being a nun had never come up between them. It never came up with most people, actually. People never assumed someone was once a nun at one time. Not wearing the habit had been a hard change when she'd been asked to leave the convent. She'd purposefully picked a convent that continued to wear traditional attire. She'd wanted the uniform. It had reminded her of who she was and why her calling was important. She hadn't wanted anything to ever let her forget it.

Alice forced herself to refocus. "It makes a lot of sense. Our society puts a lot of weight on how we present ourselves, what we wear, how we abide by expectations. We're conditioned from the first pink or blue baby blanket, and our identity is formed around it. So, yes, it makes complete sense."

Taylor's anxiety not only seemed to fade, she became almost exuberant. Alice had never seen her so animated. "I picked Taylor to replace my birth name. I even used it when I applied for my place at Oceana. I was so afraid they'd find out it wasn't my legal name, but Gem didn't even question it. It doesn't matter, anyway, right? As long as I pay my rent."

"They have a knack for selecting who to trust," Alice said, knowing it would matter if it were anyplace else. But Gem and Tripp, and now Rose, used a better system to select residents than a federal background search. They used the gift they'd been born with: being able to sense a person's true essence. Taylor's essence was genuine. Even Alice could sense it, and she didn't possess the gift.

But this wasn't the time to get into that.

"It's legal now. It only takes a couple of months to get a name changed in California." Taylor took a sip of water as the server delivered their food. "Anyway, I just wanted to make sure you knew who I really was. And…" She looked up and then back at her food. "Thanks for not asking what my old name was. That's usually the first thing people ask. If it isn't about medical procedures."

"I'm interested in who you are now, not who you never really were. I'm honored that you trust me. Knowing the real you is a gift." Tears blurred Alice's vision. "I already know who you are. You're Taylor, a kind and loving person. Everyone you meet is lucky to know you."

The young woman who'd always seemed a little on edge now exuded a peace that Alice hadn't seen before. Her eyes even sparkled. "I don't know why I was so nervous about this. I knew you were going to be cool. It's more than that. You're understanding and accepting. I mean, it sort of comes with the territory, but not everyone is cool just because they're gay."

A sense of being caught doing something she shouldn't caused Alice's heart to lurch. She swallowed a bite of carne asada. It seemed to grind down her throat, and she wasn't sure it would go all the way down. Finally, it did. She took a drink, hoping Taylor hadn't noticed her struggle. "I'm not gay."

"Wait. What? You're not?"

Alice shook her head. "Nope."

Taylor's pale cheeks flushed red. "That's weird. I mean, you never said you were, but I just..." She slid down in her chair, the peace nowhere to be found now. "Well, now I'm embarrassed."

"Don't be." Alice patted Taylor's hand. "I'm flattered. It's better than assuming everyone's straight."

Taylor smiled again and pushed herself up. "And that's exactly what I was talking about. You don't judge people. You talk about kind, but you're the definition of it. I'm so glad we're friends."

"Me too." Alice smiled and continued to eat, but inside, she was judging herself. And she wasn't being kind.

Why had she corrected Taylor? Just because she refused to think about her sexuality, let alone talk about it, didn't make it not a thing. Just like if she closed her eyes, it didn't mean she couldn't see. The thing was, her sexuality, one way or another, had always been easy to ignore when it didn't come up. It didn't come up because she didn't date, and she hadn't felt attraction for someone in decades. None of this made her any less gay than she was when she'd been kicked out of the convent for "unnatural behavior with someone of the same sex." Not that she saw that time in her life as particularly gay. To her, it had been about love and expressing it, two things she'd never experienced before or after, although she felt in her deepest heart that she was capable of both. And if it did happen again, it would probably be with a woman.

So why had she denied it? Was it shame? She didn't think so. Many of her friends were gay, and she didn't think any less of them about it. In fact, she didn't think about them in terms of their sex lives at all. She celebrated their love for one another. Not their *gay* love. Just their love. God's most precious gift. The connection and devotion between two people. Her life was about her as a person, how she tried to be a catalyst for positivity in the world, how she embodied God's love for the world and every being in it.

It had never been about the girl she'd once loved and certainly not about the private things they had done together to express it.

But as soon as Taylor asked, she had replied that she wasn't gay. Like it mattered; like it was the most truthful thing in the world.

Taylor had no idea how much she judged and how unkind she could be but only toward herself. Even so, she still heard the voice of God, in his gentle way, telling her that the mistakes she made were what made her human. They kept her humble. They helped her learn.

They reminded her to pray for guidance to be better. Still, she couldn't bring herself to correct what she'd said.

Chapter Six

The sun glinted like a million diamonds off the Pacific as Bridge turned her car west onto Cassidy Street, and the expansive ocean came into view. She'd been cruising around town, checking out what had changed in the years since she'd lived there. Most of the houses were still the old stucco, bungalow style homes she remembered, although most of them were better maintained with more elaborate landscaping. The multitudes of palms and eucalyptus trees loomed higher in the blue sky, and where thick-leafed ice plant used to cover everything, fragrant star jasmine and wisteria grew. Most of the border shrubs of white oleander had been replaced by vibrant bougainvillea, while small water features gurgled in gardens filled with hibiscus and hydrangeas mixed with succulents. The laid-back beach bum vibe she remembered had changed into more of a chaotic tourist vibe, which was disappointing. Short-term rental properties now lined the one-way street the locals had always called the Strand. It was the frontage road that used to open onto easily accessible beaches that were now for near-exclusive use by faceless property management companies. Still, the area retained a unique feel to it that had always called to her.

Recently, San Diego had been a frequent destination for her business trips because of the large medical research and development industry it supported. Before that, many years ago, the small northernmost part of it, a little town called Oceanside, had been her second home after leaving her family in San Francisco to go to college and become a nun. Overall, she liked the energy and all-around vibe of the beachfront town. The weather wasn't bad, either.

Before this move back, she'd spent most of her business trips in San Diego proper. There hadn't been much to call her back up to North County, to Oceanside, where she'd spent her convent years. It was merely part of a scenic drive on her way to Los Angeles to visit a client if she didn't choose to fly. But out of sight had never been out of mind in the case of Oceanside, the city in North County where Bridge had spent almost five of the most surreal years of her younger life. Not a day had gone by in the last twenty-five years that she hadn't thought of her time there, specifically in the Blood of the Crucifix Convent, where she'd lived and trained as a nun while going to school at Santo Benedictine College, a period of her life that seemed like a lifetime ago. A period of her life that hadn't been her own, except for her secret love.

Bridge didn't tell many people that she'd once been a nun, but when she did, they usually waited for the punch line. It was understandable, their disbelief. She wasn't the same quiet, slightly timid person she'd been back then. Not that she was loud and out there now, but she sure didn't give off a single clue that she'd once willingly left everything in her life behind to dedicate her life to the church. Why would she? Her religion had deserted her, not the other way around.

And turnabout was fair play, as the proverb so succinctly put it. She was agnostic at best, tilting toward atheism more than faith, and she wasn't circumspect about her views. Not that she pushed them on others, but when asked, she told the truth. If she even engaged. Most of the time, she'd simply leave a conversation if it tipped toward religion. In her mind, if others were entitled to their religious views, she was entitled to her anti-religious views. It was hard, even for her, to believe that she'd once been a devout Catholic who'd renounced her worldly everything to become a bride of God. It was one of the things that made her tell everyone who would listen that an eighteen-year-old person had no business making life altering decisions that they couldn't get out of. Signing up for tens of thousands of dollars of student debt? No. Joining the military and possibly losing their life? No. Getting married without sampling the goods? No. Becoming a nun or priest without knowing who they really were yet? No. No. No. No.

Why was she thinking about this now? Was it just nostalgia? Or was it a little of the old bitterness and jaded views she'd developed based on her expulsion from the Church and the loss of someone she'd loved? Did it matter? In her heart, she didn't think so. It just was.

Were her views controversial? She knew they were. But she stood behind them. She'd gone through a lot to develop them. At eighteen, young Bridge Moore had been absolutely certain that she wanted to live as a servant to her religion. A religion her family had only been practicing for four years before she'd chosen to serve. Her father had taken a job at a Jesuit hospital in Oakland, California and decided to convert from Lutheran, the religion he'd been born into, to Catholic to be considered for more promotions.

Little fourteen-year-old Bridget Moore had fallen hook, line, and sinker for the dogma she'd been taught in catechism class. When she'd mentioned that she wanted to be just like her favorite teacher, Sister Katherine Mary, she'd received so much encouragement because her tomboy demeanor had caused a few raised eyebrows. Little had Bridge or Sister Katherine Mary known that Bridge's intentions of being *like* Sister Katherine Mary had really been intentions of being *with* Sister Mary Katherine. A small but important distinction and one Bridge hadn't been able to fully decipher until she'd fallen hard for another young nun during the four years they'd spent studying together.

That was when she'd figured out that her heart belonged to women, not some male-identified deity who made rules and laws that actively dehumanized and minimized women insidiously and intentionally.

Some who knew her might say Bridge was bitter about organized religion. But in her heart, she was positively rancorous.

With all of this on her mind, it didn't surprise her when she realized she was less than a block from the Blood of the Crucifix. And it wasn't simple nostalgia that inspired her to take a drive by her old convent and college a day after moving back to Oceanside. She felt a need to connect with her past, to somehow integrate what felt like a different lifetime to who she was now. She hadn't known she needed it, but here she was, and the desire was strong as she pulled up the to the old campus.

To her surprise, the college had moved, as had the convent, and the buildings were currently in use by a military academy. She still received alumni mail from Santo Benedictine College, and she should have known about the move, except she never read the stuff. It went from mailbox to the trash can without being opened.

She parked her car on the street in front of the wrought-iron fenced campus where young men in military uniforms moved, presumably between classes. They walked with purpose, none of the casual interaction one was used to seeing at a public high school. The gardens were gone, and a set of flagpoles had been erected in their place. The tall water fountain was still working, and the circular area featuring the stations of the cross was still ringed with rose bushes. Other than that, the school looked very much the same with bright stained glass decorating the thick limestone walls. The grand bell tower pierced the bright blue sky.

Surprised by an overwhelming sense of nostalgia, she envisioned it as it once was, where novice nuns in long white habits walked quickly behind nuns in black habits who always looked like they were in a hurry to get somewhere. The nostalgia came and went quickly. None of her best memories had occurred near the front of the school. She'd arrived and ultimately left via a door in the back near the kitchen, and aside from going to various classes, she'd spent most of her time either in the gardens or in the dormitory and chapel near the back of the school.

Still, there were memories from that time that made her smile, but she doubted that the school would allow her to visit the row of confessionals she and Sister Mary Alice would sneak into for a longing kiss or the laundry room where they would slink away to for a few stolen moments of groping beneath their heavy garments. They'd definitely not let her peek into the pair of adjacent rooms they'd called cells, where long nights of almost fully clothed sex would occur when one or the other of them would dash furtively between the side-by-side doors whose hinges had been silenced with purloined Crisco oil.

Memories laced with longing swirled in her head while she sat in the car in front of the school. With a sigh and a straightening of her shoulders, Bridge pulled away and drove to the cliffside fish and chips restaurant she's always wanted to try. She wasn't ready to go to a place where she and Mary Alice had once gone. Not even the grocery store a block away. Sometimes, it was the memories of the most ordinary things that they'd done together that caused the most poignant ache. The ghosts of regret and longing were already seeping back. Visiting their genesis would have been too much.

Sitting by herself under the ridiculous fiberglass replica of a great white shark hanging from the ceiling, the flaky white halibut encased in crisp, deep-fried beer batter was just as good as she'd always imagined, especially when dipped in the homemade tartar sauce. The coleslaw that came with it was a delightful surprise, some of the best she'd ever eaten. Even the fries, wide and long but not too thick, were delicious. She wanted a beer to drink with her meal, but it was a little early in the afternoon, so she opted for lemonade. It was probably the better choice because the beer and sunshine might have made her want to take a nap, and this day was too pretty to sleep through. There was something relaxing about eating lunch in the ocean breeze, looking out over the water.

The drive back home took her by the local Franciscan mission, if one were to consider the two and half mile detour up a scenic highway along the side of the lazy San Luis Rey River "along the way." It wouldn't have been a complete trip through her memories if she didn't visit the old mission. She had spent a lot of her time there as part of her service work during theology school.

Initially, her work had been inspired by the desire to spend more time with Sister Mary Alice, who'd unwittingly led Bridge to many places she would have never gone otherwise. So, while the historical and architectural aspects of the mission had always been interesting to her, if it weren't for the memory of Sister Mary Alice, Bridge would have simply pointed her car south on the I-5 after lunch without even thinking about Mission San Luis Rey.

"Mission San Luis Rey, built in 1815, is the largest mission and the second on the mission trail from south to north of the twenty-one missions established by Franciscan missionaries and built by the ancestors of the original Californians. Still in use today by Franciscan monks, services in both Latin and English are held..."

Recognizing the voice, Sister Mary Bridget dropped a stack of weekly missalettes on the table next to the holy water font near the massive main doors to the church and slipped in to join the tour. The soft-spoken nun from her seven-a.m. divinity class at the college guided the tour group to the first enclave of the stations of the cross that were beautifully depicted through artistic renderings along the walls of the beautiful church. When the tour was over, Sister Mary Bridget approached the nun from her class.

"You sound like an expert."

The nun bowed her head, and her cheeks grew pink. "I studied the history of the missions when I was notified of my acceptance to the convent. When I found that it was a tourist destination, I'd hoped to get to offer tours and here I am." She looked grateful, pleased, and proud all at once, and Sister Mary Bridget couldn't stop looking at her radiant face. She seemed to be lit from within.

"I'm Mary Bridget. We have class together with Friar Thomas."

The pretty nun nodded. "You sit in the back. I'm Mary Alice."

The idea that Sister Mary Alice had noticed where she sat sent an exciting tremble through Mary Bridget.

"You sit in the middle."

"Yes."

Bridget found the rule of silence they observed in the convent difficult and was surprised to find it even more difficult to talk now that she had a chance outside of the convent building. Mary Alice had an air about her that made Mary Bridget want to know her. It was hard to describe, but the best she could say was that it was her confidence without ego or timidity, not too strong but still evident. All of it, but especially her genuine kindness, drew Mary Bridget to Sister Mary Alice. She wanted to know her, be her friend, absorb some of the amazing self-assurance.

"Do you give tours regularly?"

"Every afternoon at three to the public and at other times when there are schools or scheduled tours."

"Maybe I'll come back to take the full tour."

"It will cost you seven dollars."

"Seven dollars?"

"Yes, that's the suggested donation to take the tour. But I won't charge you today."

"I'll bring my wallet."

"I'm just kidding. The tours do cost seven dollars, but I won't charge you. We'll just say you're training as my backup."

Bridge remembered the twinkle in Mary Alice's eyes as she'd teased her. It had taken her a while to realize that what she'd felt for the pretty nun was more than friendship, but that was the first time she'd felt the compelling draw that had led her to seek her out at every possibility.

For a long time, she'd believed the depth of her feelings was due to the taboo of the desire she'd had no name for at the time. But over the years, when the memory of Mary Alice remained vivid and never faded, she'd known there was a power that had drawn them together and had kept her love for Mary Alice alive. Her attraction wasn't religion, faith or even God, but it had moved her spirit, as it had other parts of her body, if she was to be crudely honest.

Shaking herself from her reverie, she put her car in park, got out, and stood to stretch in the newly paved parking lot near the mission. The building looked exactly the same. Whitewashed adobe brick in the Spanish Colonial style. Every emotion she could name, and then some, rushed through her as the fragrant scents of eucalyptus and pepper trees overtook the smell of fresh asphalt, enveloping her.

The place looked deserted. As she recalled, most Monday afternoons were quiet. She decided to take a quick peek in the church if the doors were unlocked, and they were. A tickle of anticipation teased her as she stepped into the dimly lit narthex. The smell of burning wax from the prayer candles in the by-altar to the left of the nave tickled her nose, initiating the first of three small sneezes, a reaction she had every time she was near a burning candle. She stepped into the aisle and looked around.

"God bless you," a woman's voice said quietly from the pew just behind her. A weird sense of déjà vu descended upon her as she turned. A very old nun with a small Bible clasped in her hands resting in her lap sat on the gleaming wooden bench.

Without thinking, Bridge bowed her head when she noticed her ring. "Apologies for the intrusion, Mother Superior."

"No apologies required. I was just resting." The old nun stood and with a small wave, left the church.

Stunned by her unexpected response to being in the presence of the Mother Superior, who was not even the one she'd known back in her convent days, Bridge shook her head and let out a long breath. She hadn't set foot in a church in twenty-five years, yet the ingrained responses remained. She took a long look around and left the building. She was on her way back to her car when it occurred to her that she should get something from the gift shop for her brother. Despite being a lost sheep like herself, he collected decorative crosses that he hung in the entryway to his mission-style house on Nob Hill.

There was no one behind the small glass counter when Bridge entered the gift shop that looked the same as it had when she'd last visited twenty-five years ago. Religious jewelry filled the glass case. Necklaces with crucifixes, rosaries, medallions, and other religious pendants hung from spinning displays. Stacks of books, laminated prayer cards, and a display box depicting scrolls of all the saints stood among the candles, small statues, and various religious icons. Items blessed by the Pope were displayed behind the register, incense burned in metal balls with inscriptions of religious verses, and every size and color of Bible was available for purchase, from giant leather-bound editions to the small Bibles that were found in hotel room drawers. All around, mounted on the walls, was picture after picture of white Jesus, white Mary, white popes, and white saints from every century after Jesus's birth. She rolled her eyes. Even as a nonbeliever, she was embarrassed about the whitewashing of history. It wasn't her usual passive anger for organized religion, she realized. Active rancor was bubbling within her. Maybe coming here hadn't been such a good idea.

Bridge slipped past the magnet carousel to the one wall where all the ceramic and wooden decorative crucifixes hung. She chose a fancy one with tile inlay depicting the San Luis Rey Mission from different angles. Her brother would love it.

Bridge put the wall hanging on the counter, and still, no one had come into the store. There was a service bell next to the register with a sign inviting customers to use it to call a clerk, but she was always reluctant to use them, thinking it was rude, ringing a bell and summoning service. She wasn't in a hurry, so she decided to give it a little more time. While she waited for someone to show up, she browsed the keychains that featured names on one side and the mission on the other. She didn't need one, but she always looked.

"Are you looking for a particular name?"

Bridge laughed as she spun the display carousel. "Just looking. It seems you're well-stocked with Bridgets. Hey, but you actually have a Bridge. I guess I have to—" She slid the keychain off the peg, turned toward the clerk with it in her hand…

Her whole world cranked to a violent halt.

Fawn brown eyes with specks of gold she hadn't seen in twenty-five years met her gaze.

Gravity lost its hold on her, and she was at risk of floating away. She swayed, steadying herself by putting her hand on the glass countertop. "Mary Alice." Her voice was breathy.

"Just Alice now." It was said matter-of-factly but with a definite tone of disbelief. Or maybe it was the wide eyes that indicated the disbelief.

Bridge's heart hammered in her chest. "Wha—" She shook her head slowly, never breaking eye contact. "I…I…They wouldn't tell me where you were. Where you went. Have you been here all this time?"

Mary Alice's—wait. No. *Just* Alice's eyes remained on her. Unblinking, unmoving, pinned to her face, as if whatever was going on in her head had frozen her body.

A moment more passed where they simply stared at each other before Alice blinked, seemingly coming to after being held captive by the unreal moment. "Here? At the mission?"

It took a few seconds to realize Alice was responding to the question that Bridge had forgotten she'd asked. "Not *here* here. But in Oceanside?" She had a hard time reading her. Everything about Alice seemed like the same woman she'd known only under a shell, a thin veneer that kept her contained. "Are you, I mean, you're not still a nun, are you? Do you work here?"

"I'm not a nun. Not s…since…that morning, no." Her smile faltered and reappeared, but it didn't show in her eyes anymore. In fact, she looked almost scared. Terrified, even. "I work for the historical society now."

Bridge smoothed the short hair on the side of her head, a nervous habit. "This is intense. Can you take a break? Is there somewhere we can sit?" She was a little lightheaded. "Maybe get some water?"

At the mention of sitting, Alice seemed to...thaw. Not relax entirely but settle. "How about coffee? A cup sounds good. Decaf, though." She rubbed her stomach. "I'm not sure caffeine would be a good idea right now."

Bridge could relate. Her own stomach was doing flips. "Is there somewhere close?"

Alice nodded. "The panadería. We can walk."

Bridge's mind flashed on the little Mexican bakery just down the hill. "It's still there?"

"Yes. But...but maybe..." Alice looked around her. "I don't know..."

"Can you leave?"

"That's the thing. I don't know." She sounded more than a little distracted. Was it hesitation? She had to be shocked.

Bridge was shocked herself. And excited and elated but also scared. She'd lost all hope of seeing Alice again, and here she was. Almost exactly where Bridge had left her. She reached out but dropped her hand before touching her. "I can't believe it's you," she said, not realizing she'd said it out loud until Alice nodded.

"I know. I almost feel like it's not real." Alice also lifted her hand and then dropped it as if she thought better of it. As if each believed they were seeing a ghost.

"Seriously. It's a little scary," Bridge said. "I don't know if I should smile or cry."

Alice laced her fingers together in front of her. "I'm not sure how to feel, either. It's making me act weird. Which is saying a lot." She huffed.

Bridge huffed in return. "You're not acting weird." But, then again, did she know what not-weird Alice was like anymore?

"Just a second." Alice retreated through a heavy wooden door into what Bridge assumed were offices in the back. She returned in less than a minute, during which Bridge wondered if she really would be back.

"I had to let someone know I was taking a break." She still looked haunted, but Bridge followed her out of the gift shop and down the terra-cotta sidewalk toward the garden path that would take them to the little restaurant she and Alice had sometimes gone to on the rare occasions they were given breaks at the same time.

The scents in the garden conjured up a sensation that held her in a sort of half sneeze, making her eyes water. Or was it an emotional reaction? She couldn't tell. She was just glad that Alice was ahead, walking so quickly, Bridge struggled to keep up even with several inches of height and longer legs. They didn't talk, just snuck glances as if to check to see if the other was still there. It was so disorienting walking the familiar path with a person who seemed so much like the person she'd known but also so different. It wasn't just the civilian clothes. Grown-up Alice wore what was almost a force field around her, separating her from the world. From Bridge.

"Do they still serve those sweet breads? Conchas?" Bridge finally said as they neared the panadería, and the familiar scent of sweet bread baking surrounded them. Her senses were reeling. Was this really happening?

"Yes."

"I haven't had one since I left. I'd die for a strawberry." She hadn't thought of the colorful sweet bread in years, but now, her mouth watered, and her stomach filled with butterflies. None of it had to do with the bread but the memories it evoked of stolen kisses that had taken years to work up to but had become a frequent thing the times they'd gone to the panadería to bring back a treat.

"They'll have it." Alice smiled at her and almost looked like the Alice she'd known. She opened the door, and it was like falling into another time. Nothing had changed inside the shop. They had the same diner-style tables with chrome edges and matching chairs. The same tile. And there they were, the conchas, piled in colorful mounds of pink, yellow, green, and brown. She wanted one of each, but she settled on just one pink one for her and one yellow one for Alice, plus two cups of decaf that they took to a table by the window. Even the corrugated mechanic's sheds across the narrow street still stood, dilapidated and rusted, large bay doors open displaying a row of cars in various stages of repair.

"I almost wish for the marine layer right now so I could have hot chocolate," Bridge said just to say something.

"You could have it now," Alice said, sitting stiffly across from her, her hands in her lap.

"It wouldn't be the same. Hot chocolate is for chillier days."

They were quiet for a few moments as they sampled their bread and sipped their coffee; the combination of Alice's proximity and the food brought a wave of nostalgia crashing over Bridge. She was at a loss about how to act naturally.

"I like the way you do your hair now," Alice said, staring into her coffee cup.

Bridge ran a hand down the back of her head. Her neck was damp with sweat. It was a warm September day, but the heat wasn't only because of that. "It's easy."

"It's fashionable, the short cut and slightly tussled style."

Bridge coughed to cover a laugh.

"What?" Alice asked.

"It makes me look older." She wasn't sure why she said it. She'd never been concerned with aging before. She might have been in her mid-forties, but she felt a decade and a half younger.

"You look exactly the same, only with shorter hair. It was to your shoulders back then. You don't even have any gray."

Bridge ran her fingers along the side of her head. "Oh, they're there. They just blend in with my highlights." A sparkle of electricity tingled down her back. Mary Alice's hair had been long and thick, and she guessed it still was, even pulled up as it was now. A memory of her letting her hair down in the bathroom of the dormitory flashed through Bridge's mind in high-definition.

Bridge had been in a stall, nervous to leave because she could see Mary Alice through the space next to the door. Bridge had wanted to say good night but didn't want to interrupt as Alice washed her face. It wasn't until Mary Alice had dried her face that Bridge had the courage to open the door just as Alice's thick hair fell in a cascade down her back. A current of sparkling heat had passed through Bridge then, and she felt its ghost pass through her now.

"Do you still keep your hair long? I can't tell with it pinned up."

Alice nodded, her cheeks turning pink, and Bridge was twenty years old again, brushing Mary Alice's hair at bedtime before they knelt to say their prayers. "It's a pain sometimes, but I liked to comb my mom's hair when she let it down when I was little, so… but you probably remember me telling you that once upon a time." Her eyes went distant.

Bridge wanted to tell her what she remembered. It wasn't about her mother, either. But they'd never been good at expressing that kind of thing to one another, saying the things that they felt in their hearts and bodies. Saying it out loud would have turned the magic into sin back then. If they didn't speak about it, they might have been able to pretend it wasn't happening.

Mostly, they just did things. Touches. Standing close. Letting their eyes hint at what they were thinking, wanting, needing. Until things had happened. Yet, still, they hadn't spoken about it. Kneeling next to one another during prayers, so close that when they turned to face one another, their lips had brushed mid-prayer. Soon, their breasts had pressed together, softness upon softness. Their hands had wandered, discovering what they craved to know. The words they'd used to find the stolen times they had together hadn't been direct. Neither of them had been able to say things like, *I'll be in the laundry room before afternoon prayers, and I'd like you to find me and lift my skirts.* Or *my door will open with a push if you decide to visit in the night and kiss my aching breasts.* Or *are you aware how you affect my body with the pressure of your leg when you lie atop me?*

No. The words were never said, but their eyes had conveyed it. That was all they had needed to let it happen.

Until they'd been caught.

What had happened to Mary Alice after that? It wasn't the time to ask. It seemed as if Alice was just one wrong question from running away. It reminded Bridge of how Alice had been after their first kiss, when the ecstasy of the touch had electrified them both, but the idea of the actual sin had terrified them more than getting caught. It had been one of the very few times they'd spoken about how either of them had felt.

Bridge wondered if Alice was back in that place, when their hearts and bodies were in Heaven, but each of them had also felt like they had one foot in hell, the other close behind. She'd felt like it was worth it but had hated being the cause of Mary Alice's self-persecution. It had taken weeks to get comfortable with one another again. And when they had, without talking about it, they'd both seemed to decide that the feelings they had for one another were inevitable, and they'd slowly given in to them, timidly advancing their physical relationship while continuing to pursue their religious duties as if it was all part of their daily lives. Mary Alice had warned her that if they discussed it, it would break the fragile bubble of bliss. So they hadn't. They'd worked hard to protect their safe harbor by leaving it all unspoken.

In the days after Bridge had been sent back home, the only thing she could think about was Mary Alice living in a hell of her own making, believing she'd caused shame or punishment or religious guilt for Bridge when, in reality, being released from the convent was the best thing that had ever happened to Bridge. Except for losing Mary Alice. She'd wished it hadn't happened the way it had, and she'd had no idea about what she would do with her life, but she'd dreamed of finding Mary Alice and making a life they could both be happy in.

Over time, when she hadn't been able to find Mary Alice, she'd thought she'd have gladly stayed if it meant they could have been together. A wall of emotional pain crashed over her in that moment, and she was afraid it would come pouring out of her.

"I'll be right back." She managed a smile and hoped it didn't look forced. "I have to visit the ladies' room."

As soon as she turned, her eyes blurred with tears. Thankfully, she remembered where the restroom was. She made it there before she made a fool of herself.

Curiously, except for the tears, the image in the mirror didn't reflect the feelings churning within her, each of which slashed through her vibrant and hot. The foremost being the yearning and passion from their past, then the scalding heat of anger. No. Rage. The waves of impotent despair that had hung over her for years as she'd railed against an institution that could so callously rip apart the hearts of innocents. The roiling need for retaliation for taking away the well of love she'd never known until she'd found Mary Alice. All for what? Obedience. Enforced by men feigning to be holy, who were gluttons for power, who tortured and deprived their willing servants in the name of fake piety. She hated the Church. She despised it. It was impossible that all of that wasn't etched on the face that stared back at her. She had the practice of maintaining a facade from her sales job to thank for that. She took a few deep breaths and splashed water on her face to regroup before she went back out to Alice.

But when she returned to the table, Alice was gone. The pain of losing her washed over Bridge with the force of the first time. She waited for several moments, but she knew as soon she sat down that Alice had left. A gale of grief swept through her hollow heart.

❖

The walk back to the mission was a complete blur. Seconds after Bridge had excused herself to the bathroom, Alice's calendar alarm had gone off, reminding her about a scheduled tour. She hadn't wanted to disappear on Bridge, but something had prevented her from interrupting. In a daze, she'd returned to the mission, half hoping that Bridge would come find her and half hoping she wouldn't.

The last hour felt like a fever dream. Vivid memories and emotions swirled around her. How had Mary Bridget just shown up out of the blue after all these years? Alice had stayed, even worked in the same place, but twenty-five years later, long after all her hope had been depleted, the scariest yet most beautiful specter had just shown up, reigniting old emotions. She wasn't sure she could cope, awash in insecurities about how she wasn't dressed appropriately, her hair wasn't covered, how different she must seem, and how disappointed Mary Bridget must be that Alice wasn't the person she remembered. The last was almost paralyzing, consuming her thoughts.

Over the years, she'd imagined seeing Mary Bridget in countless scenarios, yet she hadn't been ready for this. Not even a little bit.

Chapter Seven

The tour bus rumbled off, and Alice went back into the church, wondering what Bridge was doing, how she was feeling, whether she'd come find her again. Alice was dazed, feeling foggy, wondering how long Mary Bridget had waited in the panadería after she'd run away. She'd walked, but the way her heart had raced, it might as well have been a run. She slid into the back pew, barely remembering to make the sign of the cross. Shame and loss filled her to the point of feeling numb.

It had taken her years after leaving the church before she'd found peace sitting among the polished pews, the beautiful artwork, and the accouterments of her old religion. She found it calming now. Tours were easy. She simply recited the history she knew from heart, a relating of the past as it pertained to now, giving California residents and tourists a peek into how the state had come to be, the bad, the good, and the in-between. She'd never held back on explaining how cultures had clashed, and people had been displaced, but she left it to the tourists to reconcile the history she gave them with the various other versions they'd been taught. The history of the mission was a brutal subject no matter how one saw it.

She knelt on the padded kneeler, her dead grandmother's rosary wrapped around her hand. She paused before she started the prayers she could recite in her sleep.

History, in general, was a brutal subject.

Her own history included.

Mary Bridget was back. Bridget. Bridge. No matter the name, it was the same person, the same spirit, the same woman.

The numbness that had fallen over her at the realization that she was face-to-face with the one and only love she'd ever known started to crumble, and all the emotions she'd felt stirring inside but wouldn't let out were battling to consume her. Her hands tightened on her rosary, trembling.

Alice had felt her presence as soon as she was near. The gift shop was Cheri's domain, but she'd been on her break, and Alice had volunteered to watch the monitors and help any customers who might drop in. It wasn't hard. Between tours, it was usually empty. She'd seen the person come in on the closed-circuit video in the back office, and something in the grainy gray and white feed had felt familiar. She'd told Cheri to keep reading her book with the dragons on the cover, and she'd gone into the gift shop.

When the customer had turned, brutal history had reared its thorny head, and Alice had gone numb. She had no memory of what she'd said, how she'd ended up walking down to the panadería, or what she'd managed to talk about once they got there. All of it had remained a blur when she was left alone after Mary Bridget had excused herself, and when the alarm on her phone had gone off, the spell had broken. That was when she'd ran.

Kneeling in the back pew, her arms resting on the back of the one before her, she felt like she was still running. Running from shock. Running from her marauding emotions. Running from ghosts. Now she was grasping at the comfort of devotion, stroking the worn black beads of the rosary that knew all her secrets, wishes, and fears.

She made the sign of the cross and began the Apostles' Creed. "I believe in one God, the creat…"

She felt it then. It was back. Just a whisper now, but she knew the signs. The crisis of faith she'd worked so hard to overcome, when simple love had stolen her dreams, and in the name of God, she'd been cast away, labeled a sinner and a traitor to her religion. For almost two years, she'd wandered, lost and lonely;

she'd mourned the loss of her family, both heavenly and earthly, but mostly the love of the woman who'd opened her heart. Having been told her sin was the worst possible besmirch upon the church, she'd reached her darkest day two years after losing Mary Bridget. Without hope, without God, she had nothing.

She'd gone to the church to give her last confession, to say she was sorry, and to say good-bye. She owed her life to Father David. When he'd heard her confession, he'd taken her to see Reverend Jessica at the Unitarian Universalist Church within walking distance of Oceana. He'd told her that the name of her religion didn't matter in the eyes of God and that Reverend Jessica might show her a new path. Through Reverend Jessica, she'd made peace with her faith a long time ago when she'd learned that God was not her enemy, that her God did not test their believers. It was the creators of religions that invented the tests, some out of the intention to strengthen faith, but some to instill fear in the name of obedience. Her God was with her now. Her God said she was a beloved child and was loved no matter how she presented herself in this world.

So why was she afraid all these years later?

She knew exactly why. She didn't know God's plan for her, and she wanted it to contain Mary Bridget. But if she let Bridge into her heart, she wouldn't survive losing her again. She prayed for a sign and returned to reciting the rosary. As usual, the meditative act of moving through the beads grounded her. She was between worlds now, praying in the church that didn't want her. She was a visitor in her former home. Her real home was the Unitarian Universalist Church that had welcomed her with open arms all those years ago, but she loved the smells of her former church, the wood, the polish, the candles, the incense. It was the combination of the meditation and her surroundings that centered her, so when a presence entered the space, she was aware even as she was focused on her prayer.

When her fingers returned to the centerpiece of the necklace, she prayed Hail, Holy Queen and finally offered up her usual prayer of blessings to her friends and family before asking for a sign to know what to do about Mary Bridget. When she opened her eyes, she was refreshed, as if she'd just awoken from a restorative nap. Crossing herself, she stood and turned to go back to work.

The sight of Mary Bridget sitting in the pew across from her was the sign she'd been looking for. Her prayers had been delivered.

Mary Bridget rose and moved down the pew toward her. When she didn't genuflect upon leaving the space between the benches and crossing before the alter, Alice flinched internally.

"I'm sorry. I had to make sure you were okay. I stayed at the restaurant wondering what to do, not wanting to leave in case you came back. When you didn't, I couldn't help myself. I came back here. The woman in the gift shop said you were here. When I saw you praying, it reminded me so much of when we would use private prayer time to be together."

The mention of private prayer time made Alice blush. The two of them had done nothing but pray during the period of midafternoon when all the nuns had retired to their rooms for private prayer, but they had, more often than not, met in one of their cells and knelt together on kneelers meant for one. Alice had spent many of those sessions relishing the press of Mary Bridget against her side. She'd been certain that it had amplified her prayers.

Once again, Alice wondered how anyone could call the love they'd shared a sin. Their devotion to the religion when they were young was more than Alice could conjure now. "I remember, too," she said, her voice hardly a whisper.

"Look, I know this is a surprise. Believe me, I'm feeling a bit like I'm in a dream right now. This wasn't planned, but I'm so happy to see you. When you left today, I wanted to honor your wishes, whatever they are, but I don't know how to get hold of you. I couldn't forgive myself for not at least trying to see you again. Can I leave my number? If you don't call, I'll understand." Mary Bridget handed her a card. "That's my personal cell number. I hope you call."

Alice took the card and looked at it. Bridge Moore. Bridge. She liked the sound of that. For a long time, she hadn't known her last name. They gave that up at the convent. By the time she'd learned it, too many years had gone by.

"I'll call." The hard ball of regret for leaving that had been in her stomach was gone now, replaced with something else. Was it anticipation? The problem was that she didn't know how to be, how to act, how to protect herself. Not with Mary Bridget. Not with the subject of long ago. Not with herself. It was as if separate parts of herself were meeting for the first time, and she didn't know how to introduce them.

One thing she did know was that when she'd asked God for a sign, he'd made sure that she heard.

"I guess I should go," Mary Bridget said. "Please call. You said you would, but minds change."

"I'll call. Are you here for work?" Alice asked, looking at the card again. *Bridge. Her name was Bridge now.*

"I recently moved back."

"Where were you before?"

"I've lived a lot of places. Most recently, Seattle."

There was so much she wanted to know about Bridge, the first being how she could act so comfortable when Alice felt like she was falling apart. "I'll call you this evening. Is that okay?"

"Anytime is okay."

Alice looked at the card again. "You go by Bridge now."

"I never felt like a Bridget."

"How about Mary Bridget?" The question probably revealed more about herself than anything else. At one point, she ached to be called Mary Alice again. She barely remembered that Alice now.

Bridge paused. "I did at one time, but it was a different me. Someone I no longer am. You said you were 'just Alice' when I first saw you today." She shrugged. "I'm just Bridge."

Alice wondered if she and Bridge could be friends again. Friends? Not a subject she could think about right now. "So much was left on Mother Superior's desk that morning."

"God. That day."

Alice held up her hand. "Please let's not talk about that now." As she said it, she dropped her rosary and bent to pick it up, but Bridge got to it before she did.

"You still have your—"

"Grandmother's rosary," Alice finished, taking the beaded necklace, wanting to take Bridge's hand when it briefly brushed hers. "I had it repaired once, but it's withstood the passage of time with more grace than I have."

"You're just as beautiful as ever. I like what time has gifted you with." Bridge's voice was a little deeper now.

The words cascaded down Alice's spine, leaving a trail of shivers in its path. Alice had been a skinny farmgirl when Mary Bridget had known her. She wasn't nearly as thin as she'd been back then, but she was in better shape with all the yoga and walking she'd done all her life. She blushed and looked away as soon as she saw the raw emotion in Bridge's eyes. It embarrassed her to see it, especially directed at her.

"Speaking of gifts. You were going to buy something at the gift shop. Do you still want it?"

"Um…oh yes…a gift for my brother." Bridge seemed to regain her composure, and Alice was able to breathe again.

"Follow me," she said.

Alice was aware she was walking faster than most would call comfortable, but the church was no place to have the conversation they were having…or the feelings she was feeling. Also, she didn't want Bridge to leave. As awkward as their discussion had been thus far, she craved the nearness.

When they got back to the gift shop, Cheri was ringing up a customer from the tour. It seemed so long ago now. Relieved, Alice saw the wall hanging and the key chain were still on the counter.

"I see you found her," Cheri said to Bridge when she finished with the customer.

Bridge nodded. "I did. Thank you for your help."

Alice admired how Bridge could switch from one situation to another so seamlessly. It was something she'd admired all those years ago, too. It had saved them embarrassment on a few occasions. Mary Bridget had been able to explain why they were where they were discovered—usually narrowly having been caught kissing—while she'd regained her own composure. It seemed that part hadn't changed because here she was, rattled to the core while Bridge seemingly maintained her cool.

"I can ring her up," Alice said, sliding around the counter.

Cheri shrugged. "Sure. I need more water, anyway." She stepped out with her comically huge water bottle.

Alice slipped around the counter and rang up the purchase. "Cheri gives a new meaning to the word hydration. I'm giving you my employee discount," she whispered after looking toward the back door where Cheri had gone.

"You're a peach," Bridge whispered back, and for a second, looking into each other's eyes, they were twenty again. Alice was hit by the sense that all things were possible and that the future was a blank slate. When the idea began to fade, she tried to grab hold of the wisps of it to hold on to it for just a second longer, but it slipped away, leaving her longing. At least it wasn't replaced by regret, but as soon as she thought it, shards of regret rained down on her, casting its shadow over her mood. The weight of it was immense.

Alice knew she wouldn't call. She'd get home and find every reason not to. Before she could overthink it, she ripped the receipt from the register and wrote her number on it.

"I won't call. I know I won't. I want you to. If that's okay."

Bridge read the handwritten number under the name "Just Alice." She smiled. "I've never stopped wanting you, too," she said with a wink.

Without saying good-bye or waiting for a reply, Bridge left the gift shop, and Alice knew Bridge would call. And she would wait by the phone until she did. There was no way she could do anything else with those last words floating out there.

Chapter Eight

At home later, leaning on her balcony, Bridge could not stop thinking about finding Alice. Walking out of the gift shop had been one of the hardest things she'd ever done. What if that was it? What if she'd been given one last chance, and she'd blown it? After two and half decades of longing and regrets, she'd been offered the chance to revisit the single most important thing in her life and all she had to show for it was a plastic keychain and a religious totem she'd purchased as an inside joke for her brother. In a way, the items summed up her entire existence.

But she had Alice's number.

Her hand shook with the phone in her palm. She'd been in countless situations where her nerves were beyond strained—she was in sales, after all—but this kind of nervousness was beyond anything she'd ever felt, even her nerves as a young nun preparing to not only have sex for the first time but having it with a woman… in a convent…during the holiest of seasons when they were celebrating the resurrection of God's only begotten son.

Funny how much of her inner dialog had religious undertones lately. And cynical. God, it was ridiculous how cynical she was. It was obvious on all levels why she felt this way. She was back where her life had taken unforeseen turns. Not only had she been forced from what she'd once considered her life's calling, a path she'd never expected to be on but just as quickly had been denied the love it had led her to. In a strange change of circumstance, it felt like she had a chance to get back on track. At least with Alice. The path toward faith had ended forever, and she was more than happy with that.

First, she had to call her.

Aw, for fuck's sake. She hit send on the number taunting her from the screen. Part of her expected the call to go directly to voice mail or even ring several times with no answer. She wouldn't blame Alice if she didn't answer. The encounter had been a lot, from elation to terror and everything between. She was exhausted and imagined Alice was the same.

"Hello?" Alice picked up on the first ring.

A trill of glee fired through Bridge. "Hi." She could barely hear her own breathy voice, her relief was so enormous.

"Mary Bridget. I mean, Bridge. Darn. This name thing is going to be hard for me."

"Me too." How many times had her mind been consumed by thoughts of Mary Alice? Too many to count and the name always accompanied the picture in her mind.

A pause stretched out, and Bridge wished she'd had something in mind to talk about before she'd called. Getting up the nerve had been her only focus. Now, she struggled with the swirl of emotions that had been stirred up within her. Rarely was she ever at a loss for words, but Alice seemed to short-circuit her brain. "Is this a good time?"

"Even if it wasn't, I would work with it." This Alice was not the same one from earlier. In fact, this Alice was even more confident than the original. That Alice had also been smart, witty, and sometimes a little goofy, but there'd always been an air of reservation to it. This Alice was all of that except the reservation and with a new level of confidence. It was more than a little appealing.

Appreciation flared in Bridge. What other little differences would Alice reveal to her? "Are you free to talk? I can call back when it's more convenient."

"I was just finishing up yoga. I'm completely free."

Bridge laughed. Yoga? "You sound a lot more relaxed than earlier."

Alice blew out a breath. Bridge heard the flow of water into a glass. "It's the yoga. The glass of wine I drank when I got home probably helped, too, if I'm going to be honest." Alice laughed, and Bridge added wine and yoga to the list of how different Alice was now. "I'm sure you noticed I was wound up tighter than a spring. I admit, it was a lot seeing you after so many years. It's silly, but I just couldn't stop thinking about how I'd never seen you in anything other than our habits, or…" Alice let her words hang, and Bridge's mind filled in the rest. "See? I'm having a hard time even talking about something so simple."

Bridge understood. A checklist of memories had flooded her mind at the sight of Alice. What did Alice see when she looked at her? Had she changed too much? Similar features disguising a total stranger? Appearance was only part of who she was. Could Alice see who she was as a person? A terrifying idea occurred to her. Did Alice blame her for losing her religion? That was more important to her than knowing if Alice liked her hair being longer or shorter.

"Bridge? Are you still there?"

Alice's voice startled her from her fears. "I'm sorry. It's stupid. I was worried that you might not like my short hair." She wasn't ready to discuss the rest.

"That's like asking me if I like sunsets, coffee, or breathing." This was the Alice Bridge remembered. "It did strike me as very different but in a good way. I think you wear it short more naturally than when it was longer. Your clothes are very fashionable, too. It's all very attractive on you."

The words caused a fluttering in her stomach. "Thank you. I wasn't fishing, I promise. I was just…well, yeah. Anyway." She shook her head and swept her hand through her hair. This kind of self-consciousness was a new feeling. She was used to being the person who reassured others, not the other way around. But Alice had never been like others.

"Did I embarrass you?" Alice asked.

"No. No. Not at all."

"The multiple 'no's and the very telling 'not at all' indicates I did." Alice sounded amused, again reminding Bridge of the playful Alice she remembered.

"It's kind of…it's just that…well, I care about how you see me." Truth was better than being cool. Bridge felt like she was eighteen again, worried what people thought of her.

"If that's all it is, I saw you today as I always did. You're beautiful inside and out. I'll bet you turn heads when you walk into a room, but I know how kind you are. I know how gentle and patient you are. Those are the things I think about when I see you. That and your eyes. Your green eyes like constellations and hidden glades." Alice cleared her throat, and Bridge's own throat constricted, remembering those very words spoken over twenty-five years ago. Before they'd ever touched. "They say that the eyes are the windows to our souls. And by 'they,' I mean William Shakespeare, who drew his inspiration from the Bible, Matthew 6:22-24."

"I didn't know that." Bridge realized that Alice was the only person she'd tolerate reciting Bible verses to her. There was a pause where memories and dreams of the future blended in her mind.

"It seemed easier when we all looked alike," Alice said.

"I remember how you just wanted to blend in. I'd know you anywhere by your smile, your eyes, your perfect skin." Bridge had almost described how much she was drawn to the lines of her jaw and the definition of her cheeks, different from before, the things that indicated a few years had passed. They only made Alice more attractive. "I remember when you walked, it was as if you were gliding."

Alice snorted. "I've been told I walk like a soldier."

Bridge laughed. "I saw that today. On our way to the panadería and when you took me back to the gift shop from the church. It seems you do march when you're in a hurry. We were rarely in a hurry in the convent. I used to watch you glide a lot."

"I suppose it might be that the uniform enhanced our appreciation for aspects of each other that are far more important than physical appearance."

"That's the Alice I…remember." She'd almost said love. She did love the Alice she remembered. With all her heart. It was hard to think about that now. The longing it caused left scars on her heart. Was this Alice as easy to love? "You have a way of getting to the soul of things. You've always noticed the important things."

She imagined Alice on the other end of the line blushing. She also marveled at how they hadn't seen each other in decades, and here they were, six hours after running into each other again, skipping over the getting-to-know-one-another-again steps and jumping right back into a version of them that picked up where they'd left off. It was a lot like how they had started, but then again, being a nun meant there was only one important topic. There was no polite getting-to-know-you period.

"Sometimes, I notice things. Lots of times, I don't," Alice said.

"Always when it matters."

Alice sighed on her side of the line. A pause drew out as they both seemed to muse over what was happening between them.

"There's something I can't figure out," Alice finally said.

"What's that?" Bridge asked.

"Us. I can't figure us out. I mean, after all this time. Here we are. You still feel…the same. Important to me. Is that okay to say so soon?"

Alice had often wondered aloud about the uncontrollable pull they had. For her, everything had a reason. Except for them. God, were they jumping right back into it like this? When Bridge got out of her car at the mission, she'd have never guessed this moment would be happening. But here they were, and it felt like her heart was beating for the first time in two and a half decades. "What happens if you can't explain it?"

Alice was quiet for a few beats. "Have you ever hoped for something, and when it happened, it wasn't what you'd expected?" she finally asked.

Bridge mulled it over. "A few times, I guess. Are you afraid that will happen with us? Are you worried about being disappointed?"

Alice blew out a shaky breath over the line. "You were always direct."

Bridge chuckled. "Are you worried that seeing each other again won't live up to what we've built it up to be after all this time?"

Alice didn't respond at first, and Bridge wondered if this was the point where Alice decided to pull back. "You can't see it, but I'm nodding over here."

"What did you expect?"

Another pause. Alice had always been a thinker. "What… what we had inside the convent, I'm not sure there are words for it. Is it possible to have something like that outside of the convent? It seems…almost impossible."

"What we had in the convent was impossible. I think it would be easier on the outside. Infinitely easier," Bridge said.

"I don't know about that."

"Explain?"

"It was like we had almost no choice then. We have all kinds of choices now." Alice breathed out.

"Having choices would make things easier."

"Not for me."

"Explain?"

"We were basically assigned to each other," Alice said. "We had the same classes in school. We were matched on work details. It was only natural for us to become close."

"You're saying that we wouldn't have become close if we weren't put together?"

"I don't know, but if I had a choice back then, I might not have allowed myself to…"

"To what? Become intimate?" There. She said it. They'd rarely talked about it then because Alice had been worried they'd ruin it if they did.

"I was going to say fall in love. Had I not fallen in love, I wouldn't have become intimate with you. Does that sound harsh? I don't want to hurt you." In a refreshing development, Alice wasn't talking around it either.

"Not harsh. Truthful. It's useless to think about what might have been if things had been different. I wouldn't change the past. Even with the pain. Even without a future. If I had a choice, I wouldn't give that up." Bridge needed to know. "Would you?"

She heard a sharp intake of breath and then a slow exhale. "Sometimes…sometimes I did. It hurt so much to lose you that I used to wish we'd never met. Even if you'd asked me at the beginning of this call, I think I would have said the same. But having you come back, talking again like this has…has changed my mind."

Bridge's heart ached. "I've missed you, Alice."

"I've missed you, too." Alice's voice was so quiet, Bridge barely heard her, but her answer made her heart skip a beat.

"Where have you been the last twenty-five years?" she asked.

"Right here."

"In Oceanside?"

"When Sister Mary Caroline escorted me from your room, she sent me to Mother Superior's office and then went back to gather my things while I was told that my conduct was 'incompatible with the views of the church.' There were a lot more words spoken, but those were the only words I remember. I never had a chance to speak. I don't know what I would have said if I did. It all happened so quickly. Next thing I knew, I was at the bus station with a one-way ticket back to Topeka." Alice uttered a sound between a heavy sigh and a forced laugh. "Sounds like the title of a country song."

She paused again, and Bridge wondered if it had been that simple for her. Did she simply go back to Topeka and pick up where she'd left her previous life? How had she ended up back in Oceanside?

"I never called my family," Alice continued. "But I couldn't go back. Mostly, I couldn't leave you. It was kind of like that advice about being lost. Stay where you are. Let rescue find you. I prayed about what I should do, and God answered. A woman asked me if I needed help, and I accepted it. She and her husband gave me a place to stay, and she found me a teaching job at a local school. I eventually found the job at the historical society, and coincidentally, it took me back to the mission. I've been here all along."

Alice hadn't been able to leave her. Bridge barely heard the rest. She wished she'd had the presence of mind to stay, too. Instead, she'd simply followed the directions of Mother Superior and taken the train home to San Francisco. Would they have found each other sooner if she'd stayed? "Sounds a lot like what happened to me. They wouldn't tell me anything about you. I didn't know your last name or if Alice was your birth name or your taken name. Mother Superior said it wasn't my concern, even when I begged. I came back a few months later, but they wouldn't see me. I flew to Topeka about a year later, but all I could do was wander around the city. It was much bigger than I expected. No one knew a girl named Alice who'd gone to California to be a nun. I mostly sat in diners watching crowds, hoping against hope that I'd see you."

"You did all that?" Alice's voice was little more than a whisper.

"I did. Here, I stayed at that little motel on the street between the convent and the grocery store. The one on the block that rented by the hour, the day, or the week, and we always avoided because of the dangerous clientele."

"The one where the woman always asked us if we wanted to party with her?"

"That's the one."

"Why on Earth would you stay there?"

"It was the closest one to the convent, and I figured it would be the best place to run into you if you were still in the area. Topeka was harder. I stayed in a Motel Six and visited churches. There are a lot of Catholic churches there."

"How did your family react? Did you tell them…details?"

"They were worried about me. I told them what happened. They took it much better than I expected. How was your family with the news?"

Alice didn't answer.

Bridge sensed she was struggling with something. "I know you're there. I can hear you breathing," she said.

"Sorry. I never told my family."

"Didn't they question why you left the convent?"

"I haven't talked to my parents since well before I left the convent. I didn't want them to be ashamed, and I could never have told them why I left."

"Surely, they've tried to contact you or check in."

"Maybe." It was clear from Alice's tone that she didn't believe it. "Once I became a nun, they were satisfied I was safe and cared for."

It came back to Bridge how, when she'd first gone home after leaving the convent, she'd realized how truly bizarre the whole convent experience had been. They'd renounced their previous lives for a life dedicated exclusively to God. Going back into the world prior to that had been surreal. It had taken her a while to feel comfortable again. It had to have been even more so to Alice, who'd been groomed her entire life to become a nun. She had nothing to go back to. "I didn't realize."

"How could you?" Alice sounded preoccupied. "Nevertheless, it took a while before I had the courage to go back to the convent. Mother Superior wouldn't see me. I stood on the office steps like a vagrant, and they simply ignored me. To them, I was a leper in the village near Galilee before Jesus came. I was invisible."

"I'm sorry." Bridge's heart filled with pain for her.

Alice sighed. "I expected it. Still, I had to try."

"I get it. I stopped by when I came to San Diego for work. I wasn't sure what they'd tell me. But like you said, I had to try. Do you ever run into any of the sisters in your work at the mission?"

"By the time I got my job there, things had changed. There were no more work details assigned there. It's been years since I saw anyone I knew from the convent."

"So you run the gift store?"

"I work for the historical society that co-runs the missions in California with the Roman Catholic Archdiocese. We're loosely linked to the parks service, and my work centers on preservation, tours, and nonreligious event programming."

Bridge was impressed. "The mission looks like it's being maintained better than when we were at Santo Benedictine."

"Thank you."

"Can I ask you a question?" Bridge worried that her question might be seen as judgment, but she was legitimately curious.

"Sure."

"How can you reconcile staying with the church after what happened? Did they threaten you with excommunication, too?" Bridge remembered awaiting an official notification. When it never came, she had to ask about it, and that was when she'd discovered there was no formal way to quit the church. At one time, there had been a process called defection, but it didn't exist anymore except in old doctrine. It frustrated her that the church had ways of making her feel insignificant and lacking, but she had no similar recourse, reinforcing her decision to leave. Not knowing Alice's feelings, she decided not to go into all of it, but some of the old anger made her stomach sour just thinking about it.

"They did but never followed through with it. However, I'm not part of that church anymore."

That was a surprise. "But you were praying the rosary."

"I consider myself catholic with the little 'c.' I often pray in the mission church. It's beautiful, and it gives me peace. The smell alone takes me to a reverent place in my heart. It's also close to work, so it's convenient."

"Do you attend Mass?"

"Not since the last Mass I attended with you the night before they 'excused us from our vows.'"

Bridge was surprised by the huge wave of...relief? Vindication? She really wasn't sure what to call it. But hearing that Alice wasn't still a practicing Catholic pleased her more than it should have. She didn't want the institution that had treated them like criminals for simply loving one another to have a place in Alice's heart when she wasn't even there anymore.

That last idea chilled her. Was it true? Did she honestly believe that Alice didn't hold her in her heart like she did Alice?

"Are you still there?" Alice asked.

Bridge shook herself. She'd slipped back into old insecurities. "Sorry," she said as if coming to from some sort of anesthetic. "I haven't set foot in a church since that last Mass until today, when I was looking for you."

"Do you miss it?" Alice asked.

"That's a loaded question."

"Believe me, I know."

Bridge didn't doubt it. "At first, I had no idea what to do with myself. There was this big hole in my life. I mean, the church was literally our entire life." It felt good to talk to someone who understood exactly what she meant.

"I was lucky to find a Unitarian church."

"But the rosary is Catholic with the big 'C.'"

"For me, it's like yoga. It helps me meditate. I'm not Buddhist, Hindu, or Jain, but I do both yoga and meditation. I figure reciting the rosary is okay, too. The Unitarian Church accepts everybody."

"Does that make you Unitarian?" Bridge didn't know why it mattered. She would have preferred it if Alice wasn't affiliated with any church. To her, they were all problematic.

The laughter over the line sent shivers of pleasure up and down Bridge's spine. "Alice. It makes me Alice."

Bridge chuckled. "You know what I mean. Are you religious?"

"There's something about the ceremony and tradition that appeals to me and having been raised in Christianity, I lean toward it, but I can't bring myself to call it the one and only religion when there are so many good things related to the others."

"So much bad, too." Bridge felt her cynicism well up as they talked and hoped it didn't push Alice away. "I don't want to offend you."

"I'm not offended. I'm aware of the bad, too." Alice paused. "I…I know religion can be problematic. But it got me through some very hard times. I feel like I can balance the good with the bad."

Bridge had spent so much time feeling betrayed by the Church that she couldn't understand how anyone saw the good in it. And balance? To her, it was like accepting abuse because the abuser was sometimes nice. It was hard to hear Alice talk about the good, as if that excused the bad. But she didn't feel like arguing. Not with Alice. Who had stayed in Oceanside because of her.

"I'm so glad I came back and that you stayed," she said.

"So am I." Alice paused. "Scared as it makes me."

Bridge remembered their conversation earlier. "About things not working out the way we want them to?" They hadn't actually shared what it was either of them specifically expected, although, she knew what she wanted.

Alice didn't hesitate. "Yes."

Despite her fears, Bridge was willing to take the chance. "I know so much has changed. Our lives are different now. We're different now. But I miss you. I want you in my life."

Alice made a noise like all the air had been pressed out of her. "You do?"

Bridge wondered if she'd revealed too much. "All I know is that there is no way I can't at least try."

"What does that mean?" Alice sounded uncertain.

Bridge wished they were in the same room so she could see her. Better yet, hold her hand. They hadn't touched earlier. It had seemed too much, too soon. Now she wished they had. "I don't know. I want to spend time with you. I know that."

"That's what I want, too." Alice's voice was almost a whisper.

Nearly vibrating with everything they'd shared tonight, "What do you have going on tomorrow after work?"

"Nothing I can't change. What do you have in mind?"

That answer caused a flower of hope to bloom. It seemed to say that Alice put their reunion high on her list of priorities. Bridge didn't want to seem too eager, but she was open to wherever this went, and she couldn't remember feeling so excited at the prospect of spending time with another person.

CHAPTER NINE

The heart rate monitor on Alice's watch held steady at one hundred and ten beats per minute as she strode through Oceana. Being a work from home day for her, she was getting in her power walk before she started her day. She'd barely slept the night before. Surprisingly, her energy level was high despite tossing and turning most of the night. She loved the way the ocean mist clung to all the vegetation. When the sun rose higher, its evaporation would release the scents of magnolia, star jasmine, and the multitude of roses that grew among the pathways and in the scattered little parks nestled among the meandering streets lined with mobile homes. It was her favorite part of the day.

Most of the residents of Oceana who worked in offices had already left, and the traffic in the park was next to nothing, which was a good thing because her mind wasn't on avoiding getting hit by cars.

Bridge was back.

The call from last night played on repeat in her mind. Bridge had missed her as much as she'd missed Bridge. How had they not found each other in the last twenty-five years? The sheer amount of wanting should have made it happen before now. But it had happened. God moved in mysterious ways.

And they had plans to see each other that night.

What was she going to do with herself for the next eleven hours? She already knew work wasn't going to be enough to distract her. Maybe she'd visit with Shia, Mikayla, or Tripp. Taylor was probably at work. Having lived at Oceana for two and half decades meant she knew quite a few of the residents. She had options.

"Are you ignoring me?" A figure ran up beside her. Taylor. *Speak of the devil.*

"Heavens, no," she said, worried that she'd hurt Taylor's feelings. "I was just thinking about you."

"You must have been thinking hard. You walked right past me."

"Sorry. Just deep in thought."

"Sounds legit."

"Beyond legit," Alice said, glad that Taylor understood. She glanced at her. "Shouldn't you be on your way to work right now?"

"I sort of quit." She slowed her jog to a walk, and Alice slowed to a regular pace.

"What happened?"

"You know at lunch on Friday, I said I sort of hated working there? Well, when I went back, I took one look around the cruddy office, and I decided that I couldn't stay somewhere that made me so unhappy. I wrote up a letter of resignation on the spot and gave my boss Arlo two weeks. Instead, they cut me a check and let me go that day. Turns out, they have to pay me the two weeks since I offered it. So I have two weeks to find a job."

Alice couldn't imagine just quitting like that. When she'd left her teaching job to take the job at the historical society all those years ago, not only had she lined up the new job, she'd finished out the school year. Taylor, however, was positively beaming. "I don't know if I should be happy or scared for you."

Taylor grinned. "Both, I guess. But I'm not worried. Things will work out."

She sounded so positive that Alice believed that they would. "Would you like to come over for a cup of coffee? I made cookies last night." They were only a couple of streets away.

Taylor's smile was immediate. Maybe this job situation was a good idea. "Sure. What was the occasion? Or was it just for fun?"

"Both, I guess," she teased. The inspiration for baking cookies often came to her at any time for any reason. "Actually, I just had a lot on my mind." That was an understatement.

"That's the second time you mentioned you had a lot on your mind. What's going on? Is work getting to you, too?"

She was a perceptive young woman, Alice mused. "Besides being a little bored, work is fine."

"Then what is it? I mean, no pressure if you don't want to talk about it. It's just that you always help me, and you've shown me how talking through things sometimes helps make things a little clearer, you know?"

Alice cocked an eyebrow. "That's nice, but I wish I was as wise as you when I was your age."

Taylor just waved. "Don't give me all the credit. Like I said, I have you as a role model. Plus, my therapist reminds me of it all the time when I don't talk enough."

They climbed the steps to Alice's deck, and Taylor turned to face the ocean. "Just three blocks away from mine, still in Oceana, but it feels like a completely different place."

"That's what happens when you're one of the first residents of a place, you get the best location."

"How long have you lived here?"

"Twenty-five years. You weren't even born when I moved in." In some ways, it felt more like yesterday. In others, it seemed like she'd lived in Oceana her entire life. Riding the harvesters on the soy farm her dad worked at seemed like a different lifetime ago. She wondered how her family was doing. After talking to Bridge—something she'd lost hope of ever doing again—her family was on her mind.

A current of sadness swept over her about how easy it had been for her to leave home and how easily they'd all lost touch. It was expected. One of her aunts and two of her older cousins had joined convents. Once the convents had taken them in, they'd been remembered with pride but had never come back. It was a little different when her father's brother had joined the priesthood. He came home at least once a year. The difference was that priests actually received a salary and were freer to travel.

"You really do have a lot on your mind, don't you?"

Alice realized she'd been staring out over the ocean for several minutes. "Sorry. I promised you coffee." She opened her front door, and they both went inside. She'd opened all the curtains and windows earlier when she'd seen the weather was going to be in the mid-seventies, so her front rooms were flooded with natural light, and a cool breeze was moving the air around. It was the kind of day that made her happiest to live in southern California.

Although Alice took her coffee very seriously, she still used a basic Mr. Coffee, no frills, not even a clock. She'd had the same one for years. In her opinion, it made the best and most consistent cup of coffee she'd ever had. She hoped it would work forever. She measured out the exact right amount of fresh beans, ground them for exactly fifty-three seconds, poured them into the filter she'd already slipped into the basket, filled the water reservoir, and hit brew. In just under five minutes, a pot of perfect coffee would be ready. She joined Taylor at the scarred but highly polished dining table as she was flipping through a missalette from the mission.

"Taylor, have you ever had someone from your past show up in your life unexpectedly?"

Taylor looked at her with one perfectly shaped eyebrow cocked. "God, no. I'd hide."

"Why?"

"It depends on who it was. Some of my family are horrible transphobes. The ones who aren't wouldn't come out here without telling me first. My friends from school are all jocks, and I don't have anything in common with them anymore."

"You were a jock?"

Taylor nodded with a grimace. "Captain of the football team and anchor on the swim team."

"I would never have guessed."

"Thank you." Taylor beamed. "Who are you afraid will show up?"

Alice considered her response as she got up to pour. Should she play down Bridge's appearance, pretend it wasn't happening, or tell the truth? She remembered Taylor's comment about seeing things clearer when you talked about it. She needed clarity in a big way.

"They already did," she said from the kitchen. "The last time I saw them was twenty-five years ago when we were separated through no intent of our own."

"Sounds like someone you cared for quite a bit, and you don't know whether you should get involved with them again. Maybe you're afraid to get hurt again? Or maybe you think one of you has changed and aren't the person you remember?" The last was said right behind her, startling her. She sloshed a little coffee onto the counter.

Alice gaped at her as she mopped up the spill with a dishcloth. "How on earth did you get all of that from two short sentences?"

"Am I right?"

Alice handed her a cup, and they went back to the table. "Yes."

"Well, you told me once that you moved here with nothing, and the Helmstaads took you in. Whatever happened to separate you two must have been traumatic to keep you from going home to Topeka. And if you didn't have intent to separate, it was probably heartbreaking. Plus, you asked me what I would do, which tells me you're looking for advice. So I assumed."

Alice wagged a finger at her. "You're good. You should look for a job as a detective."

"I try." Taylor batted her eyelashes. "Who is it? Not a high school sweetie? What were you doing before you came here? I've heard rumors, but I don't gossip."

"What rumors?" Alice could guess.

Taylor raised her chin. "I said, I don't gossip."

"It's about me. I should know."

"Don't you?"

"When did you become a reality show host?"

"I am not."

"Tell me."

"The rumor on the street is that you used to be in a religious cult." The shock on Alice's face must have been apparent because Taylor pointed at her. "The look tells me it's true, and you're surprised that people know…or at least strongly suspect."

"I am shocked. I wasn't in a cult. I was a nun for five years, but I never told anyone." It was good to get it off her chest. "Why do people think I was in a cult?"

"I don't know. Maybe it's the way you used to dress until Mikayla did that makeover, the religious stuff you do, and how you carry a crucifix sometimes. I mean, you work at the mission, too."

"It's a rosary and working at the mission means nothing." All the other stuff was legit, as Taylor liked to say. In fact, Mikayla had gently told her that the clothing she used to wear until recently gave off an air of some kind of fundamentalist religious organization; that had been the catalyst for her new wardrobe purchases. "But I guess it makes sense. Why has nobody asked me about it?"

Taylor comically rolled her eyes. "Excuse me, ma'am? Were you at one time affiliated with a religious cult? Just curious." Taylor acted like she was pointing a microphone.

Alice had to laugh. "Fair point."

Taylor gave her a look saying she knew. "So what was it?"

"Pardon me?"

"What caused you to be booted out of the cult?"

"It was a convent."

"Did you have an affair with a priest?"

Alice put her hand to her chest. "My God, no."

"What was it?"

"I fell in love with one of my classmates, another nun."

Taylor held up her hand, palm out. "Wait. Where are the cookies you promised? And you told me on Friday that you aren't gay."

Alice got up to get the cookies. "I lied. It was an automatic response, and I regretted it immediately."

When she came back with the plate, Taylor smirked and nodded knowingly. "I knew it."

"What?" Alice pulled the plate back just before she could take a cookie.

"You don't have a poker face. I knew you were lying. Was she the first?"

Alice put the plate next to Taylor and sat. "The only. In fact, it was easy to lie because I have only ever been in love with her. I wonder if I'm just a one-person person. Brandi once told me about romantic and sexual orientation and all of the iterations, and I've wondered if maybe I'm just demisexual."

Taylor nodded enthusiastically. "I don't know Brandi, but I know demisexual is when you can only be attracted to someone who you've formed a deep connection with."

"Yes, but I've had connections with men, and I've never been attracted to one. I think I'm just a one-person lesbian." Alice felt her checks flame. She'd never talked so openly about her own sexuality before. Not even with Brandi, who happened to be an expert.

What had happened to her and Bridge had happened over time and kind of evolved. They'd never spoken about it, even with each other. It wasn't supposed to happen. It was against the rules. It was against their religion. If they had talked, it would have meant they were admitting to doing something wrong.

The only time it had been spoken of was when Sister Mary Caroline had walked in on them. Mother Superior had called what they'd done "egregious homosexual acts." The interesting thing was that, while they had engaged in "egregious homosexual acts" many times prior, they hadn't been engaging in anything other than sleeping when Sister Mary Caroline had discovered them in Sister Mary Bridget's twin bed. They'd been exhausted from heavy gardening work the day before and had fallen asleep during nightly prayers. They'd almost always done their nightly prayers together, and most of the time, they'd fallen asleep together. Their error that night was that they hadn't set the alarm.

"This other nun, your one and only love, has contacted you?"

Alice nodded, images of long ago still rotating through her mind. "We serendipitously met yesterday. She came into the gift shop at the mission."

Taylor squirmed and dropped her chin into her propped-up hand. "What did you do when you saw her?"

"I lost control of my mind."

"You glitched out?" Taylor seemed to understand.

"Completely."

"In a way that sent her packing? Or some other way?"

"She didn't run. She's not a very timid person. She seemed excited to see me and asked if we could get coffee. I had a hard time thinking or talking, but I agreed to the coffee and…oh my goodness." Alice got up quickly. "I left the carafe on the counter. The whole thing has me all cattywampus."

Taylor followed her to the kitchen. "Keep talking. I want details. What did she look like? Was she different than you remembered? Was there still a spark?"

Alice continued to relate what had happened. Bridge was beautiful, fashionable, and sophisticated. So different on the outside from when they were in the convent together but so much the same on the inside. Alice purposely didn't answer the spark question because that would lead to other questions that she wasn't ready to talk about. Her skin grew hot just thinking about it. She did say they were meeting again that evening.

"Are you excited or nervous?"

Alice tilted her head back and squeezed her eyes closed. "Both."

"You ignored the sparks question, but there were sparks. I can tell. I'd tell you not to be nervous, but you will be. So go on this date, and if you both have fun, arrange another one and so on. Just like regular people."

"What if…something happens?"

"Enjoy yourselves. Go with the flow. You're both grown-ups, and there are no religious rules in your way now. Have fun. Hump each other's brains out."

Alice could have burst into flames with embarrassment. "There will be no humping."

"Don't disappoint me, Alice. I need this…I mean, *you* need this. Go get you some."

"Well, I certainly won't be reporting back to you about anything if something does happen, which it won't. I haven't seen Bridge in a very long time. There will not be any getting of some or humping or any other sexual euphemism."

"Whatever." Taylor looked into the depth of her mug. "What do you put in your coffee, anyway?"

Alice explained the magic of Mr. Coffee while a herd of buffalo careened in her stomach. As much as she knew there would be none of the intimate stuff Taylor had encouraged her to do, the idea of it still caused her heart to race and her temperature to soar. Memories of stolen moments from their past served to fan the fire even more.

Chapter Ten

W"here are we going?" Alice asked.
"It's close." Bridge pulled into the parking lot near the south jetty at Oceanside Harbor Beach. The butterflies she'd been feeling since the previous evening when Alice had agreed to spend time with her today were doing nonstop aerial gymnastics in her belly.

"Is this a sunset thing?"

Bridge smiled. She and Alice had often sat in the courtyard of the convent and watched the sunset. During the summer, sunset had usually occurred during a period of silence just before bedtime, and they'd never been able to speak. She was looking forward to sharing the experience without the constraints of silence.

"It is. I brought a picnic. It's in the back."

They got out and walked around Bridge's black Lexus LX, her one splurge when she'd received her promotion to regional vice president of sales two years earlier. She'd imagined the luxury of it for road trips, although she hadn't gone on many. When she'd put the dinner in the back, she'd daydreamed about how she might go on some with Alice. But today, she was going for making Alice feel special by remembering some of her favorite things. She popped the rear hatch and turned.

"You look beautiful. I meant to say so when I picked you up, but you asked me about my day, and I got caught up in telling you about how much fun I had sailing this afternoon." Bridge smiled at the coral nail polish on Alice's toenails that peeked out from her sandals. "For some reason, I imagined you as a skirts and blouse person. Is that weird? But the flowy linen Sundance vibe really suits you."

Alice's checks turned pink as she looked down, smoothing the front of the cream-colored linen tunic she wore over khaki green pants. "Thank you. Sundance, huh? I didn't know there was a name for this. To me, it's kind of a dressy-casual thing. It's funny you say that. For a long time, I was the skirts and blouse type. I only recently switched it up. Ironically, it was only after I switched it up that I was told that my previous fashion choices made me look like a member of a cult."

Bridge shook her head and lowered her sunglasses. "A cult? Really? Harsh."

"Tell me about it." Alice laughed. "My friend Mikayla has been taking me shopping. I'm going for a beachy aesthetic."

Bridge pushed her sunglasses on top of her head and looked Alice up and down. She hoped it looked appreciative and not creepy. Alice's blush and shy smile seemed to point to the former. "Beachy *aesthetic*, huh? Well, it's a good statement on you."

"My friend Taylor introduced me to the word. It's the new way to say trendy. It sounds so sophisticated, which is what you are with your stylish pants and funky button-ups."

Bridge moved some of the things she'd brought. "It's interesting. I almost miss when we simply had to layer on the same robes, bibs, and sashes everyone else was wearing. We didn't have to have shoes and belts to complete different outfits. It didn't take up a ton of closet space. So much less complicated."

"Baby blue suits your gorgeous eyes."

Bridge looked at her tailored button-up with French cuffs. It was white with a pattern of little blue forget-me-nots all over it. She hadn't chosen it for the meaning the flowers possibly presented, but it occurred to her that it suited the nature of their reunion. She broke out in goose bumps even in the warm sunshine.

Alice peeked into the pile of stuff. "A picnic, huh? I was almost sure you were going to take me to a swanky restaurant with candles and mood music."

"I would never be that predictable." Bridge smiled at how close Alice had guessed as she handed over one of the smaller bags and hefted the other over her shoulder as she carried an old-school wicker basket. She'd almost taken Alice to Tableau, but she'd wanted it to be just them. No staff hovering. No pressure to give up the table for the next reservation as soon as they'd finished.

Alice's excited laugh was almost a giggle. "I'm intrigued." She looked at Bridge through her lashes as they walked. "There's something a little more…confident about you now."

"Oh yeah? As opposed to yesterday or in general?"

"In general. I think we were both a little unsteady yesterday. I know I was. At least before the phone call. I really like this confidence on you."

They'd reached the picnic area, and Bridge turned as she set the basket on the bench next to a table. "I can honestly say, I don't feel so confident right now. I'm afraid I'll wake up to find that this has been a dream."

"It's not. You feel too real." Alice placed a hand on her arm.

Bridge's world froze, and every bit of her awareness abruptly centered on the weight on her bicep. The rest of the world melted away. It was just her and Alice and the heat through her sleeve that was almost cataclysmic. The first touch they'd exchanged in twenty-five years rushed through her like a tsunami.

She stood still for a minute, even after Alice took her hand away. Her mind had either been wiped clean, or it was overwhelmed by the sensation. Either way, she couldn't catch a thought, find any words, or remember what she was supposed to be doing. As her senses came back to her, she noticed Alice looking like she felt. Her eyes were wide until she blinked a couple of times and took a deep breath.

Ah yes. Bridge was getting the picnic ready. Feeling the weight of Alice's gaze, she spread a red-and-white checkered tablecloth over the concrete table under the expansive pergola. There were at least a dozen tables, but they were the only ones there in the pre-dusk. A few other couples were sitting out on the sand. September on a weekday felt like they had the entire beach to themselves. Next came the wineglasses, a corkscrew, and a special bottle.

"Oh my gosh! That's the wine Father Gregory liked so much. How did you find it?"

Bridge held up the red blend, pleased that Alice remembered. "They make it in Temecula. He probably bought it by the case from the vineyard."

"I drink it, but I'm a wine illiterate." Alice took the bottle and studied it. "Is it good? I can't remember. We only had that one taste when we were invited into the rectory, and he commended us for the Easter Mass. We were so nervous, neither of us took more than a sip." She laughed. "I thought it was special religious wine because of the angels on the label." She handed the bottle back.

"I haven't tried it yet. I went for a drive over the weekend and saw a sign for Santo Gabriel vineyard and had to check it out. Lo and behold, I found this. I think it was an omen that I was going to see you the next day." She could feel Alice's gaze and proximity as she poured. When she offered her a glass, Alice's eyes were shining with tears.

"Here's to finding each other again," Alice said. They clinked glasses, their eyes glued to one another. Bridge felt the sting of tears, too.

She barely tasted the wine, she was so moved, but Alice's glistening eyes spilled over. Bridge stepped closer. "I know. I feel it, too."

Alice squeezed her eyes closed. "I hate to say it, but it's awful. I can't..."

What was happening? Bridge stepped back, trying to work out how Alice went from giggly to dejected so quickly. "I don't understand."

Alice dropped her chin, looking into her glass. "I mean, it's so sweet of you, but this is horrible."

Although it was a warm day, Bridge was swallowed in a vacuum of bitter cold and utter isolation. The beach, the waves, the sunshine…all of it was beyond an invisible barrier, leaving her small and vulnerable. "Horrible?" She could barely feel her lips as she spoke. She couldn't breathe. How had the moment gone from…

"I don't know how he could drink this." Alice was still looking at her glass. Swirling it. Giving it a sniff.

When those words made it through the static of disappointment, Bridge's limbs grew weak. Literally. She'd always considered that a figure of speech. "The wine. You're talking about the wine." The layer of crystalized separation that had hardened over her began to crack. Oxygen filled her lungs again. The snap back between such opposite emotions almost made her dizzy.

"What did you…oh no…did you think I was talking about…" Alice waved her hands between them. "God, no. I love that we're… no, no, no. It's the wine. It's terrible. How did Father Gregory drink this? How did we?"

Giddy with relief, Bridge took a deep drink that tasted as if the fruit had gone bad before it was able to ferment and that more than a little pine scented floor cleaner had been added to it. Sputtering after forcing herself to swallow it, she poured what remained in her glass into the sand and buried it. "Gah! I remembered that it wasn't great, but this is…yuck." She wiped her mouth with the back of her hand. "It's all coming back to me now."

Alice wiped her cheeks. "It made my eyes water," she said as she poured the rest of her wine out, too. "I must have developed a slightly more sophisticated palate, after all."

"Lucky for us, I brought a backup." Still feeling the effect of the wide emotional swings, Bridge pulled another bottle from the bag, a vintage she knew she liked. "This will be much better. But just to be safe, we'll let it breathe a bit."

"The other was just for nostalgia's sake?"

Bridge shrugged. "I may have bought half a case."

Alice's smile was helping to right her tilted world. "It's the thought that counts. It's a shame you bought a case."

"Half a case."

"Still, very sweet."

Sweet on you. She used to say it back when they'd dared to flirt when no one was around. It had been one of the ways she'd been able to let Alice know she had more than sisterly feelings for her. Feelings that were rapidly reemerging. Initially, she'd worried the feelings were more hope than reality, but after their call the night before—and seeing her again like this—Bridge knew it was more. Her feelings were real. She'd missed Mary Alice: talking to her, seeing her across the long table at mealtimes, exchanging looks, anticipating the next time they could be alone. And not just to kiss, or more, but to study together, to sit quietly, to pray.

Alice's eyes still sparkled when she talked about things that made her happy or excited. Her hands still drew shapes in the air. She still did little dancing steps as she walked. But most of all, when Alice looked at her, Bridge felt seen. For who she really was. Alice saw the good, the bad, her potential and dreams. The way Alice saw her made her want to be the best person she could be.

The memories of her had made Bridge pursue the life she had. She'd wanted to make Alice proud, and along the way, she'd found pride in herself.

It didn't hurt that Alice was the epitome of unvarnished beauty, even though beauty had never impressed Alice as much as it did Bridge. They'd spoken about it quite a bit back in the convent when they'd debated theological philosophy, from the concept of beauty that was skin-deep to people who were beautiful inside and out.

When Alice complimented her, Bridge knew it was for much more than her appearance. Alice saw souls.

Bridge wanted to be like that. This very concept had allowed them to think of what they'd had together as more than a physical thing. Rather, an ethereal concept, transcending the outward trappings of gender and social constructs.

Goose bumps traveled up Bridge's arms and across her shoulders. Remembering the transcendence they'd experienced brought back heady times of conversations, companionship, and their emotional and physical connection.

She hadn't come close to sharing that with anyone else. Ever.

And she'd missed it.

"Wait until you see the rest." She meant the dinner, but she was thinking about all that seeing Alice again foretold. Swallowing back emotion, she lifted two foil-covered dishes from the insulated bag, followed by a wrapped baguette and two smaller dishes with salad.

Alice stepped toward her. "I just got a whiff of oregano. Is that garlic?"

"It might be." Bridge smiled as she stacked the food containers and began to lay out two fancy dinner plates with intricate ivy patterns along the edges, followed by two matching salad plates, and real silverware rolled in linen napkins that matched the tablecloth. Finally, she lifted out a candle in a tall glass container, lit it with a long match, and placed it in the center of the table. "Have a seat, madame. Dinner is ready."

Alice did, and Bridge served her. "Chicken parm! My favorite. And is that chopped salad?"

Bridge was pleased at her reaction. "It is. I got the food from Woody's."

The restaurant had been the place they'd gone on their one outing that had been closest to a date. It was rare that the nuns had been allowed to go anywhere unless in a group or running an errand. Alice never knew the contortions Bridge had gone through to pull it off.

Emotions played behind Alice's eyes "I haven't been back since…well, in a lot of years."

"We're both in for a treat."

After plating their food, Bridge tucked the containers back into the bags and stored it all under the table. She poured fresh wine before taking a seat. She was about to offer a toast when she noticed Alice's head bowed in prayer. She bent her head out of respect, but that habit had left her many years earlier. Right about the time she'd left the convent.

Right about the time she'd last seen Alice.

To her surprise, the usual silent swirl of resentment she experienced toward overt religious gestures didn't swallow her this time. In a way it was familiar. And over quickly, thankfully.

"This is so nice," Alice said after lifting her head. "I expected we'd be sitting on a blanket in the sand."

"That might be nice another day. This evening, I prefer my dinner without sand in it." Bridge lifted her glass.

"Indeed," Alice said, lifting her glass in turn.

"To the mysteries of life that lead us back to the people we treasure."

"Amen." Alice's eyes were glistening again. She hadn't sampled her new wine yet, so Bridge knew those tears were from her heart.

She pulled up an app on her phone that played cello music.

"Candlelight, music, Italian food. If there's tiramisu in one of those bags, I'm going to have to marry you."

Bridge cut into her chicken. "Whose last name are we going to use?"

Alice tipped her head. "What does that mean?"

Bridge's face flushed, something she rarely felt. Maybe her little joke had gone too far, too fast. "It means you guessed correctly about the tiramisu." Alice's delighted smile and clapping put her worry away. "How could I bring Woody's without your favorite dessert?"

"You remembered."

Bridge had never forgotten. "Do you remember when we would sneak off to that little Italian deli next to the grocery store when we were supposed to be shopping for Sister Mary Charlie?"

Alice nodded, smoothing the cloth with both hands. "This tablecloth makes me feel like we're right back there. I can't eat a meatball sub without thinking about that place."

"We'd split one so we could finish before we got back."

"We thought we were so slick until Mother Superior handed you a handkerchief and asked how you enjoyed your sandwich."

"Secret snacks always taste so much better than ones you get to enjoy in the open."

Alice raised an eyebrow. "I haven't had to sneak anything in so long, I forgot about the tickle of anticipation. Would those sandwiches taste the same today?"

"This reminds me of our conversation last night."

Alice stared at her wineglass, a smile quivering on her mouth. "Are you comparing our past...relationship to meatball subs?"

A flutter of anticipation erupted in Bridge's chest and floated lower. Alice calling her out revealed that she was probably on the same wavelength. "Secret sandwiches, Father Gregory's wine, novice nuns praying passionately in pajamas."

A giddy sort of tension filled the air as they ate and exchanged glittery-eyed glances. Alice was quiet for a moment, and Bridge suspected she was thinking about them kneeling, side pressed to side. She wondered if Alice had ever prayed for kisses, too.

When Bridge stood to get the tiramisu, it was because she needed something to distract her to keep from exploding from the feelings building inside her.

"The lure of the forbidden fruit." Alice looked up, contemplating her. Her gaze carried a heat Bridge had rarely felt, and it had never seeped into her soul like it was doing now. Not even back then, when their actions could have, and ultimately did, cost them so much. Something told her that they didn't have to worry about things not living up to what either of them had built up in their minds.

She opened the dessert, placing it on plates. When Alice got up, Bridge gestured for her to take one. Alice continued to walk around the table without a word, finally resting a hand on her arm. The touch reignited that heat Bridge had felt earlier. Their five inches or so of height difference was even more pronounced so close.

Alice's eyes pierced her as she reached up and pulled her in, kissing her. It was a brief kiss, almost chaste, but the electricity was off the charts. When Alice let go, and Bridge opened her eyes, she saw shock in Alice's expression.

"That was unexpected," Bridge said.

Alice took a long breath. "For both of us. One second, I was sitting over there thinking of secret sandwiches." She glanced at the other side of the table. "And the next, I was standing here." She was staring at Bridge's mouth, and Bridge felt it like a physical touch. Not as tantalizing as Alice's actual lips but enough to make her insides feel like liquid. She wanted to wrap her arms around Alice's waist, but she was frozen solid, afraid to shatter the moment.

Bridge breathed in, unable to do anything about how uneven it sounded. "It seemed like you knew exactly what you were doing."

Alice wouldn't look her in the eye. "I don't think I was controlling my body. All I remember thinking about was whether kissing you would be the same if it wasn't secret."

"Was it?"

Alice shook her head. "There's nothing keeping us from doing it. No one we need to hide from." Her eyes drifted skyward for a brief second before drifting across Bridge's face, landing back on her lips. "It was better."

"Absence makes the heart grow fonder?" Bridge asked, and Alice shrugged. Bridge nearly laughed. "If you were looking for God a second ago, I don't think they care."

Alice's eyes grew slightly haunted. "Old habits."

"So?"

"I think I need to let it marinate."

"Me too." Bridge felt off-kilter. "I didn't expect there to be kisses tonight."

"I've been thinking about them since the moment I saw you again."

A shadow of something familiar filled Alice's expression. An innocent desire, the one Bridge used to be familiar with, mixed with a new need that had gone from innocent to intense over the course of so many years apart.

Bridge looked at the plates she'd prepared. "Shall we finish eating and talk about this unexpected turn of events?"

Alice stepped aside and smoothed the front of her top, seemingly nervous. Bridge couldn't help but think that the women she'd dated after Alice had been so very different, but none of them had affected her this way.

Not that she and Alice were dating.

Or were they? Was this the first of others?

As Alice went back to her seat, Bridge considered the passion she wielded. Bridge ached to see the very soul of the woman who didn't know how to hold back once she let go. That was the Alice she knew, the Alice she remembered, the Alice she'd missed with a longing pain that had never diminished.

"I want more," she said. When Alice's fork paused halfway to her mouth, Bridge realized she'd said it out loud. "Kisses, I mean. I've yearned for you every day since that morning when everything happened."

Alice placed her fork back on her plate, clearly surprised. "I try not to think about that morning. I'd hoped they wouldn't punish you."

"They had to punish us. It was obvious what was going on."

"They caught us in an innocent embrace that morning. I wanted to tell Mother Superior it was all my fault. That I'd climbed into bed with you while you were sleeping. That I'd had another nightmare. Or even that my desire for you was unrequited. But she did all the speaking. I was mute. I couldn't find any words."

Bridge was moved. "It wouldn't have worked. I told her you'd had a nightmare, and I lured you into my bed because I had a secret crush on you."

Alice laughed. "We really did have plausible deniability. You heard my cries after my first nightmare and comforted me. After that, we didn't bother to make excuses."

"I just don't want you to think you failed me. Do you still have the nightmares?"

"They've gotten better over time." Alice took a bite of dessert. "I hoped you hadn't been expelled, too. But when I visited the convent after everything, you never came out. I sent a letter that came back with 'not at this address.' Still, I hoped that maybe they'd sent you to another convent."

Bridge was glad she'd been kicked out. There was no way she could have stayed without Alice. "It was cruel not letting us know what happened to the other."

Alice's shoulders slumped, and she looked at Bridge with tortured eyes. "It killed me not to know. I went to the convent all the time in the hope that I'd hear something about you." She smiled ruefully. "When they moved with Santo Benedictine College to the new campus in the hills, I started going to the mission, hoping I'd see you there. I'd sit in the last pew, praying you would walk in. One day, Sister Mary Caroline came in. She seemed shocked to see me and asked if I would take a walk with her. I didn't feel like I had a choice, so I followed her. We sat on the bench near the giant pepper tree. She told me she was sorry."

"For what? What we did was not her fault."

"Turning us in. I don't think it was her fault, either." Alice blew out a breath. "I can't say I didn't want to shoot the messenger for a long time, though."

Bridge laughed, too. "It was her duty. A mortal sin is a transgression she couldn't ignore,"

Alice shrugged. "She was sorry for how things turned out. She said we were both good nuns and should have been offered alternative consequences. She insinuated it wasn't the first time nuns had been caught in…compromising situations."

Bridge wanted to argue that they'd both been fully dressed and sleeping. She wanted to say that it was simply their superiors' dirty minds and was surprised how this fresh anger rose inside her. It was almost as if it had just happened. She had to remind herself that they'd had sex many times before then. And it was against the rules to sleep in anyone's bed but one's own. Any arguments were simply rhetoric. "Were those nuns kicked out, too?"

"No. She hinted that we were used as an example."

Bridge was shocked. She tried to remind herself that she was happy that things had happened the way they had. Except for losing Alice. That part had been unbearable. It still was. It seemed impossible that they were here now, after all this time. "What did you say?"

"I told her I'd forgiven her."

"Had you really?"

Alice nodded. "I certainly had my moments, but she was simply performing her duties. She regretted that Mother Superior wouldn't give us any information about each other, so she said you had gone home to your family. She told me your last name, too."

"That's it?"

Alice nodded.

"She randomly ran into you at church, gave you this information, and left? Did you ask her why?" Anger rose in Bridge again, the swiftness and volume continuing to catch her off guard. She reminded herself that this was new information. She might have made peace with what had happened long ago, but the ache of losing Alice had never fully healed. "I'm not angry with you. If my tone seemed…I'm just…I'm not angry with you. I never was."

"Of course. It may have been years later, but I'd been left at a bus station, brokenhearted, confused, and with no option or desire to go back home. I was forced to rebuild my future with nothing but the clothes I'd entered the convent in, and two hundred and fifty dollars in a white envelope. I had lots of questions."

"What did she say?"

"It was her day off, and she'd visited the mission to get some variety." Alice laughed, and Bridge wondered if they were thinking the same thing: that nuns had no concept of variety, something that had become wholly evident when she'd returned to a secular life. "She said she wanted to talk to me when I'd come back seeking information, but she wasn't allowed. She wanted me to know she didn't share the Church's views about homosexuality. It wasn't a thing she'd thought about until we were punished for it. Of course, it was too late at that point, but she was trying to make changes from the inside in the small ways she could."

"Too late for her to do what? Mother Superior made the call."

"But Sister Caroline was the one who'd turned us in."

Bridge sighed. She was tired of talking about it. It wasn't going to change anything. "I suppose you're right. I'm just disappointed in Mother Superior."

"Why?"

"She knew about us sneaking to get sandwiches, and she never scolded us."

"Sandwiches and breaking our vows are two very different things."

"I know. But she'd always been cooler than that. I guess this just proves that I was never meant to be a nun. I've always been a rule follower. I feel safe when there are rules that protect us and make society run smoother. But seriously, what good is served by preventing two people from loving one another? Who were we hurting?"

Alice gave a half laugh, half groan. "That's a very deep question, and the sunset is just starting to get good."

Bridge glanced over her shoulder at the western horizon. Soft pink was beginning to tinge the sky. "You're right." She looked at their plates. "It looks like we're both finished. How about we watch the sunset?"

Alice smiled, and Bridge was once again nearly destroyed by her beauty, especially in the golden light. "That's a great plan."

Bridge gathered their dishes and stored them back in the picnic basket. "Would you like another glass of wine while we watch God paint by numbers?"

"I believe I could be talked into another, yes."

Bridge poured them both generous refills. "Sit on this side. We can lean back against the table. Are you chilly? I brought a blanket."

Alice smiled affectionately. "You came prepared."

Bridge was transported back to when they were younger. Alice would almost glow when Bridge had done anything nice for her. It was as if she wasn't used to it. Because of that, Bridge would have done almost anything to make her smile like that. "I just wanted tonight to be nice."

She spread a blanket on the seat and gestured for Alice to sit, leaving several inches between them. She laid another blanket over their laps. When their eyes met, they both smiled and scooched a little closer. Not touching, but close enough for Bridge to feel the minimal space between them. She wasn't one to fill silences, but the proximity and the romantic sunset were almost too much to take. She reached back to get their wineglasses. "Tell me about what you've been up to since that fateful day."

Alice rolled her shoulders, something she'd done a few times now, a mannerism she hadn't had before. A shadow of regret passed through Bridge at having missed out on Alice's life for so many years. She'd like to have seen her transformation into the woman she appeared to be now, who looked much the same except for a few more smile lines and features that had grown more defined over the years. Bridge experienced a small thrill realizing there were new things to be discovered about Alice, softening the earlier pang of regret.

"Let's see," Alice said. "I told you already that I couldn't bring myself to get on the bus home."

"Feel you there," Bridge said, breathing out a long breath. Getting off the train at Mission Street when it had pulled into San Francisco had been one of the hardest moments of her life.

"Were you scared to face your family?" Alice asked.

"Mostly my brother. He'd been the most surprised about me joining the convent in the first place. When he and my parents saw me off, his last words to me were, 'I give it two months, tops.' It had been almost five years, but I was still worried he would tease me."

"Did he?"

"Surprisingly, no. He'd grown up. He was unnaturally kind to me." Bridge sighed and waved in a "give me more" gesture. "We were talking about you. Why didn't you go home?"

"It wasn't my home anymore. I became a guest in our house the minute I was accepted into the convent, with the full expectation that I wouldn't be back. After the first year or so, I'd fallen out of touch." She spoke without a trace of emotion, good or bad.

Realizing that Alice had truly lost everything when she was expelled from her calling forced a torrent of sorrow through Bridge. And placed yet another brick of bitterness in the wall she'd erected between her heart and the Church. "I remember you telling me about the tradition where the oldest daughter in your family always became a nun. You'd been so proud to be the chosen one. In my eyes, you were Catholic nobility, ordained from above." Alice had seemed to be a living angel in almost every essence back then. All that reverence Bridge felt was still very much in place, although the light was one hundred percent from Alice, and the Church held no stake in it.

In a way, that made Alice that much more ethereally divine. God, her heart ached with gratitude for having this second chance. Everything contributed to the swelling of emotion within her: the sunset, the breeze, the smell of the ocean, the overwhelming energy of Alice merely centimeters away. A symphony of everything in existence that was right.

Alice chuffed. "Embarrassingly enough, in a way, I felt like we were, too. I knew I would be a nun before I could even walk."

Bridge's former awe about Alice's family tradition turned sour. It seemed cruel that they'd taken all agency away from those daughters before they'd even known who they were. "The sacrificial lamb."

"Pretty much. Going back home would have added insult to injury to me, but it would have devastated my family."

Bridge wished she'd known Alice had nowhere to go. They'd known each other so deeply in so many ways, but they'd known nothing of each other outside the constructs of the convent.

Imagining Alice thrust alone into the world ripped her heart open. Her eyes blurred with tears. "What did you do?"

Alice's eyes were focused out over the water and didn't seem to notice her reaction, thankfully. "What I always do. I prayed for a sign. No sooner had I said amen than a couple in the bus station offered me a place to live."

Bridge remembered her saying a little bit about this before. "They helped you get a teaching job, right?"

"At a nearby middle school. I taught there for a few years until Santo Benedictine and the convent relocated, and the historical society took over the tours and oversight of the mission property, and then I went back to doing the tours. I'm now the assistant to the executive director of the historical society. My boss, Chandra, runs all the missions in California. I still live in Oceana. I bought my own place several years ago."

Bridge swayed closer, pressing their shoulders together, shocking herself by how easy it was to slip back into their old familiarity. In the same breath, it made her self-conscious, and she wondered if Alice minded. The way she leaned, too, made Bridge think that she didn't mind. She didn't want to overthink it and just relaxed into it.

"You just had a full-on internal debate about whether it was okay to touch me, didn't you?" Alice asked, shimmying against her.

Bridge couldn't help a half laugh. "I used to wonder if you could read my mind, now I know you can."

Alice patted her leg. "You've always been an open book. At least to me."

"That's scary."

"I'd never abuse my power."

"That's good to know," Bridge said, warm waves of happiness rippling through her at the nearness. "You still haven't seen your parents in all these years?"

Alice shook her head. "It bothered me for a while. Still does, if I'm honest. When social media became a thing, I looked them up. I looked you up, too. I found a few of them, but I never found you."

"I spend enough time on my computer for work."

"I wish I could say the same. I probably spend too much time on it."

"So you're friends with your family on social media?"

Alice shook her head. "I don't use my real name, and my accounts are all private. Mostly, I just check to see if everyone is okay."

"I'd probably do the same if I didn't talk to my parents and brother all the time." Bridge realized what she'd just said. "I'm sorry. That was insensitive of me."

"What? That you're close to your family? Even when I lived at home, I wouldn't have called myself close to mine. I grew up knowing I'd leave and never see them again. My interest is not out of longing to know them." She shrugged. "It's hard to explain."

"I sort of get it. I'd be curious, too."

"My mom and dad are still alive, living in the same house. He's retired from the mill. She's still a housewife. Most of my siblings live in the general vicinity of Topeka and are married with kids. Some of the kids even have kids. You'd think I'd be sad about not being part of their lives, but it's like watching them through thick glass. Interesting but not relatable. They're all very Catholic, and all the posts revolve around holidays and church events. My youngest brother became a priest. The last I heard, he's at a church in Colorado. He shows up in my other siblings' posts sometimes when he visits. My mom brags about him."

Bridge held back a few cynical comments. God. Sometimes she wished she hadn't lost her rose-colored glasses. It hurt to have so much anger boiling away inside. "Do they ever mention you? Does your mom brag about you?"

Alice nodded. "They mention me, mostly in prayers to protect me as I fulfill my calling as a nun. Maybe they think I'm cloistered away or something. In a sense, I guess I am. I have my community here, and aside from a few business trips to other missions in

California, I don't go anywhere. I'm a bit of a homebody. Besides, it's perfect here. Who needs to travel?"

Bridge couldn't understand how a family could be so blasé about never seeing a relative again. It felt dystopian. Alice, in comparison, seemed not to be bothered by it but was worried to have disappointed them. Bridge decided to play it safe. "I wouldn't say it's perfect here, but I can't complain about the weather or beautiful views." She looked pointedly at Alice, who swatted her. "The area has changed quite a bit, hasn't it?"

"You probably notice it more than I do because I've watched it happen slowly. You moved away for a couple dozen years, and then, bang, it's all rental properties and tourists."

Bridge had made more than a few trips to the area over the years, far more than her work schedule warranted. And the weather wasn't what drew her back, even after she'd lost hope of finding Alice. It had never occurred to her that she might not recognize her if she did. She needn't have worried. Besides looking mostly the same, Alice *felt* familiar. Even the way she was currently relaxed against her side. They melted together like their bodies remembered how they were supposed to fit.

"So much has changed, yes." *But not you.*

"You haven't changed much."

Bridge stared at her in disbelief. "No?"

Alice shook her head. "You're still bold, brave, and kind. Sure, the exterior is more sophisticated in your trendy getup and snazzy haircut, but if we threw a habit on you, you'd be the same Sister Mary Bridget I used to know."

"I might look a little like her, but I am definitely not the same Sister Mary Bridget."

Alice studied her, making Bridge's skin warm. "I suppose not. I mean that I feel the same when I'm near you."

The last sentence settled into Bridge's heart, completely unexpected but a piece of knowledge she needed to know. "What do you mean?"

"Safe. Seen. Accepted...other stuff, too."

Bridge pressed her shoulder more tightly to Alice's. "Other stuff, huh?"

Alice flapped a hand at her. "Yes. Other stuff." Bridge opened her mouth to ask what kind of other stuff, but Alice put her fingers on her lips. "Be polite."

"This is coming from the woman who laid a big old smooch on me just a little while ago?" Her lips still remembered the soft warmth of Alice's mouth against her own. Too brief, but long enough to reignite a swarm of emotions and familiar sensations.

Alice buried her face in her hands. It reminded Bridge of how tentative and shy she had been back in the beginning, when they'd both realized how the touches and gazes were more than just deepening friendship. They'd been doing it unconsciously for a year before Bridge had noticed. And another nine months before she was sure Alice was aware, too.

By then, they'd often fallen asleep curled around each other, always on top of the covers, nightclothes on, waking in the early morning before the bells rang. Alice would bury her face in her hands before rolling her eyes in a, "How'd that happen?" kind of way. Then, one would leave quietly, depending on whose room they'd fallen asleep in. They'd grown more self-conscious over time about what it meant as they'd woken with hands tucked under shirts or resting on a breast or with a thigh pressed against...

Parts of Bridge stirred as the memories of their dawning desire sketched sensations across her body. "I'm sorry if I embarrassed you. I loved that smooch."

"Loved?"

"Not as much as I love y...ou." Bridge held her breath. She hadn't meant to say it out loud, but there it was, out there, hanging between them, and not even the steady wind from the ocean could blow it away. The teasing little joke they'd used to say to each other had evolved into a simple telling stare they'd used during silent hours or when they were among others.

The look Alice gave her now.

Bridge continued to gaze into her eyes. "Can I hug you properly?"

"I mean, I kissed you earlier. A proper hug is…yes."

Bridge faced her more squarely and lifted her arms, inviting Alice closer, but the angle of their legs and the weird, stiff way their arms went around each other made it hard to know where to rest their hands or heads. They sort of pulled back and tried again before Bridge had to laugh. "This is not how it's supposed to go. We need to stand."

When they did, everything changed. Alice moved seamlessly into Bridge's embrace, and she delighted in the way their bodies melded to each other, filling in the spaces. Alice's head nestled perfectly under Bridge's chin, the warm air of her breath against the vee in Bridge's shirt. She inhaled the scent of Alice's hair and felt as if she hadn't taken a breath in twenty-five years. She closed her eyes against the fading colors of the sunset and relaxed, reveling in a comfort so deep and relaxing, she never wanted to let go.

CHAPTER ELEVEN

Alice took Bridge's hand and stepped into the small inflatable motorboat tied to the end of a much larger boat at the end of a dock in San Diego Bay. She did this carefully while watching a couple of harbor seals swim up looking for a snack. When they didn't get one, they flipped over like synchronized swimmers, dove under the inky water, and surfaced closer to a fisherman sitting on the rocks near a dock several yards away.

Alice took a seat, and Bridge sat near the back, leaning expertly to distribute their weight as they settled into the small craft. It had been a week since their fateful reunion at the mission, and they'd seen each other every day. Alice had never been so happy. She loved the little adventures Bridge kept finding. One day had been dinner in Del Mar, where they'd watched the hot-air balloons travel south along the coast. Another had been an after-hours tour of the San Diego Zoo Safari Park, where they'd watched the keepers feed the animals, and they got to pet the elephants. They'd also toured the Humane Society Alice volunteered at and explored the shops at Balboa Park. Mostly, they'd walked a lot in the evenings and talked. They never ran out of things to talk about.

"Are we stealing this? Or do you know the owner?" Alice asked as Bridge fired up the motor, pushed away from the slip, and drove into the channel between it and the nearby dock.

"They're both mine. They used to be my dad's, but he doesn't go out much anymore, so he gave the boat to me and my brother, but he doesn't sail, so it's basically mine."

"Thus, the name, *Bridge to Paradise.*"

She grimaced. "My mom named it when they first bought it. Boating used to be her favorite thing. I loved having it named after me when I was younger but find it embarrassing now."

"You've had to explain this a few times, haven't you?"

"Once or twice. I keep meaning to change it, but it becomes less of a priority as time goes on."

Alice watched the ripples in the water and wondered who she'd had to explain it to. Clients? Friends? Girlfriends? It made her wonder what they were to one another now. "Can I ask you a question?"

"Anything." Bridge scooped a Styrofoam cup out of the water as they passed and stowed it in a net bag in the storage bin at the back of the boat.

"Do you have..." Alice paused, wondering how to ask if Bridge had hopes one way or another about them. Because she did. She wanted to spend more time together. Beyond that, she wasn't sure what she wanted, but it wasn't just a friend. She just hadn't named all the feelings Bridge inspired in her yet.

"A girlfriend?"

That idea knocked the wind out of Alice. That hadn't occurred to her. Not at all. The prospect gave her the sensation of having passed through a frozen section of air. "That wasn't what I was going to ask, but...do you?" Alice was terrified of the answer.

Bridge pulled another cup out of the water. "Not in the last couple of years and nothing very serious for a few years before that."

Alice breathed in, the briny sea air filling her lungs with glorious oxygen.

"What's your question, then?"

Alice barely registered the question in her relief and realized they had a lot more talking to do before asking what Bridge wanted out of their...what was it? Friendship? Were they dating? Just hanging out? Situation-ship? The last one was something she'd heard on a reality show. "I should have asked if you were involved with someone before I kissed you the other day. Why don't you have a girlfriend?"

Bridge looked amused. "Are you disappointed that I don't?"

Alice tipped her head. "I can't see how you don't. You're a catch."

Bridge laughed. "I suppose it depends on who's...fishing?"

And Alice was fishing. She wanted to know what Bridge's status was, what she was working with, whether there was a chance...wait. She was getting ahead of herself. She had no experience with this sort of thing. Maybe she should just be direct. "What's your status, Gladys?"

Bridge's expression was comical. "What?"

"My grandfather used to say it. It's just a way of checking in. Besides not currently being attached, what are you looking for? Do you not want to be attached? Are you nursing a broken heart? Pining for someone?" *Please don't let it be the last one. Please.*

Bridge slowed their boat and seemed to consider the question. "I'm not against being attached, but I've never really looked for it, I guess. I just haven't found...I mean, I date. Not much lately, but there have been a few..." She shook her head. "I'm making this weird." She smiled and rolled her eyes. "I've dated on and off through the years. Went a little crazy after I left the convent. Not immediately. I missed you too much."

Alice's heart squeezed almost painfully.

"Once I broke out of my shell, I dated a lot. There were three serious relationships, but none of them lasted." She paused. "Is this okay? I'm not sure how much detail you want."

"Is it weird that I want to know everything? I seem to have encapsulated our past inside a snow globe of sorts. While I've missed you all these years, I never let myself obsess about what you were doing. I just prayed that you were happy and healthy. Tell me how you love."

Bridge laughed, and Alice felt its pleasurable vibration reverberate within her. "You, more than anyone, know how I love." Those words seemed to suck the oxygen out of Alice's lungs, and she missed some of what Bridge said as she regained her equilibrium. "…and the last one was in Baltimore. Jackie. Then, I moved to Seattle. She had her career and family, so she didn't want to move. I was sad but not heartbroken. We'd been together three years, and I was getting bored. Again. We tried to do the long-distance thing. It worked well at first. It reignited a spark. Not seeing each other all the time made the time we had together feel more exciting. I didn't miss her when I didn't see her, but the reunions were pretty spicy."

Maybe Alice didn't want to know everything after all. She could do without the spice. "What happened? I mean, to end it. Not the spicy stuff."

Bridge sighed. "The spice wore off. She met someone, which was a relief because I'd started to wonder how to break it off with her."

"Was there someone you were interested in, too?"

She shook her head. "I'd started to crave life without strings. I've gone out on two dates since then. They didn't go anywhere."

"I'll bet you get asked out all the time."

Bridge smiled wryly. "Not really. I've become a bit of a workaholic. It's one of the reasons I asked to be assigned to San Diego. I've been working too much. The company has grown enough to give other sales execs the opportunity to work with the larger clients. I think it's time for me to settle down somewhere."

Alice wanted to know more about the long-distance thing. Was that what Bridge wanted in a relationship? Did she get bored in every one? It kind of sounded like it. Maybe she wasn't the type to settle down. But Alice didn't want to sound nosey. "They retired you to San Diego?"

Bridge smirked. "I think they'll cry if I retire. I make them a lot of money. But unlike most business types, the founders are interested in the well-being of the staff. They try to help us find balance."

"It sounds like a great company."

"I love what I do, and I love the impact we make on people's lives. I don't know when I'll want to retire or if I ever will. But I did decide recently to stop working at full throttle. I'd like to travel for pleasure more. Go sailing more often. I'm working on transferring the biggest accounts to dedicated teams. A lot of the others will go to the regionals. I'm going to focus on a handful of West Coast clients who have signaled they want to get more involved with research."

"It's great that you know what you want to do and have the ability to make it happen."

"I've worked hard to get here, but I got lucky along the way." She waved dismissively. "Enough about my boring work. I need to know your relationship status, Gladys."

Alice should have expected it, but she seriously hadn't anticipated the question being turned back on her. Her answer was simple, but expressing it wasn't. "I haven't…there hasn't…I mean…I don't date." She could have said: "There's never been anyone else. In my bed or otherwise. It's always been you. Only you." How sad and pitiful was that? How terrifying for Bridge. She'd surely run as fast and far as she could.

Bridge let go of the rudder, and the boat slowed, and the motor quietly hummed. "It's my turn to be incredulous. You must get asked out all the time."

Alice giggled nervously. Maybe she'd dodged scrutiny about her sexual history. But Bridge apparently considered her dating material. There was that. "Nope. No one wants to date an ex-nun. At least this one. Shia would say my vibe is all wrong. She's direct like that."

"Who's Shia? What does that vibe thing even mean?"

She sounded offended on her behalf, which tickled Alice. "Shia would never say that specifically about me. Just in general. She's all into vibes. I don't know." She had a hard time explaining it. How could she say she wasn't the dating type without sounding pathetic or driving Bridge away? "I don't put myself out there. Before Mikayla convinced me to do a clothing makeover, I didn't put a whole lot of energy into fashion or having any sort of aesthetic. I work. I go to church. I volunteer. I bake cookies for my friends. My world is very small."

Bridge's eyes grew soft. "I think you're amazing. You're the exact definition of beautiful, inside and out."

The flame of Alice's blush felt like a blowtorch. It took everything in her not to say something to minimize the compliment. She studied her hands to regroup. Bridge thought she was beautiful. A shiver played up her spine. She hated to have this kind of scrutiny on her. "To sum it up, no one's going to be upset that I kissed you," she said in an effort to close this line of conversation.

"I guess it would have been a problem if either of us had someone."

"True."

"You were going to ask me something else."

"I was?"

"A bit ago. You said you had a question, but it wasn't about whether I had a girlfriend. I guess I was projecting. To be truthful, I wanted to know if you had one. Now that we know that about each other, what was it you wanted to ask?"

Alice paused. The question she'd wanted to ask would have been jumping the gun. The fact that it had been interrupted was probably a good thing. But now, she was left at a loss for words. She was never at a loss for words. Even if it was silly or weird or random, she always had something to say.

"Well?" Bridge prompted after an uncomfortable pause.

She felt like she had to ask now and forced herself. "What do you think, I mean, we were once, you know, we were…close. Now that we've reunited, or whatever this is, what, I mean, how do you want it to go?" There. She'd gotten it out. The opposite of graceful, but it was said. She was terrified for Bridge's response. And the boat was just sitting there, drifting with this awkward weight pressing down on them.

Bridge looked at her. Really looked. With a steady, intense, meaningful gaze that pierced her. "I want to *know* you. I want to be close to you. I want to learn all about what you've experienced in the last twenty-five years. I want to be your friend and maybe… more than that, if it feels right. But more than anything, I want to be the person you can be totally you with. I think we had that once. I want that again. But next level. I want to move forward together. If you do." Bridge paused; those words that must have been mined from her deepest heart. Her eyes invaded Alice's very soul. She shook her head as if she'd surprised herself. "Um, wow. I meant every word I said, but…I'm sorry. That was intense. And a lot."

Alice wanted to move toward her, yet she was glued to the spot. Not out of fear but possibility. And maybe a little afraid of tipping the boat over. But mostly possibility. "It's what I want, too." It came out as a whisper. She cleared her throat and spoke a little louder. "I don't always have the words, and sometimes, even when I do, I have a hard time getting them out, but I'm glad there's an us again. I want to see where we go from here."

The conversation reminded her of the romance novels she'd read. Not because it sounded like one, but because she'd always wished the characters would just talk about what they wanted, and they never seemed to do it until it was too late. By then, she wanted to scream at them to just tell each other how they felt. Not the "I love you" part. That had to be held back because why else would the reader keep going?

Besides, she and Bridge had already said the "I love you" years ago. The love was still there. They just needed to know if they could start where they'd left off, and right now, it seemed like that was what they both wanted. A shiver of anticipation raced through her.

Bridge seemed to relax. At least, her shoulders dropped to their normal position, and she breathed more deeply. Alice found herself wanting to say more. How much Bridge meant to her. That she still loved her. Had always loved her. But it seemed like too much, too soon. That was one thing that was different between them now. She didn't remember ever being afraid of driving Bridge away back then. There'd been nowhere to go.

She realized they were just watching one another. Taking each other in. She reached with a sandal-clad foot and gently nudged Bridge's.

Bridge pressed back. "I'm glad we got that cleared up."

"Me too," Alice said. She drummed her hands against the pontoon. "Where are you taking me in this little rig? And will I get a tour of the bigger boat?"

"If you're lucky," Bridge said, taking the tiller again and swinging it slightly to maneuver the boat through the water. She sounded a little dazed, but the easiness was back between them.

Alice raised her eyebrows and lowered her glasses an inch to look over their frame.

"That came out wrong." Bridge blushed and smiled. "I'll be happy to show you the boat." She wiggled her eyebrows. "As for where we're going, you'll see soon. It isn't far."

Alice wondered if she was talking about the exchange they'd just had or about their actual destination but decided it didn't matter because she was excited about both. "What's in the bag?" She nodded at a zippered Yeti bag Bridge had placed on the floor near her feet.

"Something I hope you enjoy, but you'll also see soon enough."

Alice leaned to look over the side. The water was deeper and darker farther out in the bay. "It's a good thing I trust you. For all I know, it's cement boots. Or worse, more of Father Gregory's special wine."

Bridge snorted. "I promise, it isn't that wine."

"But you're not denying the cement boots?"

Bridge angled the boat toward the rock-reinforced shore at the back of the bay where kayaks and other small craft bobbed on the calm water. "Anything is possible. Hold on tight. I'm turning."

"Well, it's been a good life."

Bridge maneuvered the little boat around a grid of smaller docks and back toward the water's edge. Within minutes, she'd cut the motor and tossed a little anchor over the side. They were among a scattering of kayaks and other small boats, several feet from the rocks that constituted the seawall and the fence stretching along the periphery of this part of the harbor. Their boat rocked calmly between the rocks and a floating dock. It seemed an odd destination, but people seemed to be having a good time with picnics and drinks. She wondered if it was like a block party for the harbor residents and was about to ask what the attraction was when an announcement sounded from a nearby speaker, welcoming people to Humphrey's Concerts by the Bay, a venue Alice had only been to once many years earlier. She hadn't realized that the fence at the top of the seawall was the border.

"Is there a concert tonight?"

Bridge grinned. "I remembered that you liked Natalie Merchant, and I saw that she was playing tonight. There weren't any tickets available, so I brought you here."

Alice couldn't help but be touched. It didn't surprise her. Bridge had always been a thoughtful person. "We're allowed to listen from here?"

"Apparently, it's a local thing." Bridge gestured to the small boats. "A friend from work told me about it when I mentioned that I'd rented a slip from the harbor. She said it used to be a real party out here when Jimmy Buffet played."

Alice was already excited, but a tickle of anticipation about hearing one of her favorite artists added to her excitement. "I feel like my cool points just went from negative to slightly positive, not only doing locals-only stuff but music-related locals-only stuff. I may have just peaked." She didn't mention that doing it with Bridge added a whole new level that she was trying to understand. Doing anything with Bridge drove her to the pinnacle of happiness.

Bridge laughed, and Alice added more points for being the cause of making a beautiful woman laugh like she meant it.

Before the music started, Bridge created a little nest on the floor of the boat with blankets and pillows from a plastic container at the back. In addition, rather than cement boots, she pulled out a bottle of wine from the bag—thankfully, not Father Gregory's—and snacks in a tacklebox, using the little compartments to display a variety of finger foods.

"What a delightful use of fishing equipment. You surprise me every time I see you." Alice picked out a chocolate-covered almond. "I have to tell my friend Mikayla about this. She makes charcuterie boards all the time. Sometimes, that's all she eats for dinner."

"I've eaten my share of them. Why limit yourself to just one or two kinds of food when you can have a variety of flavors to sample?" Bridge handed her a small plate and a linen napkin. "If I remember correctly, you don't like nuts unless they're covered in chocolate, and cheese isn't your friend in large amounts."

"You remember very correctly. Impressive. It's been over twenty-five years. Although, I discovered Lactaid in the meantime."

"It's easy to remember the important things." Bridge's eyes sparkled at her. "It sounds like a long time, doesn't it?"

"It *is* a long time in some ways. In others, it feels like yesterday." Alice liked how Bridge called her tastes one of "the important things."

"Funny how it can feel like both yesterday and a lifetime."

"Yeah." Alice didn't have a lot to add as a wave of remorse flowed through her. She wondered how different her life would have been if she'd been able to spend the last twenty-five years with Bridge.

"Do you have regrets?"

The question made her wonder if Bridge could read her mind. "Regrets?" Alice asked, rolling the question around in her mind. Regret was a layered concept. Did she wish they hadn't been caught? Yes. Did that mean she'd have changed their relationship? No. Did wishing she'd had more time with Bridge constitute regret? Had she ever wished she hadn't let herself get carried away with her need to be physically close to Bridge during their convent days? To break the rules when that need had led them to more intimate pursuits? "I don't think so."

"None?"

Alice tilted her head. "I feel a lot of things about our time together and how it ended. But not regret."

"Any you'd care to share?"

"I'd gladly share anything with you." She shocked herself by saying it, but it was the truth. "But I'm not sure I have names or words for all of it."

"You've always been a person who preferred to experience the things your emotions inspired rather than talk about them." Bridge's smile was gentle, almost reverent, but something twinged deep inside Alice and not in an entirely pleasant way.

"I told you I loved you the minute it occurred to me that what I was feeling was more than friendship." Where was this defensiveness coming from? She hoped Bridge didn't hear it in her voice.

"I think about that day often. In the garden, wrist-deep in soil." Her eyes grew unfocused in the lowering sun. "You straightened, kneeling between the rows, your gloved hands on your thighs, spilling dirt onto your robes. The tie of your straw garden hat dangled from your chin. You looked at me with surprise, making me worry that something had happened. 'My love for you isn't sisterly, you know. It's not friendly, either. I love you like I love Jesus, only not at all how I love him. It's a deep inside, all-consuming kind of love.'

"I memorized your words and wrote them on a piece of paper that I carried in my Bible. They've stayed with me all this time. Your cheeks went red, and you went back to digging with a fervor and a secret smile while I sat there in shock wanting to say I loved you, too."

Alice felt her cheeks grow warm, her defensiveness gone. She remembered that day like it was yesterday. Her heart had been overflowing. She couldn't not tell Bridge what she'd been feeling. "You did?"

"Yes. But Jesus got in the way." Something in Bridge's tone blunted the reignited feeling of Alice's heart blossoming again. Maybe Bridge sensed it, because she hurried to add: "It took me a while after that to know my feelings were physical as well as heartfelt."

"I already knew my feelings were physical."

"Me too." Bridge's voice shook.

"You did?" Alice repeated, back in the moment again.

Bridge nodded. "I still believed my love for you was sisterly, only with the confusing knowledge that I also wanted more, to express what I felt with touch. I knew physical love was not allowed. But the way I felt, they weren't separate. By the time we kissed, I was ready to justify the breaking of every rule to feel the way I did."

Alice nodded. "I didn't let myself think about it at all. I would never have allowed myself to love you the way I had if I did. Something in me believed that as soon as I gave words to it, I would have walled that part of myself off. I couldn't let that happen. I needed to feel that way about you. I didn't want any rules or shame to cloud my feelings."

"I'd always believed it was our naiveté that kept us from talking. My regret is not forcing us to discuss it. Maybe we could have protected what we had."

Alice realized their regrets were the same: that they hadn't talked about what they had been doing all those years ago. If they had, they might have been better equipped to ensure their privacy. "My reluctance to talk wasn't out of shame, although I did feel that later. For getting dismissed. For disappointing my family. For playing a part in whatever happened to you."

Bridge's expression was contemplative. "I notice you didn't include breaking your vows or going against church doctrine or disappointing God."

There it was again, a tone of bitterness. Alice wondered if Bridge blamed God for what had happened. Their love for God had brought them together. She wasn't sure she could bear it if Bridge had completely lost her faith. It would be like losing her soul. "Believe me, I've had moments of crisis about that, but it always comes down to the same thing. What we shared was not a weakness of spiritual or even emotional character. Love is a pure and godly thing. I felt closer to God when I was with you in mind, body, and spirit. Your presence gave me a sense of purpose larger than anything I had ever known prior to then." She shook her head. "At most, I felt like I didn't pass an unfair test of deprivation some human came up with. What's better than sharing your heart with someone?"

Bridge's eyes shimmered in the gloaming. "When you have words for something, they're gold. You should have been a poet. I love how you think."

Alice huffed. "I wish I had the clarity you have."

"I wish I had a fraction of the deep and brilliant light I see in you. I used to think it was your unwavering faith. Maybe it is. I lost mine a long time ago. I've shifted my trust to science, devoted my life to helping others. I wish it filled me with the kind of light you have, but it drives me as strongly as my former faith used to." Bridge shook her head. "That sounded almost sad, didn't it? What I meant to say is, you help me remember what matters." She handed a wineglass to Alice and poured her own. Lifting it, she smiled brightly. "To fires that burn more brightly when they join."

Alice's heart ached for her. She couldn't imagine not having faith in God. However, it had never been her way to try to convince anyone, no matter how much she loved them. It only caused more confusion and pain. And the last person she wanted to do that to was Bridge.

She did feel a small change in their connection, though. Religion had been the thing that had united them in the beginning. But she was confident that her relationship with God could serve them both.

CHAPTER TWELVE

Bridge settled against the pillows stacked against the headboard in the nondescript hotel room in Bethesda, Maryland. For once, her clients hadn't taken her up on her invitation to dinner, and she had the evening to herself. Aside from the coast-to-coast flight at the ass crack of dawn making it a very long day, the business trip was a gentle reentry back to work after having two weeks off following the move to San Diego.

The group at Walter Reed was one of her best and oldest clients, and it was time to transition them to another person on the sales team. She'd planned to be out late doing the wining and dining they usually appreciated, but they had an early morning tour the next day with her replacement.

Closing her eyes, she went over the last week. Alice's gorgeous face filled her mind, with those liquid eyes that could melt the frostiest heart. It was still hard to believe that they'd found each other again.

They'd been so young when they'd first met, a lifetime ago. Bridge tried not to think of all the time they'd wasted. Instead, she focused on how wonderful the last week had been. Getting to know Alice again, getting reminded of the girl she'd loved, and learning more about the woman she'd become, had been a gift she'd never expected. Her stomach erupted in fluttery anticipation when she imagined where it all might lead to.

In a different lifetime, she and Alice had expressed their love in every way possible. Their inexperience had made the physical part seem almost chaste in comparison to what Bridge had experienced in the years since, but making love to Alice now would be better than anything before. Their love had bloomed so slowly the first time around. It was hard not to want to rush it now. Aside from the one kiss, they hadn't touched much. Alice seemed content to go slow, and Bridge was willing to take her lead.

It still boggled her mind that she'd set her sights on being a nun based solely on a few comments by her great-grandmother. She snorted. Although the family had called themselves Catholic and Lutheran, no one other than her great-grandmother had been very religious. In fact, Bridge's father had laughingly called their family Holiday Lutherans or Holiday Catholics after they'd converted. They wore their religions interchangeably; an accessory to show off when people were looking or for a job promotion.

Jesus. It was insidious. Flock control. The idea only poured more vitriol onto her mountain of disdain.

Bridge's great-grandmother's stories of having the calling to be a nun but not following it had had a profound impact on her, who'd already had a strong attachment to her namesake. It was one of the reasons she had eagerly attended church with her great-grandmother, who'd left her a leather-bound Bible and a pearl rosary, along with a note encouraging Bridge to follow her calling. Young Bridge had never looked back.

Until the day Mother Superior had looked at her with disappointment in her wise eyes and told her that, despite how much the church's views—especially about homosexuality and abortion—were keeping women in a position of servitude, she had to follow the rules and dismiss her for breaking her vows and bringing potential scandal on the convent. At that moment, Bridge knew the rules were defined by men, throwing her into the deepest crisis of faith she'd ever known, forcing her to reimagine her future.

The most painful part being that it wouldn't include Alice.

Until a week ago.

Bridge picked up her phone. It was six o'clock in Bethesda but only three in San Diego. She selected the number in her contacts while her stomach leaped just looking at the name.

"How's Maryland?" Alice's voice sounded like she was smiling, and Bridge couldn't help but smile, too.

"Oh, you know, east coasty."

"I've never been. Aside from eighteen years in Topeka, I've never been outside of California and 99.9 percent of that has been spent in Oceanside."

"I'd rather be in Oceanside than Bethesda."

"Are the muckety-mucks at Herman Reed not buying your bionic hands?"

She knew Alice was making fun of her own lack of travel experience by saying the name wrong; it was something new and fun about her. The old Alice had been embarrassed about her small-town roots. It was a nice evolution, sexy, even. Although Alice in any form was her favorite. "*Walter* Reed and on the contrary, I've already closed the deal."

"In one day? Could you have done it over the phone?"

"People don't want to spend nearly a hundred million via a phone call. Plus, I'm introducing them to my replacement. They weren't very happy about that, but Ethan seems to have won them over. Come to think of it, I'm a little offended at how quickly they took to him."

"I'm sure they're just being nice about it. But did I hear you right?" Alice coughed. "Was that a hundred *million*?"

"You heard correctly."

"Dollars?"

"Yep. The bona fide money kind, too, not the kind that comes in board games."

"Tarnation! That's not even a real number."

"To be honest, it doesn't feel completely real, even though I deal in those numbers all the time. When it comes down to it, it's just moving numbers on spreadsheets. They partner with us on research and development, so we all get a slice of the prosthetics pie one way or another. The important thing is that the person who lost a limb gets a chance at getting back as much functionality as science can give them."

"It's so amazing. As close to being like God as you could get."

At one time, Bridge had felt something akin to that, but it had been a long time. "We've had enough people thinking they're God, if you ask me."

Alice was quiet for a moment, and Bridge worried she'd said something wrong. "I think you're right. For as much as the Bible teaches us to be Christlike, we mortals lean toward evil when we think we have attained such status."

"Amen, sister."

"Simply Alice will suffice."

Bridge could hear the smile in her voice. "You got it, Simply Alice."

"I forgot how much I like you."

"I like you, too." They were quiet for a moment, and Bridge was sure they were both thinking along the same lines: how much time they'd missed.

Alice broke the silence. "You know, I think about what important work you're doing, and it makes what I do very insignificant."

"Comparing yourself to others is a sure way to feel like that. First, most people never talk about the unappealing or boring parts of their lives, so all you see is the amazing stuff. And second, what you do has purpose and matters to many people."

Alice hummed as if she wasn't quite swayed. "I know where you're going, and I agree. The world needs people fulfilling every kind of job. I guess what I'm saying is it's not satisfying. I love the tours, but the administration doesn't captivate me like it once did, and I do a lot more administration than tours. Honestly, I'm just bored. Working at the Humane Society helps a little but not as much as I hoped."

"Maybe you need a promotion."

"I wouldn't even know how to ask."

"How did you get raises in the past?"

"My boss just gave them to me. The biggest was when the mission and the historical society came together under one office."

"Talk to your boss about it and see what opportunities there are. And at the risk of being too presumptuous, make sure they don't take it as an invitation to give you more administrative work. You'd still be bored, just busier. And probably doing it with little to no additional compensation. You should be specific about what you want."

"I'm not sure what that is."

"Something that challenges you, right?"

"Yes."

"And that interests you?"

"Also, yes."

"Maybe something that expands your knowledge?"

"You're good at this."

"I've been there. The hardest part is asking for it. But if you know what you want and that you deserve it, it makes it easier. Also, you have skills and value that's easier to nurture than replace. Remind them of that."

"You have me all excited now."

Bridge almost responded with a sexual quip, but something held her back. They'd never been on a sexually flirtatious wavelength, at least not verbally. And although they'd skirted a few flirtatious comments in the last week, they hadn't talked much about sex. Bridge wondered if she'd gone a little far in saying she wanted more. It had been obvious what she'd meant, and it had felt right to say in the moment. But when she'd gotten home that night, she'd agonized over it, especially since Alice hadn't responded.

With anyone else, Bridge would have moved them toward sex by now. But with Alice, it felt natural to take it slower. It didn't mean that her dreams weren't dominated by furtive caresses and secret rendezvous.

Chapter Thirteen

B ridge's wide smile made Alice dance in her seat as she pulled her truck up to the arrivals curb at the San Diego airport. Before Alice could jump out to greet her, Bridge dropped her carry-on into the bed of the truck and jumped into the cab. Alice had to refrain from sliding across the bench seat and throwing her arms around her.

"I was totally serious about getting a Lyft home," Bridge said.

"And I'm totally serious about how I need to drive more often to keep old Ethel here in shape." Alice stroked the steering wheel lovingly. "I so rarely need to drive anywhere that all she does is sit in the carport."

"I would never have taken you for a truck owner."

"Not just any truck. A Ford F-150. It was the only kind of car my father ever drove and his father before him. You didn't mention the name Chevrolet unless you wanted to get an earful. We couldn't even sing that old Don McLean song about the levy."

They pulled into the traffic leaving the airport.

"I did not know this allegiance to car brands," Bridge said.

Alice nodded and held her forefinger aloft. "'A person has got to have loyalties.' If my father taught me anything other than how to clean a carburetor and to love Jesus, it was that a good Ford will last you a lifetime if you take care of her."

"Is that a real accent? Or are you exaggerating?" Bridge sounded amused.

"Accent?"

"You had a bit of a midwestern drawl back in the day, but these days, you sound a little more SoCal. You had a definite twang just now."

Alice squinted before retuning her attention to the highway. "If it's a twang, it's from my grandfather. He brought our family to Topeka by way of Tulsa, Oklahoma when my dad was a kid." She huffed. "I wasn't aware that I had an accent then or now."

It was Bridge's turn to nod. "I remember noticing it when we first met, but it was more about the words. I don't notice it much now except when you're joking. Do I have an accent?"

"You sound like they do on the radio."

"Makes sense. San Franciscans don't have much of an accent. But I also travel a lot, so who knows what I've picked up over the years."

"Speaking of, how was the trip?"

"The flight back was fine. With all our phone calls, now you're caught up. Did you have the meeting with your boss this morning?"

"Oh, yeah. It turns out that she was just promoted to executive director and has been interviewing candidates for her old job as director of administration."

"She didn't tell you?"

"She didn't think I would be interested." Alice snorted. She hadn't known she'd be interested, either, until Bridge had mentioned it. "Besides, the position is in Santa Barbara."

Bridge pursed her lips. "Are you going for it?"

Alice had dismissed it as soon as her boss had mentioned Santa Barbara. "I told her if it was in San Diego, I'd want to be considered."

"Could they let you do it from here?"

"She said she could make something happen for me here, whether it was a raise or a promotion, but she wasn't sure she'd be able to move the director position. She's going to look into it, though. So one way or another, I'm going to get a raise or a promotion." She wiggled a little. It had been hard to hold on to the news, and she was happy to finally tell. She wanted Bridge to be proud of her. She couldn't remember the last time she'd wanted that from someone.

"That's amazing. We need to celebrate." Bridge swiveled to face her within the confines of her seat belt.

Alice's face burned from the attention, and she wished she could be cooler, but she wasn't as smooth as Bridge. "I wouldn't have any of these opportunities if you hadn't suggested it. I have you to thank."

"It sounds like you're a shoo-in. Why didn't she think you'd be interested?"

"Probably because she had no idea I was bored."

"What do you want to do to celebrate?"

"How about I make dinner? Afterward, we can take a walk on the beach. I enjoy watching sunsets with you. That would be a wonderful way to celebrate."

"Your wish is my command," Bridge said with a huge smile. "Why don't we go directly to your place? There's nothing at mine I need to do, and I've missed you. I mean, if you don't have other plans."

Alice felt a rush of anticipation. "There's nothing I'd rather do. I hope you still like filet mignon."

"Are you kidding me? I love it. Steak and wine is my favorite pairing."

Alice was unexpectedly beset with nerves. She'd already gone shopping for the dinner, thinking that even if Bridge didn't want to celebrate, she'd still be able to enjoy it. She wondered if any of the bottles she had on hand would be fancy enough. She wasn't as picky about what she drank…well, at least until she'd tried Father Gregory's wine. And what if she burned the steaks? Maybe the scalloped potatoes wouldn't turn out.

Bridge's hand rested on her leg, and its warmth through her sundress stopped her racing thoughts. "Don't be nervous," Bridge said. "We're just a couple of former nuns who used to fool around under the all-knowing eyes of God, Jesus, Mary, and all the saints. Often while praying together. I'd be happy with a granola bar and a game of checkers if it meant spending time with you."

Alice couldn't help the laugh that bubbled up from her chest. She pulled into the carport and smiled. "You're bad, you know. And how did you know I was nervous?"

Bridge cradled her cheek, slowly rubbing it with her thumb. "When you get nervous, you still get those little red circles here. When you're embarrassed, your face turns scarlet. Some things don't change."

"And some things do. I've learned to delegate, and I have some potatoes I need you to peel." Despite her confident tone, Alice could feel the little red spots on her cheeks burning a hole through her skin. The way Bridge was looking at her gave her a feeling she hadn't felt in twenty-five years. It wasn't just nerves. It wasn't embarrassment, either. Or tenderness or love. It was sheer, unvarnished desire. The things going on under her new linen sundress had been escalating over the last two weeks. She knew what she wanted, but she'd fallen back into her old habit of not giving it a name and letting things happen. It was time for her to give words to what she was thinking and feeling: that twenty-five years was a long time to have gone without the touch of the woman she'd loved with every bit of her heart and soul. Two weeks might be way too soon to get intimate, but Bridge wasn't just anyone. They had history. They'd been intimate already. Being with her like they'd been before was all she could think about.

But did she have the guts to let it happen tonight?

Chapter Fourteen

Bridge cleared the dishes while Alice put the leftovers in the fridge. Dinner had been perfect. Dessert had been lovely, as well, with little cookies Alice called lavender meltaways. Bridge had been skeptical about the lavender, but the delicate taste and the delightful way they'd melted in her mouth had been almost sensual.

All that combined with candlelight and wine on the porch while the late afternoon became early evening, had Bridge brimming with desire for more experiences just like it…and more. Much more.

"Let's leave the dishes in the sink and go for that walk," Alice said as she closed the refrigerator and leaned against it.

"Sounds perfect. I really like that outfit on you." She stopped short of running her fingers along the strap of Alice's sundress, but her eyes lingered on the skin she wanted so badly to touch. She couldn't remember having a reaction to a woman's bare shoulders before, but Alice's had been tantalizing her all through dinner.

Alice looked down, pushing a loose strand of hair behind her ear. "Thank you."

"You'd look beautiful in anything, but that was made for you." Bridge held her elbow. "Shall we?"

Alice slid her arm through hers with a smile.

"Alice!"

They were walking down the street in front of Alice's place when someone called out. Bridge got the impression that Alice almost pulled away but willed herself not to. What was that about?

"Shia," Alice called back.

A young woman in board shorts and a sports bra approached, tying her long blond hair up as she walked. "Sorry. I saw you walking, and I wanted to ask if...sorry for being rude." She held her hand out to Bridge, who took it. "I'm Shia, Alice's neighbor." She pointed to the smaller home next door. Her smile and energy were high wattage, and Bridge liked her immediately.

"I'm Bridge."

Alice relaxed against her, making her feel a little better. "I should have introduced you. Bridge is an old friend of mine."

"Well, old is a subjective word." Bridge laughed. "But we do go way back."

Shia's expressive brown eyes moved between them, obviously sizing them up. "Alice knows everybody. Are you from around here?"

"I have a place in South Oceanside. I just moved from Seattle."

"Then, we'll have something to celebrate. I was just about to ask if Alice wants to help with a bonfire tomorrow night. Rose will help, but she doesn't want to step on your toes since this is sort of our thing. Are you in? Say yes. Bring Bridge. Oh, and your friend Taylor. This is the perfect occasion to meet her. The woman from your church and book club?" Shia looked down the road at a woman walking toward them. "Here comes Mikayla. I'm late."

Bridge was about to ask what for when yet another young woman joined their little group in the middle of the cul-de-sac. This one was in a light blue Oceana polo shirt and khaki shorts. Her eyes locked on Shia's. "Text me when you get back home."

Shia's slow smile said she would do more than just call. "You made me late for practice, but the sun will set soon, so practice will be short. Have you met Bridge?"

The pretty, dark-haired woman peered around their little circle and looked almost surprised when she noticed Bridge. But

Shia was the only person she seemed to really notice. She held her hand out. "Hi, I'm Rose."

Alice leaned toward Bridge and stage-whispered, "Rose and Shia are too distracted with one another to notice us common folk these days."

Shia stood a little taller. "That's not true. I've just been busy with all the competitions this summer."

Rose grimaced. "I think she's talking about me. She nearly had to tackle me the other day when I was weaving bougainvillea through the lattice on the front wall."

"You didn't notice me until I was less than a foot away."

"I was listening to music, Alice. I would never ignore you like that," Rose said with a stunning smile.

Bridge was pretty sure Rose was used to getting anything she wanted when she focused all thousand watts on someone. Shia looked like she was about to turn into a puddle.

"It's only been two months. They're still in the gaga stage," Alice stage-whispered again.

Rose and Shia looked at each other and shrugged, making everyone laugh.

"Shake your tail feathers, Shia. Light's a' wasting." Mikayla stood halfway down the street, smiling, so Bridge assumed she was used to Shia being late.

Shia dropped her chin. "Tell me why I need a manager again, Alice."

"To help you win next week's competition in Huntington," Alice said.

Shia's head popped right back up. "Exactly." She kissed Rose, fired finger guns at the rest of them, and loped toward Mikayla before turning and walking backward. "I'll text as soon as I'm home, hot stuff," she said, looking at Rose. Pointing to Alice, she said, "I'll hit you up later about the bonfire." And finally, "Bridge, remember, you're invited."

"Looking forward to it," Bridge said.

"Catch you later, Alice. Nice meeting you, Bridge," Rose said before heading to a stucco house at the end of the street.

Bridge waited until everyone was out of earshot. "Do they only allow beautiful people to live here?"

"That is, in fact, part of the HOA," Alice said with a straight face.

"My goodness. Even the woman Shia left with—"

"Mikayla."

"The one you go shopping with? Is she Shia's mom? And who's Taylor?"

Alice sucked in a breath with a grimace. "Mikayla probably wouldn't mind being mistaken for Shia's mom, but I wouldn't say that to either of them. She's Shia's manager. Shia's a professional surfer. As for Taylor, she's a newish friend from my choir who recently moved to Oceana. I want her to meet people her own age. In fact..." She pulled her phone out of her pocket and shot off a text. "You'll like her. Gem, too. She's one of the owners of Oceana and dating Mikayla."

They held hands and started walking while Alice filled her in on a few more details about who lived where. They stopped to smell a low hanging magnolia blossom. Bridge loved the sense of nostalgia the smell gave her, reminding her of the trees scattered around the convent. There weren't many blossoms left this late in the summer, but the few that decorated the massive tree wafted their lemony scent all around them.

"Is everyone here family?"

"Only Rose and Gem are related. Oh, and Tripp, Gem's father."

Bridge was confused for a second. "Family as in queer."

Alice looked confused, and then her eyes cleared up and she nodded. "There are quite a few of...of us living here, but there are a lot of regular people, too."

"Regular?"

Alice swatted her playfully. "You know what I mean."

"I think I do, but regular doesn't mean straight."

Alice's expression changed before settling on exasperated. "I honestly don't with labels, as the younger folks like to say. I also don't talk about it a lot, so I don't have the lexicon."

"But you just got finished telling me who was dating who. You're interested and invested in your friends that way, so why wouldn't you use the right words?"

"Because people aren't the sum of their sexuality or gender. I didn't describe Taylor as trans, but she is, and she expresses herself as a woman. It would be weird to say, 'Here's my friend Taylor, a trans woman.' Shouldn't I let her define herself?"

As they left the park and crossed the highway to the beach, Bridge wondered how they'd gotten on this tangent, and it didn't feel good. Like the edge of an argument. Or more likely, it was just a step they'd skipped in the process of growing in the years they'd been apart. Alice didn't seem completely comfortable with labels as they pertained to herself, rather than others. She certainly didn't seem to have any issues with her friends' sexualities or gender expressions. In fact, she appeared protective of them.

There was something complex at play, but Bridge didn't want it to ruin their night. She squeezed Alice's hand. "I'm sorry. When I came out, I slammed the door behind me and pretty much dared anyone to tell me I couldn't be who I was. It required me to label myself to anyone who even looked at me weird. I don't feel that way now, and I respect all the ways people present themselves." Bridge ran her hands up and down Alice's arms. The feel of her warm skin sent ripples of pleasure through her. She tried not to focus on it, but it was difficult. Making sure Alice and she were okay was more important than her insistent libido.

When Alice smiled, relief flooded through her. She gave Bridge a side-eye. "I'm sorry I overreacted. I think it was a mix of you meeting everyone at once and me still feeling…like a country bumpkin next to you. You're so much more socially confident than I've ever been. You just got surrounded and were cool as a cucumber. You know what family means. I just felt like you might find me…lacking, and I hate that."

Bridge hated the confused, vulnerable look in Alice's eyes. They stopped on the firm sand near the water, and she gently cupped her face. "You're the opposite of lacking. I keep discovering wonderful new things about you. Smooth is just my sales training. You have meaningful connections with people. I'm jealous about the tight community you have here. Oceana seems like a queer Valhalla. If anyone is lacking, it's me."

Alice's eyes softened. "You lack for nothing. Oceana is more than it looks, though. I mean, beyond there being a lot of family."

"Is it a lovers' paradise or something? From the way your friends are all paired off, it sounds like Cupid must be busy here."

"Oceana has a way of bringing the people who live here together that helps them get what they need the most."

"Do people apply to live here and it's a wish fulfillment thing? Like *The Bachelorette* or something?"

"You watch too much reality television."

"Wait. Do you mean, like, in a mystical way?"

Alice looked serious. Like there really was wish fulfillment going on. "It's hard to explain. Gem's dad, Tripp, thinks it might be located on some sort of ley line. I've seen it happen time and again. People come here with a problem they don't even know they have, and somehow, they get what they need to resolve it."

It was a little woo-woo, but in Bridge's mind, it was better than relying on religion to make life better. *Talk about the ultimate woo-woo.* "Like when you needed a place to stay?"

"Exactly. Shia found help through her trust issues. Mikayla found a place to heal her broken heart that led to her and Gem finding each other. Even Tripp had a community to help him get through a health scare. There's something here, and part of me doesn't want to talk about it too much or analyze it, just in case looking too hard at it might ruin it."

There it was again, the not wanting to look too hard at or label things. Like how Alice hadn't wanted to talk about what was happening between them in the past.

And now?

"I can't say that I understand, but I like the idea."

Alice looked at her with that happy, appreciating look, and Bridge's heart swelled. "You are one of the most accepting people I've ever met. I love that about you."

Bridge grinned, knowing she wasn't accepting of everything, but if acknowledging that Oceana was a special place made Alice shine like that, she was all in. "You love it, huh?" she teased.

"There are a lot of things I love about you." The look Alice gave her reminded her of the early days of their forbidden relationship.

A tingle moved up Bridge's spine. She took her hand and squeezed. Her mind was still on Alice so easily mentioning the things she loved about Bridge. It wasn't the same as saying, "I love you," but it was close.

Was it too soon to tell if they still had the same connection? It felt like it, but was that wishful thinking? Bridge hadn't even told Alice about how her religious views had changed. They'd skirted it, but with things going the way they were, it might be best to make sure Alice understood the extent. Before either of them got too invested.

In fact, she probably already was. "I'm not perfect about acceptance. I have a really hard time with religion."

"I've picked up on that." Alice rubbed her thumb over the top of Bridge's hand, giving her the courage to continue.

"After what you and I went through, I can't let it go. To me, religion isn't all that good, nor is it harmless. It's a tool that hurts people in many ways." Alice looked away, and Bridge realized this might be a major obstacle. But it felt like a necessary subject to face. "Not all religious people are bad, though."

Alice rested a hand on her arm. She could see there was a lot going on behind her beautiful but now slightly guarded eyes. "I think maybe this is a subject we might want to avoid. At least for now."

Bridge felt scolded. She knew Alice didn't mean it that way, but it stung a little. If not now, then when? "I'm sorry if I said something to hurt you. Now or before. I never want to hurt you."

Alice smiled again, but the pressure in Bridge's chest remained. "I have absolutely no doubt about that. The tide is perfect right now. Let's go sit on the jetty."

The beach was almost deserted with most of the tourists gone for the season. Bridge breathed deeply of the briny air, and Alice led them toward the rock formation that served as the northern border to the Oceanside Harbor. It went several yards into the ocean, affecting the currents so the beach didn't erode. Walking hand-in-hand here was a dream come true, even with the tension. Bridge would have gone anywhere Alice took her.

When they reached the large rocks, Bridge was prepared to offer a steadying hand, but to her surprise, Alice slid her sandals off and scurried up like a beach squirrel.

"Hey, do you think the hunk of concrete with the heart scratched into it is still here?" Bridge asked, thinking about the times they'd come to the beach all those years ago. She'd always thought of it as their heart.

"It's on the other jetty," Alice said, pointing south to the jetty that protected the mouth of the San Luis Rey River.

"That's right. It's been so long since I've been here."

They picked their way along and took a seat on one of the rocks at the end, just far enough to not get wet from the crashing waves spewing spray and foam into the evening sky. The sailboats were on their way back in, and a steady stream of other boats floated by them. One smaller motorboat that had been kicking up a wake throttled its engine when it reached the smoother harbor water and became quieter.

Bridge snapped a few pictures with her phone. "Check out how choppy the water is out there in the wind and how calm it is in the harbor. It's kind of amazing how a simple pile of rocks creates this calm."

"It's like a metaphor for life, isn't it?"

"For sure." The comment sank into her. She didn't spend a lot of time thinking back, but when she did reflect, she often saw herself as a boat plowing through the water, speeding forward, overcoming each new challenging swell. The last couple of weeks had felt like she was safely anchored in a harbor, with peaceful water all around, after thinking it had been lost to her all this time. She tried not to think about the currents beneath the surface, preferring to believe her walls could contain them.

"I had no idea how much I missed this." She turned to Alice, and the golden light washing over her was ethereal. She took a quick picture of her with the boats in the background and already knew she'd frame it and put it on her desk. "Do you feel like taking a picture with me?"

Alice tipped her head to the side. "I'd love to. I don't have any pictures of you."

"That's what I was just thinking. But I never needed one to remember you. I just close my eyes and see you exactly as you are."

They posed side by side, Bridge relishing the warmth of Alice pressed to her side. Neither moved away after the picture was taken.

"Do you see the twenty-year-old me or the forty-something me?" Alice bumped her shoulder. "When you close your eyes."

"They're one and the same. Beautiful. Brilliant. Amazing."

Alice looked away. "You're sweet."

Bridge stroked the side of her face. "I'm serious. I'm so glad I get to have this time with you. You're my lost harbor."

That was exactly what Alice was to her. She never thought they'd see each other again, but now that they had, although they had twenty-five years of reacquainting to do, Bridge's soul had found its peace.

Chapter Fifteen

Dripping wet, Bridge disappeared into the bathroom when they got back to the house. When the door clicked shut, Alice allowed the laughter she'd been holding in to spill into the throw pillow she clutched over her face. She tried to keep it quiet, worried that the sound of the shower wouldn't drown it out. But once the first roll of amusement left her lips, she felt almost hysterical and had to curl up on the couch for a few minutes with the pillow over her face to muffle the sound.

The timing couldn't have been better…or worse, depending on if you were Bridge or not. A pelican gliding past had let go of a bomb of epic proportions. The splash zone had been a full five-foot-ten and then some, striking Bridge from her toes to the top of her head and did not spare her face. When she realized what had happened, she'd descended the jetty and ran directly into the water, barely sparing a half second to hand Alice her phone.

Alice was impressed with how well Bridge had maintained herself during the entire ordeal. She was even more impressed with herself for not howling with laughter when she'd seen the shock and horror cross Bridge's face. It was priceless. Even better, she'd caught it in a picture as she'd tried to sneak a candid photo of Bridge with her eyes shut, head tipped back, seemingly soaking in the moment. She'd caught the precise moment Bridge had opened her eyes, awareness dawning on her.

By the time the shower turned off, Alice had regained her composure and was making coffee, trying to decide whether she wanted to tell Bridge about the picture. Her back was to the door, yet she could tell the exact moment Bridge entered the kitchen. The air seemed to press into her, and all thoughts of pelicans left her mind when she was enveloped in the scent of sandalwood and coriander bath soap.

Trying to remain cool, she looked over her shoulder to ask how her shower had been and beheld Bridge leaning against the door frame in a pair of low-slung sweats and a threadbare T-shirt that barely disguised the heavy swing of her breasts as she settled into the casual pose. The short tee showed off a strip of bare skin at the waistband of the sweats, with the perfect indent of Bridge's belly button displayed in the center. Alice barely contained a gasp before she turned back to their coffee.

"Thank goodness you…you had your suitcase here. I don't think I have any clothes that would fit you." Aside from the slight stutter, she was impressed with the almost normal timbre of her voice.

"I hope you don't mind. My jammies are the only casual thing I brought, aside from the shorts I had on. Which I might have to burn now."

She sounded amused, no doubt unaware that Alice was trying to still her heart as her fingers itched to touch the glimpse of bare skin that was etched into her mind.

Alice swallowed hard. "That's a long way from the granny gowns we wore back in the day." This time, her voice was a little tighter. It seemed the more she tried to remain cool and collected, the tighter every muscle in her body became. The spoon she stirred the coffee with certainly didn't need white-knuckled handling. She let go and leaned against the counter for support as she tried to relax.

Without warning, waves of desire swept over her, almost rendering her incapable of standing. Seeing Bridge in a state of casual she'd never seen before, with her hair towel-dried, rumpled

T-shirt, and barefoot, was the single most erotic thing she'd ever seen. It felt like she was standing on a cliff, high above a distant pool. Mouth dry, heart beating like a drum, a pressure started high and flowed down until it wrapped around her lower abdomen. She stood stock still, waiting for the fall. Lord, Bridge had an effect on her that no person ever had before. It reminded her of the day she'd first seen her, which was burned vividly into her memory:

Her first full day in the convent, and she was standing in Mother Superior's office after being officially welcomed. Swirls of excitement spun in her stomach about the new page in her life she embarked on. Mother Superior had left the office to attend to head nun things, and Mary Alice looked at pictures hanging on the wall, waiting for the companion who had been assigned to her to show her around the convent and the school that shared the same campus. The quiet sound of a person clearing their throat caused her to turn, and a young novice dressed in white just like her stood before her, only with the prettiest face she'd ever seen. They stared at each other for a silent moment before smiling shyly and dropping their eyes.

Alice felt like the air had been sucked from the room.

"Oh, good. You're here, too, Sister Mary Bridget. We have someone on their way for you as well. Please wait here. Come with me, Sister Mary Alice, your companion is in the hall."

Alice had a hard time not turning to keep looking at the other young novice as she walked past, following Sister Mary Charlotte from the room. As it was, she bumped into the door in her distraction, but she barely noticed. All she could see were greenish-blue eyes surrounded by thick dark lashes.

Without a single word spoken, her heart would never be the same.

"You're an angel. Coffee is just the thing I need to warm me from that frigid dunk," Bridge said, coming to Alice's side, apparently unaware of her effect. "I had the shower as hot as I could stand it, but that cold seeped into my bones. I hope it at least got rid of the stench." She stood so close that Alice could feel the heat radiating from her. Or was it the flame of her heart?

Alice put the spoon on the counter. She turned, careful to keep her eyes up lest the sight of a barely concealed breast or swath of tan stomach rendered her lifeless. Mere inches separated them, and Alice wanted nothing more than to make them disappear, but she was frozen, tortured by the electric charge between them. Surely, Bridge could feel it. It was almost burning.

"Are you okay?" Bridge's words and sparkling eyes belied the lack of concern in her voice. The way her eyes dropped to Alice's lips was enough evidence that she was coming up to speed on the situation.

"N...no." Alice swallowed.

Bridge's lips curled inward before the tip of her tongue slipped between them. "Is there anything I can do to help?"

"You're the only one who can." Had that really come out of her mouth?

The corner of Bridge's mouth rose almost barely, but Alice was hyperaware of every aspect, including how Bridge placed her hands on the counter on either side of her. The tiny rise of those soft lips stole her breath away. The number of responses firing inside her made her lightheaded, and the brain she usually used to get her through any situation seemed to be taking a break, leaving her at the mercy of her primal core. It was telling her to close the distance so she could take those lips in a kiss, triggering a whole lot of other actions that would hopefully do something about the raging storm between her legs. The things going on down there—the strength of them—were beyond anything she'd felt before. Even when she and Bridge had been sneaking off to release the tension back then. That was child's play compared to...

"I'd like to try," Bridge said, tipping her head, bringing her mouth an inch away.

Alice's mind filled with the ways she wanted Bridge to touch her. God, she wanted those lips to crush her own. She wanted her mouth and her hands. Against her, inside her, above her, behind her, beside her. She wanted. She wanted. She wanted.

And she wasn't going to apologize for thinking the Lord's name in vain. If there was ever a time that God could show her the way, it was now, and words and names were obsolete.

Warm skin beneath her palms shot lightning into her fingertips. How her hands made their way from clenched at her sides to sliding around Bridge's waist, she had no clue. They moved across the softest skin she'd ever touched. It gave under the pressure, warming her hands with radiant heat. She imagined how it would taste, how the texture would feel against her lips, how it would move beneath her tongue.

Thank you, God.

Bridge cupped her jaw before she removed her glasses. Alice didn't care where those hands went as long as Bridge brought them back to her face. Having her cheek cradled by Bridge told her things that words couldn't convey. Tenderness. Desire. Need.

Bridge swept a soft kiss across her lips and then another before she looked into Alice's eyes as if cherishing what she saw. "Before this goes any further, I need to check in."

Alice was out of breath. Her heart was hammering, and she wanted everything all at once. "I want…I want to go wherever this takes us." She fought the urge to look away, embarrassed about the naked need in her voice.

"I want to do this right. I'm afraid I won't remember to—"

"Check in?" Alice finished for her.

Bridge nodded. So serious.

Alice kissed her, pulling away with a nervous laugh. "Why am I lightheaded?" She rested her forehead against Bridge's. "I was single-minded, but now I don't know what to do. It's been so long. I almost reached for your skirts," she said, referring to the thing she'd done first when an opportunity had arisen, and they'd groped behind a door for a few minutes. "It's like it's our first time, but that happened so gradually that we didn't even realize how far it would go. Not until it happened."

"Oh, I knew." Bridge was still serious, but her eyes almost glowed.

"I felt like I was in a haze. I didn't know where I left off and you began. I didn't even know you were touching me until... until..."

"You were coming?"

"Yes. I'd never felt that way before. My body was responding in an incredible way, and you were touching me."

"Every time I started to take my hand away, you'd pull it back. I've always wished I'd thought to put my fingers inside you. I wish I'd felt your body respond the first time."

A flash of heat rippled from the top of Alice's head all the way down her body, a supernova dancing right beneath her navel. She pressed against Bridge, and those breasts that had sent her reeling before were crushed against her, and all she wanted to do was wrap a leg around Bridge, pulling her as close as she could.

"If you'd spoken to me then the way you are now," Alice whispered, "I think we'd have been discovered a lot earlier. Discretion be damned, I'd have dragged you into closets and confessionals without a single glance. I feel that way right now. I want so many things. I want you to do everything to me, and I want to do everything to you. It's so overwhelming, I don't know where to begin." Her tone was nearly pleading. "I'm scaring myself."

Bridge swept her lips across Alice's forehead. "We can stop."

"No." It came out louder than she meant. "No," she said more quietly, trembling. "I want this. I really want it." She laughed quietly. "And there's no one to hide from here. Except myself. And I'm tired of hiding from me."

"Can I take you to the bedroom and undress you?" Bridge whispered, and the warm breath against her ear made Alice shiver. A long roll of pleasure made her squeeze her thighs together. She couldn't form the words to say yes, so she kissed her. The kiss in response was both tender and demanding. Alice didn't want it to end, but Bridge pulled back just enough to say, "Does this mean yes?" and Alice nodded, still kissing her.

Bridge intertwined all their fingers. "I can't risk looking away. You might disappear." She took a step back, and Alice followed, feeling her gaze like a magnetic beam. She had no idea how they made it to the bedroom without tripping or hitting a wall, but they were standing at the foot of the bed. "Do you have any candles?"

Alice tried to think where they might be; a drawer in her bedside table. She took them out, and Bridge lit them in a small cluster on the table by the bed, sneezing three times. Alice smiled, remembering how she'd always sneezed at the scent of burning candles.

"I like this smell."

"It's eucalyptus." It always made her think of the convent that had been surrounded by eucalyptus trees. It felt fitting now, as Alice never thought of it without Bridge's memory.

Bridge closed her eyes. "Very nice." When she opened them again, Alice nearly gasped at what she could only describe as their love story reflected at her: softness and warmth, adoration and desire, hope and need, and so much more.

Alice could barely breathe when Bridge cradled her face and kissed her gently, sliding warm fingers under the straps of her sundress. She played with them idly as her lips teased the corner of Alice's mouth before kissing a line across her jaw to her neck, where she nibbled and licked.

Alice didn't know what to do with her hands while Bridge teased her sensitive skin, so she placed them on Bridge's waist, relishing the bare skin she couldn't wait to explore closer. When Bridge pushed one strap down, she caressed the unfettered shoulder before pressing kisses to it and then moving to the other, removing that strap, too, and slowly moving to the row of buttons between Alice's breasts as if worshiping what she saw.

At the first gentle tug of the top button, Alice's nipples responded with an awareness she hadn't felt since the heady times in the convent when Bridge would cradle them through her clothes. Bridge slowly unbuttoned the dress, dropping kisses on each inch of exposed skin, and Alice's breasts ached with a longing for

Bridge's mouth. Every touch, every kiss, every breath sent a bolt of need to Alice's center, building a fire inside her. She arched and moved into Bridge's caresses and kisses, impatient, although she didn't know what for. How had she gone so long without feeling intimate touch? Especially from someone who cared about her. Maybe even still loved her.

Bridge seemed to understand because she moved slower, more deliberately. The pressure built under Alice's skin as she anticipated every new movement, every light kiss. When the dress fell to the floor, Bridge stood before her with a reverent expression lighting her beautiful face in the flickering candlelight. "My God, you're gorgeous. I knew you would be, but there are no words for what seeing you is doing to me."

"I'm not sure if I should be flattered or relieved." Alice would have thought she'd feel shy, but it was having the opposite effect. "What did you expect?"

Bridge's expression changed from reverent to abashed. "I've thought about what you'd look like naked for years, but my fantasy was less about what my eyes would see and more about the feel of you. I never expected you to wear such sexy lingerie." She released a shuddering breath. "May I take it off?"

Alice's heart felt like it would beat out of her chest. "Please." Everything about what they were doing was new and exciting, and if Alice hadn't already had full faith in Bridge and feelings that ran deeper than any she'd ever had, she might have been uncomfortable or afraid. But because it was Bridge, she was able to allow herself to follow her lead.

The bra was strapless and clasped in the front. Bridge approached it as if Alice's breasts were a precious gift she was about to open. The brush of her fingertips above the satin and lace was a tantalizing tickle. When the bra opened, Bridge slowly removed it from one breast at a time, her expression worshipful.

Alice gasped at the passion rising within her under a gaze so rapt. She dropped her head back, closing her eyes as Bridge's breath moved over one nipple and then the other before she gently caressed them, taking one in her mouth while cradling the other. Clasping Bridge's head to hold her in place, Alice bit her lip as the wet warmth of Bridge's mouth alternated between gently sucking and lightly nibbling. She'd thought about what this would feel like, thinking she'd built the expectation too much but was surprised when the sensations it brought alive within her went far beyond anything she'd ever imagined. It was as if the nerves in her nipples were wired to her core; each sensation caused a flurry of ripples between her legs.

Bridge dragged a hand down the side of Alice's body that sang with responsiveness. Fingers snagged on the waist of her panties, dragging them down as they caressed her thighs, the backs of her knees, and her calves. Alice spread her legs as Bridge's fingers slid back up, tracing paths along the inside of her thighs.

"I need to touch you, Alice. Can I?" Bridge's hooded eyes glimmered darkly in the candlelight.

Alice's mind and body were swimming through a fog of sensuality. She couldn't have said anything but yes even if she'd wanted to. Her entire being had been screaming it since she'd laid eyes on Bridge in the kitchen.

"Yes. Yes. Yes. But can I..." Alice couldn't finish, so she tugged on Bridge's T-shirt. Her breath came in hitching inhales and short exhales.

Bridge stood, taking Alice's hands, helping her lift the shirt over her head, and then, without a pause, she pushed her sweatpants off. Standing before her, Alice's heart nearly stopped. There was no oxygen, no sound, no room around them. Need pulsed through Alice as she beheld Bridge's perfect form. It was as if they were floating in a bath of exquisite pleasure, and while they weren't touching, Alice felt connected in a way that was beyond joined, as if they were almost the same body. She closed her eyes and floated in the tidal wave of emotion that crashed over her, an unfamiliar, but oh-so desired situation she'd had no context for until that moment.

Bridge brought their bodies together and everything Alice had felt before left her unprepared for the cascade of sensation as their bodies pressed together from their lips to their legs. Every time Alice thought that she couldn't feel anything better, she was proven wrong. Because somehow, they were lying in bed, and touch became pressure, and pressure became friction, and friction became incandescence.

All Alice was concerned with was the sensation. If her breasts had telegraphed her need to her core earlier, her flesh was using alien technology to communicate how much she required Bridge to touch her in the deepest way.

Bridge was above her, held up by one forearm while her free hand left paths of light across her skin. It felt so good, so very good. When Bridge kissed her neck, Alice wrapped her arms around her, relishing the weight pressing her into the soft mattress. Her hips automatically lifted to arch in the familiar way they used to, their centers pushed against the other's thighs. She ached to feel the naked pressure of Bridge against the part of her that craved contact the most.

Bridge's response was to tangle their limbs and move, setting a rhythm so familiar, so missed, so natural. A shuddering sigh fell from her mouth as her back arched.

The rise to the precipice accelerated. Alice was ready. It had been so long. So very long. The occasional attempts she'd made to relieve herself had been nice, but they didn't approach the satisfaction she'd achieved with Bridge. Now, she was there and beyond.

But there was something more she needed. It escaped her ability to conceptualize, but as close as she was to bursting over the precipice, there was something...

Bridge's hand went between them. Alice spread her legs even more, making space for the touch that was already spreading fire through her body. Pressure so divine. Bridge was inside her, filling her. When they'd dipped inside each other before, it had been ethereal, gentle, like the tongue of a hummingbird seeking sweet nourishment. Now, Bridge claimed her, taking her to higher levels. Alice stilled to absorb the experience.

Bridge stopped moving, still deep inside. Her eyes looked directly into Alice's soul. "Are you, okay?"

Alice couldn't find her voice. She nodded, focused on Bridge's hand and eyes as the storm swirled around them, poured over her, through her, from her.

Bridge smiled. "You need to breathe, baby. Open your mouth and breathe."

Alice opened her mouth, but instead of breathing, she released a low moan that had been filling her throat. Oxygen flowed into her lungs, and light and fire blazed through her. They began to move again, and instead of falling over the precipice, Alice catapulted into heaven with the speed of a lightning bolt.

By the time she stilled, she was breathing in long gasps, and with every inhale, she felt the oxygen fill every cell, making her feel effervescent. Surprise held her, and she floated like a dandelion seed above the earth, rising and falling with the currents. Finally, she came to rest beneath Bridge, and the spots of light that had taken over her vision receded. The face of the young Mary Bridget looked down at her with the same expression she'd held all those years ago, amazement and reverence. Tears streamed down her cheeks, and a tremulous smile animated her face.

"I have never seen anything as beautiful than you in this moment." Bridge rolled to her side, ignoring her tears, and propped her head on one hand, swaying forward to kiss Alice, drawing her fingers across her skin in slow shapes.

Alice caught her breath and relaxed under the light touch. "What did you do to me?" she asked, only half joking. She would have thought she'd have been embarrassed by her loss of control. But she wasn't. Bridge had been there with her all the way.

"You tell me." Bridge continued to draw lazy shapes across her skin.

"I don't think I can describe it. Words wouldn't do it justice. How do you know exactly how to touch me?"

"Your body speaks to me."

Alice kissed her gently. "When I can feel my limbs again, I want a chance to make you feel how you made me feel." Part of her wondered how she'd know what to do, but she had no doubt that she'd have ample opportunity to figure it out.

❖

Bridge's plan had been to sneak into the bedroom and leave a rose on Alice's pillow. She wanted it to be the first thing Alice saw when she woke up. But when she got to the doorway, she was struck by what she saw. If she'd been an artist, she would have painted it.

Alice was lying on her stomach with both arms resting above her head, her long hair tousled, fanned out along the pillow. Her beautiful back, naked to where the sheet started at her waist, begged Bridge to run her fingers along it, to memorize the smooth, soft expanse. It took everything in her not to crawl back into bed and stretch out alongside her, to mold her body against her, to wake her with kisses, and make love to her again in the gentle morning sunlight.

But Alice looked so peaceful. Bridge stood there with the vivid memory of the taste of Alice dancing on the tip of her tongue, remembering the warmth and feel of her body beneath her fingertips, her hips, her mouth. Her mind and body played through the hours of new memories they'd made throughout the night. Yet, her desire continued to burn.

How different, yet familiar, the time they'd spent relearning each other. Years ago, the danger of being caught had hung over them with every kiss, every touch, every whispered endearment. They had never been offered the chance to savor their time together. Last night, though…

A shudder ran through Bridge. Last night had been a revelation on so many levels. There had been time to savor, freedom to experience, safety to focus on nothing but what they were doing.

Last night, they had been able to give themselves to each other without reservation, and that had been everything.

The sting of tears threatened to make Bridge cry thinking about the gift they'd been given by finding one another again. This time, she wouldn't let anything tear them apart.

"Some people would be creeped out waking up to a person staring at them like that." Alice hadn't moved, but her eyes were open.

Bridge sat on the edge of the bed. Nothing short of brute force, and maybe not even that, would have stopped her from placing a hand on Alice's naked back. She needed to prove to herself that she hadn't been exaggerating to herself how silky-smooth Alice's skin was. "Were you creeped out?"

With a languid stretch, Alice smiled and rolled to her back, not bothering to pull the sheet up. "Not even a little bit. What time is it?"

Bridge's pulse raced at the vision of her breasts. "Just a little after nine."

Alice covered a yawn. "I'm usually up around seven. But someone kept me up way past my bedtime." To Bridge's disappointment, she pulled the sheet up before she sat. "Where'd you get that flower?"

Bridge looked at the red rose in her hand and smelled it. "It's for you," she said, handing it to her. "I hope you don't mind that I stole it from one of your bushes."

"Not at all. I love it. Do I smell bacon?"

Bridge nodded. "I made a frittata and some fried potatoes with a side of mixed fruit."

Alice rubbed her stomach. "It sounds heavenly. I'm starving."

"Can I bring you a plate?"

"I'd rather get up and eat on the porch if that sounds good to you."

Bridge leaned forward to give her a quick kiss on the cheek. She really wanted to lay Alice back down and have her way with her again, but she, too, was starving, and she hadn't brushed her teeth yet. "I'll go fix our plates. I'd tell you to not bother with clothes, but if you want to eat on the porch, you might want to put something on. It depends on how snooty your neighbors are."

Alice appeared to consider her options. "No doubt the sheet would be the talk of the cul-de-sac. And I reckon complete nudity would compel the neighbors to ask for a wellness check."

"I guess we should clothe you, then, if only to preserve the peace of the community."

Another quick kiss on the cheek and Bridge had to leave before they were both lying naked in the bed again.

Alice emerged from the bedroom a few minutes later in shorts and a sleeveless button-up shirt, her hair still lying in waves down her back. Bridge had never seen a prettier sight.

CHAPTER SIXTEEN

A lice pulled her standing mixer to the edge of the counter and tossed in the ingredients for chocolate chip cookies as her mind wandered through the events of last night and that morning.

Something major had shifted in her life.

Well, it was obviously Bridge. But there was a whole slew of facets she'd once thought of as individual aspects that were now joined into a single, comprehensive entity. Once a cacophony of attributes with no rhyme or reason now happened to add up to who she was and made sense now. She'd opened her heart to allow entry to something she never thought she'd have again. Not only Bridge but also the acceptance of herself but all of the rules, judgment, and subsequent condemnation in the name of human-constructed morals were not things that she was constrained by anymore. She'd shed those shackles at the first touch from Bridge last night.

If she'd been the one to write the Book of Revelation now, it would have been a drastically different prognostication: rebirth, fulfillment, peace, and love. A shiver coursed through her at the shift she felt within her soul, her whole existence. She felt cleansed. Baptized in a whole new breadth of understanding.

But there was still something underneath it all. Something new was trying to speak to her. The promise of what it was happened over twenty-five years ago when she and Sister Mary Bridget had whispered their first "I love you," but she hadn't been free from the consequences of back then. Not like she was now. God reveled in their pure love, and she'd imagined golden scripture exalting the joining of their spirits. She'd seen it, even if the Church hadn't. And as much as Bridge claimed that religion held no shackles on her, her continuing struggle appeared to prove just the opposite, showing she was held in place by it while Alice had found her freedom.

Last night had been an awakening; she knew this as she preheated the oven. Back then, God was her whole existence, woven into the fabric of her very purpose. Now, God walked with her, but not everything she did was solely in the name of God. She was free to have her own life, her own love, her own pleasure, and it wasn't taking a thing away from God.

With this knowledge, she relished the memory of her night. She couldn't wait to tell Bridge. Maybe it would help to free her, too.

The clock told her it was almost five when she pulled the last batch of cookies out of the oven and moved them to the cooling rack. Shia and Rose were taking care of the ice chests and wood for the bonfire. The only things she was responsible for were Bridge, cookies, and a bottle of wine. After she and Bridge had pried themselves out of bed, she'd gotten dressed in one of her new outfits. As embarrassed as she was about the collection of clothing she'd amassed in the last month or so, it gave her a new confidence. Not just confidence. Presence. As if she'd found her way into a more prominent position in her own life.

Not that she'd ever felt like a background character, but she'd always been more comfortable as an observer who occasionally performed quiet actions in the background to move the action forward. Now, she was ready to be part of the main action. This idea had started before Bridge had come back into her life, but now it was evident. She was ready to be her own leading lady.

Another epiphany!

"Hello? Anyone home?" Bridge's voice startled her from her thoughts.

A glance at the clock told her she'd been standing in the pantry for at least twenty minutes. "Back here," she called as she straightened the containers of flour and brown sugar and closed the door.

"I felt weird letting myself in, but it didn't seem like you heard the doorbell."

"It hasn't worked for a few years." Seeing Bridge amplified the almost overwhelming feeling of connection and desire. For a moment, she forgot how to breathe.

"I can probably fix it for you," Bridge said as she came close with a smile that confirmed she was making polite conversation while more erotic topics played in her mind.

"It's weird that we're talking about a broken doorbell when all I can think about is what we did last night," Alice said, taking her hand.

Bridge brought the hand to her lips. "And most of today. Are you okay? I know we talked this morning, but I had a feeling you were playing hostess and processing on the inside."

Tingles spread through Alice's arm at the warmth of Bridge's lips and breath against her fingers. "How could you tell?"

"Remember the garden shed?"

At once, the image of a wooden shed painted white with blue trim filled her mind. The ghostly scents of earth and fertilizer tickled her nose. Garden tools had hung neatly along a wall. With the door closed, the only light had seeped in through a small square of corrugated plastic fitted into the roof, casting a green hue over the dim space.

She'd first kissed Sister Mary Bridget among the garden tools and scents. First cradled her breast through her clothes. The first time she'd bitten her own fingers so she wouldn't cry out when she'd trembled and shaken as waves of pleasure roared through her.

Oh, she remembered.

"You always needed time to let things settle after we visited the shed," Bridge said.

"Not always."

"After we discovered something new."

It was true. She'd retreated each time a new boundary had been breached. She'd had to talk it out with God, who had always shown his favor, whether it was a bountiful tomato season, a salient point in Father Gregory's sermon, or the one time the Lavender Orpington had laid an egg within an egg. "You were always so patient with me."

Bridge looked down and shook her head. "Believe me, it wasn't natural. The convent was a strange bubble where time didn't exist, and personal space wasn't a thing. I suppose if we'd been in a place where you could have physically withdrawn, where I didn't have the benefit of seeing you several times a day without the pressure of talking, I might have been less patient. But you were right there. I could see you and know it was just a matter of time."

"You were so kind last night, making sure I was doing okay."

"Your heart is important to me."

Alice pressed Bridge's hand to her chest. "My heart is doing magnificently. So is everything else."

Bridge's cheeks flushed. "And then you go and say something like that. Sometimes, you throw me for a loop."

"Does that bother you?"

"Only in a good way."

Alice felt a crackle in the air that grew infinitely more pronounced as Bridge stepped closer.

"I wanted to sweep you into my arms when I saw you."

"What's stopping you?"

"Nothing." Bridge wrapped her arms around Alice, and tingles exploded throughout her until Bridge's incredibly soft lips pressed against hers, and the tingles became fireworks. Lights and flares exploded behind her eyelids.

Alice spread her hands across Bridge's back, pulling them closer, and as their curves and valleys molded together, Alice opened her mouth to explore Bridge's more freely. She lost track of who ended and who began. She reached to touch Bridge's face.

"You have no idea how much your kisses affect me," Bridge whispered.

"Do they make you feel like you're floating one minute and in a free fall the next?"

"Yes."

"Do you have a hard time distinguishing where your body ends and mine begins?"

"Yes."

"Does your mind stop thinking in words and revert to images that take your breath away and send your senses reeling?"

"Yes."

"I think we might be on the same page, then."

"I think you're right."

"We should probably head over to the park before I beg you to take me into the other room."

"You wouldn't have to beg."

Alice kissed her again but found the strength to resist dragging her down the hall. When she pulled back, she put a hand on Bridge's chest and pushed her gently. "I promised to bring cookies. Plus, I want you to meet the rest of my friends."

"Silly question, what do I say when they ask how we know each other?"

Alice was taken by surprise. "I guess it's not a strange thing to ask."

"You told Shia I was your friend. Your *old* friend, to be precise."

Alice giggled. "You're certainly not just a friend, and we're not old. But that was before…well, before last night." She blushed. "I guess there are two things at play here. You're going to think they're both silly. The first one is that none of them have ever seen me with a romantic partner. It's going to be a bit of a shock."

"Is that a bad thing?"

Alice giggled again. "Just the opposite. They'll probably interrogate us. At least, that's what I would do. I'm always in everybody's business."

Bridge's eyes shined with amusement. "Should we come up with a bizarre story. Or should we tell the truth?"

Alice curled her lips in and bit them before responding. "I think our story is both bizarre and truthful. They don't know I used to be a nun. Well, Taylor does, but she hardly knows anybody."

Bridge's face froze. "I was thinking more along the lines of we met in prison or something. They don't know you were a nun?"

"It never came up."

Bridge squinted one eye, and Alice thought it was the cutest expression she'd ever seen. "It's not something that comes up. You have to say. Why haven't you?"

"I don't know. I just haven't."

"Do you not want them to know?"

"I'm not hiding it, really. It'll make things interesting at the bonfire." She worried that they might be a little miffed that she'd held back something so fundamental, but she didn't think they'd be very surprised.

No matter. It wasn't anything a few batches of cookies wouldn't make up for.

She hoped.

CHAPTER SEVENTEEN

At the little park at the end of the street, Bridge felt all eyes on her as she and Alice approached the already blazing bonfire. Shia crouched next to the inferno, adding pieces of wood that looked as if they'd been part of a pallet.

Alice handed Bridge the plate of cookies and sprinted forward. "Shia! What have I told you about not getting so close? You're going to hurt yourself before the competition next weekend."

Bridge laughed over Alice's watchful ways, a trait she remembered well from the convent. She took a step to follow when a woman gently intercepted her. "Hi there. I'm sorry I didn't stop to introduce myself yesterday. I'm Mikayla." She held out a hand. She had a unique air about her; at once appearing exceptionally put together yet laid back, an unusual combination.

Bridge took her hand. "I'm Bridge. Alice told me you're Shia's manager."

Mikayla squeezed her hand while looking toward Shia and Alice with amusement. "Sometimes, I wonder who's managing who. One thing's for sure, she certainly listens to Alice."

A pang of something Bridge couldn't name hit her. She and Alice had known each other for almost three decades, but there was an ease between Shia and Alice that Bridge wished she had.

"How come I haven't seen you around before?"

"I just moved back to Oceanside." She and Mikayla walked toward the picnic table next to the fire, near Alice and Shia. Bridge added the cookies to the growing assembly of food.

A tall man with an affable smile winked at her before he lifted the edge of the clear wrap and stole one of the cookies. "I can spot Alice's cookies from a mile away," he said.

"Leave some for the rest of us." Mikayla wagged a finger at him, and he pretended to take the rest of the plate. Mikayla turned to a lovely woman standing in front of the grill near the table. "Gem, tell your dad to behave. Also, I have someone to introduce you to. This is Bridge. She's Alice's friend."

Gem slipped her arm around Mikayla's waist while expertly wielding barbeque tongs that she threatened her father with. "Dad, if you eat all the cookies, you won't have room for Harper's wings or Mikayla's chicken kebobs."

"Don't worry, Angel. I skipped lunch. There's room for all that and then some." He took another cookie and made his way down the table.

"There's your warning to not dally about getting your plate filled. That man has no shame." Gem snapped her tongs in his direction with a smile and offered Bridge her hand. Handshakes had never felt so welcoming before. "Welcome to the bonfire."

Bridge took in the sense of friendship displayed all around her. "Looks like a good time. It's nice to meet you."

Gem smiled, giving Bridge a weird feeling they'd met before, although she'd have remembered. Yet, something gave her the impression that Gem knew *her*. Like, really *knew* her. It wasn't threatening, but it was a bit unnerving. Under normal circumstances, she'd have felt a little wary about the naked way she felt under Gem's gaze, but she didn't. She felt seen.

"Bridge makes prosthetic hands. The kind that operate like real hands."

Hyperaware of Gem's focus, Bridge had to deliberately look around to recognize that Mikayla had spoken.

"You amaze me." Gem kissed Mikayla on the cheek before returning her attention to Bridge. "She's a consummate host. Always the first to say hello and get to know the newbies. What's it been? Ten minutes?"

"You're easily impressed." Mikayla gently pushed the bill of Gem's cap down, and Gem good-naturedly took it off and plopped it onto Mikayla's head. She simply adjusted it and smiled.

Their banter gave Bridge a little more time to get used to the strange feeling Gem's knowing gaze had given her, leaving her with an off-kilter sensation. She glanced toward Alice, who seemed engaged in a serious conversation with Shia. Rose and another young woman joined them. Maybe the interrogation Alice predicted had begun.

As if Alice had sensed Bridge watching her, she looked over, making Bridge's stomach flutter. Alice said something to the others, and the next thing Bridge knew, all four of them made their way over. She wondered again if there was a rule that required everyone in Oceana to be gorgeous.

Her entire body tingled when Alice took her hand. "I see you've met Mikayla and Gem," Alice said, gesturing to them. It was amusing and a little sexy that Alice was using her tour guide voice. "The distinguished gentleman on the other side of the table riffling through the food is Tripp, the owner of Oceana and he's Gem's father. And this is Taylor," she said, gesturing to a woman Bridge hadn't met yet. "Rose has met her, but she's new to the rest of you. Everyone, this is Bridge, who is new to the group today, as is Taylor, who moved to Oceana recently." Alice beamed. "There will be a quiz at the end of the evening. Did I miss anyone?"

"Let me take a shot at the quiz," Taylor said, rubbing her hands together.

"I was kidding." Alice tilted her head with a gentle smile, causing Bridge's heart to melt. It reminded her of the infinitely patient and kind young nun she'd been drawn to like a bee to a flower.

"But I love a challenge," Taylor said, then proceeded to name off the people. When she had successfully ticked off each one, including the relationships they had to one another, Taylor finished with: "Bridge is Alice's friend from back in the day."

"Challenge defeated," Rose said, giving her a high five.

When Taylor finished celebrating, she turned to Bridge again. "Okay, I can easily see Alice as an ex-nun, but no way in a million years would I have guessed you were one, too."

Gem and Mikayla wore surprised expressions. "Wait. What?" Mikayla said. "Did you just say nun?" She looked at Shia and Rose.

Gem shook her head as Mikayla sputtered out questions. "I think we need more details." She didn't seem as astounded as Mikayla, but she looked at her father with a questioning brow. It was almost comical. Bridge had never lived in a small town, but Oceana seemed like a place where everyone knew everyone else's business. Alice's worry about having kept secrets made a little more sense. People who lived in small communities were invested in each other. Much like the convent, where the nuns would whisper discreetly among themselves anytime a juicy bit of news came up.

Alice breathed out. "I told them you and I were in convent together when they asked how we know each other." She gave her a smallish smile, and her eyes said she was relieved to have this over with. "I wanted to make sure it was okay with you before I said more."

Bridge squeezed her hand. "I'm fine with it if you are."

Alice shrugged. "How about we all get a drink first? I'm sure you have questions."

Chattering with anticipation, the small group disbanded, and Bridge leaned toward Alice after getting a bottle of wine and a couple of glasses. "You sure?"

Alice nodded with a small smile. "It just slipped out. No one seemed mad about me not saying anything before. I think it will be fine. Although, I'm surprised Gem seemed surprised. I thought she'd have picked up something with her gift."

"Gift?"

Alice's smile grew wider. She swiped one of the wineglasses and took a long drink. "I'll fill you in on that later. I need wine, and everyone is coming back."

Bridge refilled Alice's glass while everyone reassembled, pulling up chairs. Alice sat on the seat of the picnic table with her back against the tabletop and Bridge next to her.

Shia sat closest to Alice and slid a can of Pepsi into the drink holder on her beach chair before resting her hand on Alice's. "I know you, woman. You're probably overthinking not telling us about you being a nun. I wasn't angry at you about my mom, so I won't be angry about you keeping something about yourself private. Should you be ashamed for not telling us? Only because it answers so many questions about you. But should you be ashamed about your past? No. What I'm saying is, we love knowing about you because we're your friends, but it's your business."

"Exactly," Gem said.

Bridge had never been among so many loving and supportive people. It made her happy to know Alice had such great friends.

"I'm surprised you didn't already know," Alice said to Gem. "I mean, with your gift and all."

Gem shook her head. "That's not how it works. I can't wait to hear about your secret past."

Bridge wanted to hear Alice's version of the best part of Bridge's life. A host of tingly-tangly fluttering wings filled her stomach.

"Well, about twenty-five years ago…" Alice looked at her, and she nodded. "Most of you know I moved here from Kansas to go to school, but the school was attached to the convent, and I was sent to become a nun. It's no secret that I'm somewhat religious."

Shia snickered, then covered her mouth. "I'm sorry. No disrespect. It's just a bit of an understatement. Though, now that I think about it, compared to a practicing nun, I suppose you're a lot closer to 'somewhat' than 'super' religious."

Alice chuckled. "Considering that you just now learned I was once married to God, I can see how it's a bit of an adjustment."

Several people laughed. Bridge admired Alice for keeping the conversation light. It was something she wasn't sure she could have done. Talking about religion always got her hackles up. She wondered if she should have sought out therapy or something. Her family just pretended it had been a "phase."

"This story is about how Bridge and I met," Alice said, "but when I was separated from the convent, I took it as a personal failure. That part made it difficult to talk about. I'd broken my vows."

The fluttering was still there in Bridge, but a little of that old disappointment joined it.

"With Bridge?" Taylor asked.

Although the sun had mostly set and they were all illuminated rosily by the bonfire, Bridge saw Alice's face flame red. If she touched her, her skin would be hot.

Alice took a long drink. "Yes." She gave the abridged version of their time together. To Bridge's surprise, she didn't fade to black, but she didn't give many details, either. The way she told it made Bridge long for those days of patient yearning, secret meetings, and fervent joining. Even more surprising, Alice didn't portray it as forbidden. Instead, she described it the way Bridge remembered it: natural, almost unavoidable.

Alice explained her faith as creating deeper connections and passionate feelings, how their love amplified the passion they had for religion. The emotions that swept through Bridge transported her back, repainting their past in a new light, one that wasn't as barren of humanity as she'd come to remember. She'd never suspected Alice of having such a complex awareness of her religion and how it colored everything else in her life. She was a bit embarrassed to admit that she'd assumed it was more surface for Alice, a simple but faithful acceptance.

But when Alice talked about how their friendship became a desire for more, Bridge could almost feel the undeniable pressure, the compulsory need to show Alice how much she meant to her. It was easy to see how Alice might have taken that to be an outside force, something like the Holy Ghost, guiding them toward one another.

"When Gem's parents found me at the bus station," Alice said, "I honestly thought it had been a mistake. That if I'd had a chance to explain, Mother Superior would have understood. Instead, I withdrew. I didn't fight for my place in the convent. I had faith that God would bring Sister Mary Bridget and me together again. I had to rebuild my life. I never lost hope, but as the years rolled by, I tried to stop thinking about it. It hurt too much. Of course, I often thought of bits and pieces but in a way that was separate from who I'd become. It didn't seem necessary to tell people because it wasn't who I was anymore."

"I notice you use Sister Mary Bridget when you talk of the past and Bridge when you talk about now," Mikayla said.

"I guess I do." Alice looked at Bridge. "To me, we're both so different now."

Bridge nodded.

"You're still a bit of an enigma," Taylor said.

Alice laughed. "You know as much as I do now."

"I somehow doubt it."

"I think the story of Alice and Bridge calls for a dance," Tripp said, picking up a Bluetooth speaker and his phone.

"You don't dance, Dad," Gem said. "He's always said it's banned in Sweden so he lost the gene. Even though he was born in California."

Tripp snapped his fingers to a song and turned it up. "That was correct until about a month ago. My physiotherapist said dancing is good for you, not only for your physical health but for your mental health. Also, it's not banned in Sweden."

Gem shook her head and laughed. "It is. I looked it up."

"Of course you did, my smart daughter." His eyes gleamed. "But no one abides by it. It's like the law that all Christmas lights must be down by February in San Diego. It's on the books, but it's not enforced." He shimmied his shoulders. "Now, let's boogie!"

People made their way to the nearby half basketball court and began to dance. Alice continued to sit and stare into the fire. She wore a soft smile, and the light was doing its own dance in her eyes.

Bridge took her hand. "I liked how you described the passion of our faith as the propellant of our emotional relationship. That's exactly how it was. How could they expect us to keep a wall between that kind of emotion and everything else in our lives?"

"I think that's the idea behind being cloistered, performing the sacred marriage to God, and putting us on a rigorous schedule of chores and prayer. I think they believed if we were too busy or tired, we wouldn't have the energy or time to stray."

Bridge felt a twinge of discordance. She wanted to laugh at the irony, but it seemed like she and Alice saw it differently, and she wondered if that was a good or bad thing. "We didn't stray, though, did we? We found each other, and we continued to perform all our duties."

"That we did. With even more fervor because of the love in our hearts." Alice's eyes met hers as if she was looking for something.

Bridge wondered what it could be and wondered if she found it or was disappointed that she didn't. She couldn't read which. "God. The power that filled my heart back then," Bridge said as she held her gaze. She wanted to say that she was feeling it now. The way that Alice's searching look continued to hold hers told Bridge that she was still looking.

Chapter Eighteen

A lice poured the brine shrimp into the tank and closed the top. She turned on the light and put it to her favorite setting that rotated through different tones of blue. Pausing to admire the artful display of the ghostlike moon jellies floating in the continuous current, she stepped down from the stool. She loved the jellyfish tank that almost covered the entire length of the wall in her combined exercise and prayer room. Just a few minutes of watching the beautiful, brainless creatures could reduce her stress to almost nothing most days.

Not that she was stressed. At least, not in a bad way. There was the job thing; that was a good stress. At a minimum, she was going to get a raise, but she was pretty sure her boss had something in mind for her as far as a promotion went. Then, there had been introducing Bridge to her friends. Also a good stress, although she'd nearly had an anxiety attack when she'd told everyone about how they'd met. Now that the secret she'd never considered a secret was out, she felt a new kind of peace. In a weird way, it was as if she'd never taken a full breath and didn't know how until she took one.

With the pressure she hadn't even been aware of gone, her mind was unconstrained. She felt like one of her jellyfish: buoyant and untethered.

"I could watch that all day."

She turned toward Bridge's quiet voice to find her leaning against the door in nothing but a pair of tight boxer briefs. The tank light accentuated the lines of her statuesque body, sculpting her. In reality, Alice knew her curves were soft, her plains silky. A body magnificent, skin rivaling the finest fabrics.

"Did I wake you?" Alice asked.

Bridge came closer, wrapping her arms around her. Her warmth in sensuous contrast to the chill air produced by the air-conditioner. Alice had been unaccountably happy to know Bridge liked to sleep in cooler temperatures for the same reason she did: perimenopause. They'd both laughed about it the first night, each professing that they didn't think they were as old as they thought they'd be when the night sweats had started, but here they were.

"You wiped me out. My bladder woke me." Bridge kissed her and moved closer to the tank. "I'm glad I used the bathroom before I went looking for you because the sound of that tank would have caused a crisis. I didn't know you were a fish person, let alone jellyfish. I didn't even know you could keep them in a tank."

"Me either, until my friend Brandi asked if I wanted it when she switched to seahorses. I had no desire to maintain something like this. But there's almost no maintenance, just feeding and swapping out some of the water occasionally. I have the guys at the fish store come out a couple of times a year to clean the filters, and that's about it."

"It's like living art, the black backdrop, the lights, and the jellyfish just floating in there. It's hard to believe something so pretty will sting the heck out of you."

"You're safe. Moon jelly barbs aren't strong enough to pierce skin."

"Are those babies?" Bridge pointed to the sand at the bottom of the tank where a few small, translucent organisms swayed in the current.

It had been a few months since the last cleaning where they'd been thinned out, so a few more had planted at the bottom. "Those are the polyps."

"That doesn't sound appealing."

"Right? The life cycle of jellies is complex. The big ones are the adult form. They reproduce like we do with sperm and eggs and create larvae that plant themselves in the sand, where they grow into a polyp that splits off clones that grow into the medusa." She pointed to one of the larger floating masses. "Since a polyp can continue to asexually produce clones, you can imagine how a tank can get crowded. When the filters get cleaned, they thin out the polyps, too."

Bridge looked stunned. "You have to kill them?"

"I think of it as trimming seaweed. Jellies don't have brains. They're just slightly more complex than plants. They don't even know they exist. They just...are."

Bridge pursed her lips. "Aren't they still one of—"

Alice put a hand up. "Don't say it. There's a reason I have the fish store do the upkeep." If she thought of them as God's creatures, she couldn't do it.

"I'll bet you spend a lot of time in here."

Alice tipped her head. "At least a few hours a day. Morning and evening prayers and an hour or so of Pilates or yoga, depending on the day."

Bridge looked around. The room was cast in a blue hue, the hardwood floor gleaming in the pale light. Alice felt Bridge tense and guessed she was looking for the kneeler. She rarely knelt to pray, preferring to sit on a yoga mat, but she did have a large wooden cross on the back wall, with a long table that held her Bible and two candles.

She could have called it meditation, and she wondered if she should have, what with Bridge's anti-religion views. She knew people were uncomfortable with her faith. Sometimes, it bothered her, but it was as much a part of her as her arms and legs. She prayed the same morning and evening prayers she'd done when they were in the convent. To her, they weren't specific to the Catholic Church, although they were catholic in nature, just for her spirit, not the Church.

Her prayers were between her and God. Bridge didn't need to be part of it if she didn't want to. It would be nice, but it wasn't necessary. It might just take some time to get used to this change in who they were without the religion binding them. Even so, Alice longed to talk to Bridge about this shift in her belief system, but she wasn't sure Bridge would enjoy a theological discussion anymore.

Bridge's glance landed on the crucifix hanging on the wall, and Alice wondered what she was thinking. It was the same one from the convent, one of the only relics she'd kept. What would Bridge say if she knew there were locks of their hair hidden inside a compartment on the back meant for candles? She'd braided them back then, giddy to have a piece of Mary Bridget for herself.

"I like this space. It's very Zen."

Bridge's quiet voice brought Alice back from her thoughts, only to make her wonder how they would have reacted back then if they'd known that, in twenty-five years, they'd be in this room after making love, barely dressed, unconcerned with anyone walking in.

A surge woven of desire, love, and gratitude filled Alice's chest as she wrapped her arms around Bridge's waist from behind. "Thank you. I love having you in here."

Bridge studied the plain wooden cross. "I was surprised earlier."

What about? The bonfire had been fun. They'd stayed until the younger crowd had started to get a little more boisterous, and then they'd said good night. Alice had already known Bridge would spend the night, and she'd spent much of the evening looking forward to going back to her place, wondering what the others would think if they knew she couldn't stop thinking of having her mouth on Bridge, maybe one of her favorite things ever. Just the thought made her mouth water and her lower region do that lazy rolling throb that made her want to press herself against Bridge's thigh.

"Are you meditating right now?"

"Sorry. I was trying to figure out what surprised you when I went on a mental tangent about how much I like to go down on you. It feels kind of dirty saying it, but I really love doing that." The look of disbelief that crossed Bridge's face almost made her laugh. "Just thinking about it got my motor running again. Do you remember how we would disappear into small rooms to kiss and rub until we shook?" Alice had meant to tease, but her mind went right back there, and her motor really was revving up.

Bridge rotated until she was behind, brushing Alice's hair from her neck, gently pulling it around so it fell down her left shoulder. Bridge nuzzled the right side of her neck while opening her robe. When Bridge's hands slid down her belly and along her thighs, a tremor made its way through her, and she pressed backward, reaching up to hold Bridge's head where it was. "Your hands are so warm."

"So are you," Bridge whispered against her neck, and her kisses continued to make Alice tremble while her hands moved between her legs.

Alice spread her stance, and her hips rolled. A low moan poured from her throat. Bridge ran two fingers through Alice's aching folds, driving her passion higher as she skimmed her fingertips around her inner lips, dipping inside just a bit before teasing the outside edge even more. Alice wanted Bridge to put them inside her, could almost feel them slipping in, feel them fill her. A strong pulse of desire rolled down her innermost parts while Bridge traced around the most sensitive part of her. The suspense elicited sensations she'd never experienced before, slowly spiraling her need higher and higher. Her legs could barely support her, they were shaking so much. She held herself up by clinging to Bridge's neck.

"Lean into me, baby, I have you," Bridge whispered against her ear.

Alice leaned back, turning her head toward Bridge, not as comfortable talking during such an intimate moment but loving Bridge's words. It was new, hearing Bridge speak about what she wanted, what she was feeling, and it added to the exquisite and swift heights her body was taken to.

Bridge found her lips, kissing her, her tongue moving the way her fingers were around Alice's throbbing center. When Bridge broke the kiss to go back to her neck, her fingers slid inside, filling her exactly how she knew they would. Bridge's other hand, held flat, pressing against the hard knot of aching nerves until Alice was rocking along with the broad strokes.

Bridge replaced the pressure with two fingers along each side and massaged the area around it with one hand while continuing to slide her fingers in and out. Alice squirmed, rolling with huge waves of pending release. She wanted to let go so bad. She knew she could if she let herself. But the building pressure, the tremors, and the electric tingling that teased her from deep within were glorious. Every time Bridge moaned or breathed against her ear, Alice almost let go, but she held on. Held up by Bridge, Alice had almost no control of what her body did. It ebbed and flowed with the sensations building within her. She put a foot up against the low table and let her knee drop to the side as she stood on one leg and leaned heavily into Bridge, whose fingers continued to slide against the sides of Alice's rigid need.

"I'm about to come, and you're not even touching me," Bridge's rough voice and ragged breathing tickled Alice's ear, ramping up the pleasure coursing through her body.

"You have…no…idea…" Alice began but didn't finish as a bolt of pleasure ripped through her, arching her hips up and then back. She rolled them in time with the rhythmic swells of tension rippling outward through her limbs, coalescing until the pressure surged outward. Her hips twitched and pulsed. She clutched at Bridge's hair. She bit her lip so hard, she wondered if she drew blood. And her raised leg flexed, her toes pointed, pressing into Bridge with all her might. Finally, a shudder ran through her, and her muscles relaxed. If Bridge hadn't been pressing her forward, curved around her back, she would have fallen.

As her senses returned, she realized that all her weight rested backward; Bridge had braced her foot on the table at some point, and she was now balancing on one leg, slowly stroking Alice as she came down from her release. Sighing loudly and trying to catch her breath, Alice dropped her foot to the floor. Her knees were weak, but she was able to support herself. Bridge's foot slid from the table, too, landing with a thud against the floor. Alice spun just in time to help Bridge regain her balance.

Alice wrapped her in her arms. "I almost knocked you over."

She shook her head with an out-of-breath laugh. "Your pleasure is my kryptonite."

Alice dropped her head to rest against Bridge's chest, feeling her heart beating hard against her forehead. "I have no idea how you held us both up."

Bridge chuckled. "Long arms and legs."

"You know, you'd think that since we have the freedom to make love in a bed without fear of being caught, we'd never do this standing up again. Small, secluded spaces don't lend themselves to lying down."

"Was it disappointing?"

Alice looked up at her, gaping. "I have never experienced the likes of what just happened. It was metaphysical."

Bridge smiled. "I'm going to have to do some specific strength training. Besides, we're good at doing it standing up, even in a spacious place with pillows and mats all around."

"You stood. I levitated."

Bridge's mouth stretched into a cocky grin.

Alice pushed her weakly, putting a few inches between them. "You're entitled to that grin. My legs are still Jell-O. Are you hungry?"

Bridge rubbed her stomach. Bless it, she was sexy in just those tight boxers. "I think that's what woke me up."

With Bridge's naked breasts all out in the open for her to admire, Alice was on the verge of fantasizing again. She forced herself not to let her thoughts go too far down that route, or they might starve to death. She tied her robe closed and took Bridge's hand, leading her out of the room toward the kitchen. "What were we talking about before you attacked me?"

Bridge stopped walking and pulled Alice to her. "Attacked? You're the one who brought up...things."

Alice kissed her, and her thoughts veered right back to that train of thought. She wanted her mouth on...her stomach growled.

Bridge's eyes opened as she pulled away, and Alice had to put her fingers over Bridge's lips to keep from going right back to them as her empty stomach battled her aching center.

"Food it is." Bridge led them into the kitchen, helped collect the makings of sandwiches, and slipped into a hoodie hanging on the back of one of the barstools. The arms were a little short, but Alice thought it was cute. As much as she missed having an unobstructed view, it was probably best that Bridge's breasts were out of sight for the time being.

Bridge slid onto a barstool. "You mentioned something about a gift that the owners of Oceana have. Does it have something to do with the ley lines?"

A tingle, kind of like static electricity, spread across Alice's skin. Their gift and the ley lines didn't seem to be related, but she wasn't an expert. Whatever it was, it was a kind of miracle. It was something the Church would have considered for sainthood in ages past. She smeared a little mayo and mustard on the bread. "No one knows why Oceana affects the people who live here the way it does." She layered lettuce over the condiments. "Did you know there has never been a robbery here? Not so much as a doormat has gone missing. That alone is incredible. But it doesn't have anything to do with the Helmstaad family having the ability to tune into other people's emotions. At least, I don't think it does."

"That's what their gift is? Highly tuned empathy?"

"They sense a person's emotions as they pertain to their core essence." She placed slices of avocado and provolone atop tomatoes before folding thin slices of turkey over the cheese. Finally, she sprinkled salt and pepper, followed by a sprinkle of vinegar and oil before assembling the sandwiches and cutting them.

Bridge smiled as she accepted the sandwich. She took a bite and moaned. "This is the best sandwich I've ever had."

"I think we just worked up an appetite." Alice bit into hers and agreed that it was pretty darn good. She swallowed and wiped her mouth. "I'm not one hundred percent sure how they do it, but I think they tune into a person's basic energy. When Tripp first met me, he told me I was a good person with a broken heart. He was right." She laughed, amazed that she could without a trace of bitterness now. It had taken a long time to get here.

"The whole family has it?"

"I believe it's just Tripp, Gem, and Rose. Rose just figured hers out. Gem recently admitted to having it, but she's been aware of it for a long time. Tripp says he's always known he had it. They all describe it differently, so I think they might experience it a little differently, but the result is that they can sense a person's true nature."

"Gem said it didn't work like that when you asked her if she already knew about you being a nun."

"She reminded me that it's not like telepathy. She often makes it clear that she can't read minds. People get weird when they think someone knows their thoughts. It's all about divining emotions and intentions. Unless someone had told her, she wouldn't have known."

"You mean guilt, shame, and fear doesn't automatically scream priest or nun?"

"Right." Alice smirked. She didn't need the Helmstaads' gift to see Bridge's distrust of religion. Her heart ached. She couldn't imagine feeling that way. No wonder Bridge had walked away from her faith. But she'd done more than just walk away. Alice sensed a toxic anger. And how did that translate into Bridge's feelings for her? Did Bridge see her as guilt-ridden, full of shame and fear?

Bridge put her sandwich down and looked closely at her. "You look sad."

Alice wanted to say that it made her sad that Bridge had lost her faith. She wanted to remind her that faith came with its share of pain. Anything worth fighting for did. Suffering was part of being human. But she didn't want to challenge Bridge. She decided to change the subject. "I'm just glad they didn't think I was hiding it."

"Weren't you?"

"No. Well, I mean…" Alice sighed.

"It's interesting that I, the person who eschewed religion altogether, have no problem with people knowing I was once a nun, but you fight the urge to hide it."

"I don't hide. I just never had a reason to bring it up." It was a lie, and Alice knew it. Acknowledging it wouldn't make it feel better. She just didn't want to debate her faith. It was hers. She accepted Bridge. Bridge could accept her for who she was, too.

CHAPTER NINETEEN

B ridge adjusted her sunglasses and pulled the fabric of her T-shirt from where it clung to her damp lower back as an arid blast of heat rolled through the cab of Alice's truck. She was parked in the shade of a pepper tree in front of the main door to the business offices at the mission, waiting for Alice to get off work, and a chorus of conversational voices from across the parking lot caught her attention; about three dozen tourists poured out of the large wooden doors of the majestic white facade.

Her eyes zeroed in on the familiar form of Alice among the throng of tourists, and she waited for her to notice her. Her heart rate sped up at the exact moment it happened.

Alice's gaze felt like a hot caress, and a smile spread across her face. She gave a little wave as she led some of the group to the gift shop. Less than five minutes later, she emerged and got into the passenger seat. When she pulled back from their kiss hello, her eyes remained closed, and a dreamy smile brightened her face. It never ceased to amaze Bridge that she was the cause of Alice's joy.

"That was nice." When Alice opened her eyes, her face glowed.

"Like water after a long day in the sun."

It had only been nine hours since Bridge had dropped her off at work that morning, and she'd missed her. Before that, and aside from Bridge's quick change of clothes, they hadn't been apart since Friday when Alice had picked her up from the airport. Aside from the bonfire, most of their time had been spent in bed. Alice had even skipped work on Monday, taking one of her floating holidays, something she'd never done before. Bridge had technically been working from home but had gotten very little work done. Instead, she'd found herself being drawn to wherever Alice was: the kitchen, feeding the jellies, refilling the bird feeders, or sitting quietly on the porch reading a book. It had felt strangely domestic.

With an overlay of constant desire. As if the consummation of their physical reunion had flipped a switch to her libido, leaving it in the turbo position.

They'd agreed to staying out of bed all day Monday so Bridge could work, but they'd talked and touched and absorbed each other all day. The second it turned five, though, Bridge had grabbed Alice's hand, closed her laptop, and pulled her into her lap, kissing her hungrily. It had set off an erotic few hours that had left them both starving, having missed dinner.

After dinner, they'd curled up in bed and talked about all kinds of things until Alice had fallen asleep mid-sentence. Without discussing it, Bridge had spent the night for the fourth night in a row, but with both having things they couldn't skip on Tuesday, they'd agreed to sleep instead of staying up all night again getting lost in each other's bodies.

In the morning, Bridge had dropped Alice off at the mission on her way home, and she couldn't remember the last time she'd dreaded having to go to work. That had been a challenge simply because she'd spent the entire day daydreaming about seeing Alice all day. God. She had it bad.

"Sorry about the wait. They're a Spanish tour group from a cruise ship. They're visiting all the missions between here and Santa Barbara. Were you waiting long?"

"I just pulled up when you saw me." Bridge pulled out of the parking lot and headed for the Coast Highway.

"You looked deep in thought."

Bridge smiled. She didn't want to admit to her obsessive carnal thoughts, so she brought up a thought that had crossed her mind earlier in the day. "I was wondering if your boss had gotten back to you about what she has in mind for you." Still about Alice but less lascivious.

Alice looked away, and Bridge wondered if she somehow knew what was really on her mind. "She'll probably get back to me in our next one-on-one. I see you haven't exchanged my truck for your fancy car."

Bridge had asked to drive the truck that morning. She'd never driven one, and Ethyl was so big and badass. There was something sexy about rumbling down the highway with one hand on the wheel, elbow on the window, the seaside air billowing through the cab. She was about to disagree when she saw the teasing in Alice's eyes. It was one of the things that had first drawn her in. Something about that quiet young nun's sassy side back then, and it didn't fail to affect her these many years later. "I do have my butch aesthetic to think about." She winked. "Maybe we should swap."

"Even with the broken air-conditioning? And the Santa Anas bringing their hundred and nine winds through here today?"

"I hadn't noticed." Bridge wiped the mostly dry sweat from her brow. "I suppose heat stroke is kind of butch, right?"

"Very. If butch means future hospital patient."

Bridge nodded sagely, cocking an eyebrow. "It comes with the territory. Power tools, competitive sports, impressing beautiful women with feats of strength."

"I don't want to laugh and offend you, but something tells me you're not that person."

Bridge shrugged. "I'm not. At least, not on the regular. I don't conform to gender norms. Never have. People sometimes make assumptions based on my hairstyle and clothes, but I just do what I like."

Alice seemed to study her. "I think your confidence is a big part of it."

"I'm not that confident."

"But you display it fairly consistently, one of your most attractive aspects."

"You like confident women, huh?"

"I like confident you. But then again, I like everything about you."

Bridge would have fallen into Alice's stare had she not been driving, but she felt it's intensity across every inch of her body. She took Alice's hand. "The feeling is very mutual." She cleared her throat. "In fact, my feelings have gone right back to what they were before and have grown even stronger. I hope this doesn't scare you."

Alice grasped her hand and squeezed. Bridge imagined their feelings flowing through them. She'd never felt more connected. She stared at Alice and hoped she'd say the same. Instead, the eyes before her were closed, lips moving, then she crossed herself and kissed the crucifix she wore on a gold chain around her neck.

Bridge tried to ignore the irritation she felt. No. Not just irritation. A disconnect, sudden and piercing disconnect. Their hearts and energy had been flowing full throttle and then...nothing. She felt cast into a void. She wanted Alice to herself. To talk to her, not to...

No. Shame infused her. Alice was doing what Alice did. Bridge was thankful for her happiness. *Their* happiness. It didn't feel good, though. She wanted Alice to connect with her, not retreat to God. Bridge couldn't compete with that.

Alice glanced at her. Could she sense what she'd been thinking? "I was thanking God for bringing you back into my life." She squeezed her hand again. "I know you don't believe, but—"

"I get it." And she did. Mostly. She'd never want to deprive Alice of her faith. She was afraid that she'd sound condescending or worse, like she was humoring Alice over her beliefs if she tried to explain, so she squeezed her hand back, and they sat in silence for a few minutes, and Bridge tried not to focus on her irritation.

Alice looked toward the distant horizon. "The winds will be great for shaping the waves in Huntington this weekend. I hope they last through the following weekend when Shia is scheduled to compete."

Thankful for the interruption—but uneasy that she'd made Alice feel the need to so obviously change the subject—Bridge still eagerly took up the new topic. "I heard you talking about it at the bonfire. It sounds like a big deal."

"The US Surf Championship. There are several major events every year around the world. Until this year, she'd only been able to compete in the local meets. She keeps saying that she's just happy to have gotten this far, but Mikayla thinks she's really got a shot at this one." Alice giggled. "Listen to me. I sound like I know all about surfing. It's all just stuff I've heard from them."

"I've never followed surfing, but this sounds exciting."

"Shia won't even talk about what her hope is. She thinks it will jinx her or something. All I know is that she'll come back with more sponsorships whether she wins, places, or gets knocked out in the first round. I have plans to go up this weekend to watch on Thursday to be there for the kickoff on Friday. Do you want to come? We'd be back Sunday night."

"This weekend?" Bridge wondered why she was just hearing about it.

"It snuck up on me." Alice gave her a shy side-eye. "I've been a little preoccupied. When I saw it on my calendar today, I couldn't believe it was finally here. As it is, I have to miss the finals next weekend."

Bridge shifted in her seat. "I'd really love to, but a trip to DC came up today for this Friday. To tie up the paperwork for the Walter Reed deal. I don't get back until Saturday. I'm open next weekend, though."

Alice sighed. "October starts the busy season of the Interfaith calendar, and we have a lot to do at church next weekend to get ready for it. I'm the holiday events coordinator, so I have to be there. I feel so bad about not being there to support Shia in the finals, but I committed myself months ago. Next year, I'll know better."

This was the first Alice had mentioned the busy church season, and for some reason, Bridge was more irritated about this than about Alice's trip to watch Shia's competition. Except for Bridge's business trips, they'd seen each other every day. Up till now, church hadn't competed for their time together. This...feeling that rose in her was deep irritation and admittedly, pure jealousy.

Shame infused her again. She didn't want to excavate why she felt jealous or of what. Jealousy and resentment were not emotions she ever spent time with, so it was with a very intentional effort that she told herself to drop it. She was disappointed to miss a trip with Alice, she rationalized. And maybe how Alice had brought God into her declaration of feelings without even responding to her.

Alice looked disappointed. "I'm sitting right next to you, and I miss you already. Two weekends in a row?"

Bridge was touched by her disappointment, reducing a little of the irritation, and she tried to get some of her earlier happiness back. "Are you still up for our date to the aquarium? I've been looking forward to seeing the jellyfish."

Alice brightened. "I can't wait to show you the comb jellies. If you think the moon jellies are amazing, they'll really impress you."

"Let's do it." Bridge felt a little better.

As they merged onto the highway going south toward the world-renowned Scripps Institute, Bridge tried to figure out why Alice's relationship with her church bothered her so much. Normally, other people's religious or spiritual journeys were their business. She didn't want to be judged, so she tried not to judge others. As long as they weren't hurting other people, she really didn't care what they believed in.

Except, apparently, Alice.

Things were never that binary or that easy, it appeared.

In a moment of clarity, she saw that their past was built upon a common religion. If they didn't have that in common, what did they have? Could their connection be sustained?

The best way to figure it out was to actually talk about it. Trying to bury the emotions that were bubbling within her, she cleared her throat. "Hey. So, um, I think it might be a good thing for us to talk about the elephant in the room."

"Which elephant would that be?" She didn't seem to be feigning ignorance. Her MO was not to overthink things.

"Maybe I should have said the burning bush." When Alice didn't respond, Bridge stole a glance at her.

Alice was staring out the passenger window at the verdant hills. Quick views of the sparkling ocean shone between tree trunks and boxy, stucco homes.

"I was thinking we should tell each other where we stand with religion. You know, how as opposed to when it ruled our entire lives?"

Alice waved a hand. "Why on earth would we want to do that?"

Bridge tried to nudge her. "Is there something that makes you not want to?"

"You already know. I may not attend Catholic Church anymore, and I don't have responsibilities to the order, but I consider myself as devout as I was then. With a few crucial differences."

"Let's talk about those."

"Do you really want to? It's a little heavy for a date night."

Bridge thought about all the times they'd talked about the sermons they'd attended or the scriptures they'd read. Sharing their thoughts had moved her spiritually and intellectually. How many times had they been brought to tears during discussions that had ignited their souls? How often had they trembled with the blessing of enlightenment? Those times had brought them together, bonded them. She longed for that kind of connection with Alice again.

But without the religious aspect, was it possible?

"I've always liked talking about meaningful things with you."

Alice watched her for a moment. "You can't know how much I miss our deep discussions. This is where I worry that reality might not meet our expectations."

Bridge understood. Almost painfully so. "We won't know unless we try, right? As long as I've known you, you've always drawn people to you. You're fascinating to talk to. You were like that in the convent, and you are now. I have to suspect that you've been the same fascinating Alice over the last two and half decades."

She rested a hand on Bridge's arm. "Let's not ever say the decades thing again, okay? It sounds like a very long time."

"It has been a long time."

"Yes, but we don't have to stress it, do we? It was as if a wind swept through this car, sucked all the juices out of me, and tossed me into a sarcophagus."

Bridge laughed until she had tears in her eyes. "Point taken."

"So you want to know how my beliefs have changed."

"Yes. At one point, they seemed to be the only thing we had in common. I want to know this aspect of you now." The conflict inside her roiled. She was caught between wanting to know and support Alice in every way, but the religious thing was so hard for her.

She at least had to try.

"What if you don't like it?"

"Good question. Would that be so bad?" She honestly didn't know this answer herself.

"I don't want to run you off."

"Religion is one part of you, but it isn't all there is." Bridge said it to convince herself as much as Alice.

"True." She seemed to contemplate what to say next. "Well, it is important to me. Probably the most important thing in my life. After being released from my vows, I felt like a hollow vessel, devoid of everything I'd ever loved or believed about myself. You probably felt the same way."

Bridge wanted to say she hadn't felt anything like that. She'd been angry. Full of rage for a long time. At one point, she'd expected it to turn to grief or sadness, something that wasn't as destructive. But it hadn't. She'd simply stopped thinking about it, and one day, it was gone. Mostly. Familiar, like coals banked in ash, barely smoking, and capable of flaring up if the right fuel was added. "I was angry."

"I still miss the traditions of the Church. But I hate the power dynamic and the way it feeds negative things like greed and ego. Sometimes, I think I'd go back in an instant if they allowed me to be me. But then I remember all the other things I can't abide. Just love one another. It's simple. It's agency versus authority. A struggle to balance the authority of scripture and the Holy Trinity with the agency of humankind, but in a perfect world, humans should be allowed to make their own decisions and still live to serve God in whatever capacity we're called to do so. The rest is meaningless."

"Even if they aren't called to serve?" Bridge asked.

Alice paused, and expectation hung between them.

"Shouldn't we be allowed to question? I mean, could agency be as simple as allowing those who don't feel a call to live their lives without judgment as long as they do no harm?"

Alice was quiet as she seemed to contemplate the question. "I think so, yes."

Bridge let go of the breath she'd been holding. So much had hinged on that answer. If Alice couldn't have accepted it, there would have always been a chasm between them, an unbridgeable rift. And how could they sustain a relationship with that between them?

She should have felt peace, but something still hung between them. Alice had accepted Bridge's lack of faith, but could Bridge accept Alice's when there were so many problematic issues with religion?

Chapter Twenty

As soon as she fastened all the locks on the heavy door to her hotel room, Bridge tossed her computer bag and suit jacket onto the easy chair in the corner of the room and slid off her shoes.

As much as the team from Walter Reed liked to brag about their desire to party hard after each deal was sealed, they were tame compared to some of her other clients, who would sometimes insist on showing her the late-night spots so they could wipe out the top-shelf liquor on her company's dime. Tonight, however, the Walter Reed crew had already been yawning by ten o'clock.

And at fifteen minutes past the hour, she was back in her room. She changed out of her business clothes before she planned to drop like a sack of potatoes onto the hotel bed, happy at the prospect of a good night's sleep before she had to be at her gate at Dulles in the morning. She usually took later flights, but this time, she wanted to get back to San Diego by late afternoon, a few hours before Alice would be back from Huntington Beach.

She smiled as she thought of Alice hanging out with her friends after a day on the beach. She really wished she'd been in town to make the trip. A road trip with Alice and a weekend on the beach with new friends seemed like the perfect vacation, something she'd done very little of in the last few years. Maybe she could plan one with her.

Her cell phone rang just as she pulled on a pair of soccer shorts. Glad to be out of her suit, she flopped on the bed, put in her earbuds, and answered it, knowing exactly who it was.

"This is the party to whom you're speaking," she said as she adjusted the pile of pillows behind her head. Real feathers. DC hotels were the most consistently sumptuous next to New York City. There was no debating her on this subject.

"Then it would appear that I'm conversing with the proper party."

"Proper may be an overstatement." Bridge smiled. "What are you up to right now? Having drinks with the Oceana crew at a nice seafood restaurant in Huntington? Shooting pool with some biker types? Playing winner takes all at a seedy card joint on the outskirts of town, hoping the police don't raid the place before you get a chance to win back your grandfather's watch and the deed to the farm?"

Alice chuckled, and the sound tickled Bridge's ear in an almost erotic way. "You watch too many movies."

"But was I close?"

"Unfortunately not. I just got back to the hotel. I think I'll be ordering in tonight and finishing the book I'm reading. My version of surfing support ends when the sun goes down."

"I watched a little bit of the livestream on ESPN. It looks like a huge party. Why aren't you out there drinking?"

"Have you met me? My idea of a party is a night with friends around the bonfire. These young kids are acting like it's Mardi Gras."

"Just the kids?"

"I did see a few people twice my age doing shots and dancing." Alice paused, and Bridge could almost hear her thinking. "Do you think I'm boring?"

"Not at all. I think it would be fun to experience, just to say I did. But I've done my share of partying. I've done Vegas, Monte Carlo, Carnival, San Tropez, and the Cancun thing, among other party hot spots. But my favorite thing is to lounge on the beach or at the pool reading a book or talking over fancy drinks somewhere quiet."

"I figured that you were more of a partier because of the client dinners and that sort of thing."

"If I never had to do another client dinner again, I'd be a happy woman."

"I shouldn't feel relieved about that. But I do."

"Sounds like we're well-matched in this department." Bridge's mind went into the bedroom as another example of being well-matched, and while she'd never been shy talking about sex, she was now. She didn't want Alice to think it was the only thing on her mind. "What book are you reading?"

"A romance Taylor loaned me."

"Is it good?"

"Better than good, actually."

"Is it spicy?"

"That's part of why it's good, but the story is amazing, too. The best part is that it's a sapphic romance."

"Is that right? I suppose there would be a market for sapphic romances, but I haven't seen too many."

"I found them online a few years ago. They're the only thing that kept me dreaming."

"Who's the writer? I need to send them a letter thanking them for keeping my girl from losing hope."

"I never lost hope that I'd see you again. But you might send them a thank you for enlightening me on the various ways to please a woman. Sapphic romances elevated my game."

Bridge's throat went dry. "I can attest to that."

"With that, I think we need a change of subject before something embarrassing happens."

Bridge was all about taking the conversation to the next level, but she'd rather have the subject of her fantasies lying in her arms after a good orgasm. She shifted in bed, trying to ignore how wet she'd become. "Um, well, how's Shia doing?"

"She's having a great time. She hasn't competed in anything major yet, so she's meeting up with some friends and surfing heroes. She was a big draw at the freestyle event today. She won something, but it's not part of the real competition. She taught a couple of surf clinics this morning, too. You wouldn't believe the following she has. One of the big-name surfers was fawning all over her, and she didn't even realize it."

Shia was so down-to-earth. Bridge wouldn't have expected it. "How does Rose react to that?"

"She isn't here. There was an emergency with the solar stuff they're getting ready to install. But she's not the jealous type. Everyone knows Shia doesn't have eyes for anyone but her."

"They're so cute. Are you by yourself?"

"For now. Shia's soaking in the tub in her room, and Mikayla is down in the hotel bar talking to sponsors. Did I tell you she got us a suite? We each have our own room with our own bathrooms. I don't think I've ever stayed anywhere so posh."

Bridge glanced around her hotel room. After so many years traveling, their allure was wasted on her. The occasional bottles of wine or champagne waiting for her used to impress her, along with chocolates on the pillows, turndown service, robes, spa services, and all the elegant accoutrements the best hotels offered. Nowadays, she only slept in them and caught up on work before meeting her clients.

Alice's excitement about her room made Bridge want to sweep her off to go on a real vacation. Book a boutique hotel that only offered the poshest of experiences. Having Alice in her life was giving her a new perspective on things she'd started to take for granted. She'd merely been moving through her days for the last several years. Being with Alice gave her a new lens.

"Maybe we could take a trip sometime."

Alice's sigh over the phone made a tingle slide down her spine. "I'd love to have an adventure with you."

"Let's talk about destinations when I get back."

Alice let out another sigh. That Bridge could be the cause of that kind of sound coming out of Alice made her exquisitely happy. "I can't wait to see you."

A lovely shiver passed through Bridge. It was as if they'd leveled up in their relationship that now entailed future plans. Sensual future plans. "When do you get home?"

"Late Sunday night. How about you?"

"Tomorrow evening. I'm going to have to figure out how to entertain myself for the rest of tomorrow and all of Sunday."

Alice hummed as if she was thinking.

"If you're thinking about coming home earlier, this is Shia's big competition. She deserves your support. I can wait until Monday after you get home from work."

"I took Monday off to have some time to recover. It seems taking off a few days highlighted just how much time I have accrued, and my boss is encouraging me to take more. Do you have to work?"

"I did, but that just changed." Bridge was caught off guard by the excitement that coursed through her when she thought about another Monday with Alice. It brought back times in the convent when she'd made elaborate plans to get Sister Mary Alice alone.

Alice had always thought their trysts were moments of opportunity. She'd never suspected how hard Bridge had worked to make those opportunities happen. The heightened sense of urgency and anticipation had wrapped around and electrified those days for her. As if there was a continuous tingling current running through her, along with some of the most intense emotions she'd ever felt. A lot of it had to do with their youth and how everything was new. But they'd also had secrets. All the forbidden aspects had added fuel to their hormone-infused bodies, every moment had felt sublime, every word had carried weight, every touch had seemed potent.

Now, she knew they'd been falling in love, learning about themselves. They'd been filled with such yearning that their skins felt stretched thin, ready to burst with the slightest pressure. At least, Bridge had felt like that. She wholly expected Alice felt the same.

Right now, she felt all of those old emotions again, and it was adding a special tinge to everything. This was a feeling people would trade their souls for if they could.

"Mikayla just came in," Alice said. "I should see if she wants to order dinner with me."

"Good night, then," Bridge said. She was about to hang up when she thought of something. "Hey, Alice? Think about me when you get to those spicy parts in your book tonight, okay?"

Alice hummed deeply over the line. "I always do."

Chapter Twenty-one

A lice looked out over the ocean from her hotel window, tingling all over after her phone call with Bridge. She was excited to be on the first overnight nonwork trip she'd taken in her life, but she couldn't wait to get back to see her again.

"I heard you talking, and I thought Mikayla was here." Shia stood in the doorway, a white towel wrapped around her in stark contrast to her dark tan. She pressed another towel against her wet hair.

For the umpteenth time, the thought crossed Alice's mind that Shia could easily be in movies. Everything about her screamed California surfer. "I was talking to Bridge."

Shia leaned against the door frame. "Is she back from DC?"

"She flies back tomorrow afternoon."

Shia sat on the edge of Alice's bed. "You have it bad for her, don't you?"

Alice felt a heavy thwump, as if her upper body and head had been hit with an invisible pillow, but it was just the impact of the words, jarring and unexpected. It left her at a loss. Shia stopped drying her hair and looked at her, amused. Slowly, Alice nodded. "I do."

"Why did my question scare you? You seriously looked like you walked through a ghost or something."

"Maybe I did feel something, but it wasn't fear. I mean, I don't think it was. But that walking through a ghost was a weirdly accurate description."

"Your whole body tensed and your expression...anyway, why when I just stated the obvious?"

"What's obvious?"

Shia rolled her eyes. "That you are so into Bridge that it's ridiculous."

A thrill went through Alice, but at the same time, she realized something. "Being with her again is very much like walking through a ghost, and I do have it very bad for her. I'm still getting used to it being okay and for people to know. It was forbidden and for a second, it felt like I had been caught." But there was more to it. When Bridge had talked about going on an adventure, Alice had been reminded about her small life. How could Bridge be interested in someone like her?

"Like, PTSD or something?"

"I wouldn't blithely co-opt that term."

Shia put a hand on her arm. "You lost everything when they kicked you out of the convent. Your dreams. The woman you loved. Your safety, for Christ's sake."

Alice gave her the look she routinely gave when Shia cursed or used the Lord's name in vain.

Shia rolled her eyes again. "Jeez. You literally went through all of that for Christ's sake. Give me this one, Alice." She said it lightheartedly, as much as the topic would allow, anyway.

Alice laughed. "You know what? I'm done trying to police your language. You're a grown woman. You can say what you want."

Shia scoffed. "I shouldn't say things that offend—"

Alice placed a hand on Shia's arm this time. "It's not right for me to tell you, an adult woman, what you can and cannot say. I've been a bit of a tyrant about it."

Shia grinned. "I'll still try to watch my mouth. But seriously, you get why I said it, right?"

It was funny, but Alice pretended to scowl, which made Shia giggle, so she finally gave into a smile. "I do, and it was a good one."

Shia grew serious again. "You do have PTSD. I'm no therapist, so don't take my word for it. I'll bet Gem could tell you.

Regardless, you have trauma. But what's so fucking cool about it is that you're getting a second chance. I don't really believe in that whole, meant-to-be idea. At least, I didn't until I met Rose." She shook her head. "But you and Bridge, it's like you were destined to be together. You both have the same light when you're around each other. I don't know how to explain it."

Warmth spread through Alice's chest. "I like the idea that people notice that when they see us."

"I like Bridge for you. You're like a new person. And not because of the new wardrobe, which I really like, by the way. It's like you've come alive in the last few weeks."

"I've hardly seen you the last few weeks."

"We've both been a little busy." Shia gave a light punch to Alice's arm. "I know we haven't been doing our weekly coffee date, but I have eyes." She shook her head again, this time with an amused smirk. "I can't believe I never suspected you played for my team."

"Why would you? I've never dated anyone in the time I've known you."

"Did you date women before I moved to Oceana?" Shia seemed a little shy about the question, which made Alice giggle.

"There's never been anyone but Bridge, and in the convent, that wasn't technically dating."

"No one?"

Alice shook her head. "Men have occasionally asked me out. I've never accepted. Over time, I must have acquired a natural repellant because I haven't been approached in a while. Which is just how I like it."

"So, is Bridge like..." Shia let the sentence dangle.

Alice felt her grin spread. "The one?"

"I don't want to harsh your happy heart, but how would you know who the one is for you?"

"What do you mean?"

"If you've never...you know...been with anyone else."

Alice didn't have to think about it. "Doesn't that prove it? If I've never felt anything like this in forty-seven years. Just her then, and just her now. Doesn't that prove it?"

Nodding, Shia dropped her hands into her lap. "You really like her, then."

The warmth in Alice's chest expanded as if it would burst out of her. "She showed up, and in absolutely no time, I was right back to the feelings from all those years ago. It's only getting stronger."

"Love?"

Alice couldn't help her smile. "Definitely."

"Did you know you loved her then?"

"Oh, yes. She was everything to me."

"You two seem so different."

Alice paused. That was true. But different wasn't a bad thing. Opposites attracting was real. What did Shia mean by different, though? Was everyone exciting but her? Was it the religious differences? Was she wondering how Bridge could stay enchanted with her?

Shia seemed to study her. "You have a strange expression on your face. Like you're on the edge, just before the curl, wondering if you should make the drop onto the face of the wave."

It was a good analogy. It gave the idea of possibility and excitement. There was risk, too. She didn't like to think so much about that. "I know we have our differences. But…"

"But what?"

"But it's okay to have differences." Alice paused, and the next words tumbled out of her. "I'm not sure if I can take losing her again. Before, I had the luxury of blaming outside circumstances. Even then, there was the faint hope that we'd somehow meet again, and nothing would be in the way if we decided to try again."

"Isn't that exactly how it is now? Is there anything stopping you?"

"No. But…"

"What?"

Alice tried to define what made her hesitant. "It's almost too perfect. There's the religion thing." She had tried not to think about it, so she was surprised she said it. Ever since Bridge had wanted to talk about it in the car ride to the aquarium, it had been lurking. It was almost a relief to say something.

"Yours or hers?"

"Both. The existence of mine and the absence of hers."

"She's not religious." Shia bobbed her head. "I just assumed she would be, like you. Religious but doing her own thing about it. I mean, you were both serious enough about it at one time to become nuns. BTDubs, I have so many questions."

Alice wasn't sure she wanted to talk about her life as a nun. *Especially* with Shia, who was guaranteed to have a lot to say. "She doesn't believe anymore. Whether that's atheist or agnostic, I don't know."

"And your hopes about being together hinged on you both being the same?"

Alice eventually nodded. "Isn't that stupid? It's like I'd frozen us in time. I imagined us saying our prayers together, discussing passages in the Bible, and studying theology. All with our knees pressed together and making eyes at each other, of course."

"Really?" Shia sounded dumbfounded, and Alice felt like a country bumpkin again. "That's all you imagined you two would be doing?"

"I mean, that's how I knew her." She felt her face flame. "I'm worried that since religion was what brought us together, what will keep us together now? What do we have in common?"

Shia shoulder bumped her. "Sexy things?"

Alice's face grew even hotter. "Maybe." As embarrassed as she was about Shia's insinuations, she was glad to be talking about something other than religion.

Shia smiled coyly. "I'm here for it if you want to talk. Something tells me that you two are doing okay there, though."

Alice's whole body was aflame now. Talking about religion might be less uncomfortable, after all. "We're okay there."

"The offer still stands. But I'll let you off the hook for now. Is the religious stuff a big issue?"

"It's important to me, but it doesn't have to be important to her. Her trauma pushed her away from religion. I understand, but I'm afraid she'll somehow relate my religion to her trauma and start resenting me." Putting words around it seemed to release a cloud of doubt into the air. Alice felt ill to her stomach.

"Has she indicated that she has a problem with it?"

"Religion? Yes. My practice of it? No. But I haven't really let her into much of it. Next weekend, I'll be neck-deep in holiday planning at my church. It'll be difficult to separate it from my day-to-day. Unless I don't see her for several days, she's going to be in close contact with my church activities."

"Can you talk to her about it?"

Alice stared out the window at the darkening sky over the ocean. The lights of a few boats on the water twinkled. "I'm not sure I want to. She doesn't seem to like talking about it."

"It's your choice, but Gem once told me to be careful about setting someone up to fail."

"She was talking about your mom, right?"

Shia nodded. "I didn't trust her when she came back into my life. I also didn't want to talk about all the stuff that happened to me in my childhood because of her leaving me. I felt like she needed to prove herself before I could even think about letting her close. Gem told me that if I didn't talk to her, I was setting her up to fail. You warned me about it, too, in your own way."

Alice let those words sink in. Shia was still wary of her mother, but they were talking more and working on building a relationship again. Alice was happy for them, especially since they were getting ready to work on the new surf park together.

The difference between their situations was drastic, though. Alice didn't want to hold Bridge at arm's length. Just the opposite. She just didn't want to talk about it. Not talking about things was how she always managed difficulties. If she didn't talk, she didn't think about them. She simply prayed for what she wanted to happen. Sometimes, it took a while: like her and Bridge finding each other again, but it usually worked out. God's plans were mysterious. She was used to that.

CHAPTER TWENTY-TWO

B ridge took a sip of the very hot aromatic turmeric and ginger latte she'd picked up from the Seaside Café. It was just right for a late morning on a drizzly, gray, but not quite blustery Friday.

She loved these kinds of days in the beginning of fall. They didn't happen often in San Diego. For the first time since she'd moved back, she had to turn on the heater in her townhouse to take away the morning chill. There was something nostalgic about the smell of heated air chasing away the salty ocean coldness for the first time in the season. It was like the scent of wood burning in the bay area where her family still lived. Southern California didn't have a dramatic visual shift when the seasons changed. Just subtle changes in humidity, breezes, and the slant of sunshine that just sort of hit one day, and she knew it was the beginning of fall.

She leaned against her car parked on the street across from the café and hit the speed dial reserved for Alice.

"I was just thinking about you," Alice said by way of hello.

"I hope they were good thoughts."

"I don't know if I'm capable of having bad thoughts about you."

"That's good to know." Bridge smiled in the magical fall air. "I picked up a surprise coffee for you. I'd like to bring it by your office if that's okay."

"You're so sweet! I took today off to get some errands done. You can bring it by my house if you're nearby."

Bridge tried to ignore a twinge of hurt. Alice didn't *need* to share her calendar. It wasn't like she owed Bridge any information about what she did when they weren't together. But she'd worked at the church the evening before, and they'd spent the night apart after having spent every night together for three weeks, excluding business trips and Alice's trip to Huntington Beach. It just seemed like Alice would have said something about taking time off.

Bridge felt like she was fifteen again, and her friends had forgotten to ask her to hang out. It was ridiculous, she knew. "Are you sure? I can make it quick. Just drop off the coffee and leave so you can get your errands done."

"It's more holiday prep. I can take a break with you." Alice's voice sounded conciliatory.

Bridge got into her car and wondered if Alice sensed her up-and-down emotions. She tried for more casual as she pulled into traffic. "But it's important. It's why you couldn't go to Huntington this weekend. I hear Shia's doing well going into the final rounds."

"Mikayla says she's likely to land in the top ten. For someone who hasn't placed in the competition before, it's amazing." It almost felt like they hadn't had the weird tension just a moment earlier. "I wish I could be there."

"I'm sure she knows you'd be there if you could." Just saying it made Bridge feel a little better. If Alice couldn't be there for Shia, Bridge certainly couldn't feel slighted for herself. She decided to try the talking instead of ignoring the things thing she and Alice had touched on a couple of times. "Tell me more about your holiday planning."

"It's just minor event planning. But there are several in the next few months, so we need to plan so we don't overlap."

"Are you pulling together decorations and that kind of stuff?"

Alice sounded a little surprised that she was asking. "Well, we try to recognize all the religious holidays practiced by the congregation. I head the general planning committee, so I get the calendars synced up and get an idea of the resource needs. Subcommittees plan the actual celebrations, and I coordinate if they need it." She sounded excited, and Bridge relaxed. "My favorites are Yom Kippur, Diwali, and Samhain. Last night, all the subcommittee heads and I worked on the schedule. Today, I'll work on communications, training new committee members, reserving space, and making sure we have the officiants and special guests lined up. After that, I just oversee the project schedules and check in with the subcommittee heads.

"Sounds like a lot of work."

"But it's also fun and often quite satisfying."

"It's amazing that the different faiths share space like that."

"It was a big shift for me, especially learning about the non-Christian faiths. We didn't learn much about those belief systems in our theology classes. And what we were taught was biased." She was talking animatedly, as if she was trying to convince Bridge of something, maybe sell it to her in some way.

An immediate tension filled her stomach.

"I wonder how different the world would be if we made a more concerted effort at sharing space."

Bridge knew it was a rhetorical question, but it almost seemed like Alice was saying it was that easy. To her, it was impossible, but she didn't want to argue.

"If only it was that simple," Alice said, almost as if she'd read her mind. "Religion on its own is a volatile subject."

Bridge felt her own volatility churning inside her. She appreciated that Alice seemed sensitive to it and hoped it wasn't because she sensed her hostility. "Yet, it's intertwined with almost everything."

"True. Power. Money. Ego. Survival. Along with a multitude of other things that drive behavior. When one of them is taken off the table, there are plenty of other volatile subjects that remain. We all pick our priorities."

Bridge wondered if Alice was more aware of her discomfort around religion than she'd guessed. Was she trying to say that there were a lot of things they could disagree about, so why would religion be a deal-breaker? "I'm not sure where this conversation is going."

"My faith is important to me. But I don't feel the need to cloister myself among people who think exactly as I do. I'll always feel the scars from when I thought my faith was stolen from me. But if it wasn't for that pain, I would never have found the joy that came with knowing my faith was still there, unbroken. I get a feeling that makes you uncomfortable."

And there it was: Bridge's instinct to deny it. She'd tried so hard to keep her conflicting emotions to herself. She wanted to be a person who respected the beliefs of others. Kindness was her thing, and people were fascinating because of their differences. Despite the trouble she had with religion, she didn't want Alice to be exactly like her. Not at all.

At one time, they'd had everything in common. Now, there were twenty-five years of experience between them. And Bridge loved learning how Alice had been spending her time. She loved learning new things about her. The small community she'd built was intriguing. It was just this damned religious stuff. And it was her, not Alice, who had a problem with it. She needed time to get her old pain settled in her mind and heart.

Alice clicked her tongue. "The wheels are spinning in your head."

Bridge blew out a breath. "Sorry. I was just thinking."

"The last thing I want to do is make religion a thing between us."

Bridge snorted. "I'm not sure that's possible given the way we met."

"Do you really think so?" Alice sounded guarded again.

"I only mean that in the sense of how religion *was* our common thing."

"You don't think we have anything in common now?"

Bridge felt like her answer would either erect a wall between them or get rid of some of the doubt. She tried to forget her own insecurities as she searched for an answer. Maybe that was why Alice hadn't expressed her feelings about her yet, even though Bridge had told her that her feelings were the same, if not stronger than they'd been before. She hadn't said that she loved her, but that was what she'd meant, and there was no way Alice wouldn't have known it. In fact, Bridge's feelings had grown in the last week. It would kill her to know Alice was holding back because she was worried about their lack of a common faith. That it might one day drive them apart.

"That's not what I mean," she said. "We have a lot of things in common. We both love the ocean. Sunsets. The smell of eucalyptus. You love jellyfish, and I am a recent devotee. We both still love meatball sandwiches. You love to bake, and I love to eat baked goods. The very little we've spoken about politics tells me that neither of us like them, but we both lean liberal."

"Yes, but do you think—"

"I think we make a great team." Bridge paused. Maybe she was trying to be a little *too* convincing. "Sorry. I cut you off."

"It's okay. I think I might have caused you stress. I didn't mean to."

"I'm not stressed." Bridge lied, feeling that they had both just landed closer to some feelings that they needed to talk about, but she wasn't sure how. She turned off her car at Alice's house.

"Are you going to bring me the surprise coffee you promised?"

"I've been sitting in your driveway for all but five minutes of this conversation."

"Seriously?" Alice appeared on her deck with the phone still to her ear. "Why?"

Bridge wiggled her fingers at her. "I was concentrating on our conversation."

"We do tend to talk more when we aren't in the same room." Alice leaned on the railing and smiled.

"I'm not sure if I want to change that."

"How about you come inside, and we try to keep our clothes on this time?" Alice hooked a finger at her. Bridge didn't even remember opening her car door, but she was no longer concerned about talking.

CHAPTER TWENTY-THREE

After lots of kisses, Alice waved good-bye to Bridge as the Lyft pulled out of her driveway and drove down the street, turning out of sight on her way to another client in another city. Standing with her coffee in hand, already missing Bridge, Alice tried to convince herself that, in a way, Bridge leaving for a five-day business trip was romantic. Missing her and knowing she'd be back gave them both something to look forward to.

And Bridge's last relationship had been spiced up when it had gone long-distance. At the time, Alice hadn't seen how, but thinking about Bridge missing her, and her own anticipation of Bridge's return...it started a pleasant buzz low in her abdomen. Maybe the way she'd started missing her before she'd even left was a little pathetic, but she didn't care.

It made her think about the relocation to Santa Barbara again. Maybe she should consider it more closely. It would make it less likely for Bridge to get sick of her.

That was a weird swing. She shook it from her thoughts.

She turned back toward the house, preferring to think about how nice the weekend had been. She almost couldn't remember how she'd spent the weekends before Bridge had come back into her life. She looked forward to them now, enjoying the time with the woman who'd taught her how to love.

Over the weekend, Alice had tried to get up the courage to tell Bridge she loved her. She was sure Bridge knew, but she wanted to say it. She vowed to do it when Bridge returned Friday from her trip to Montreal. Five days. She could handle five days when she'd made it through twenty-five years.

Expressing her love should have been easy. She'd been the one to say it back then. And Bridge had told her weeks ago. The words should have slid like honey from her lips, yet, they remained perched upon her tongue, unsaid. Something kept telling her to hold off. Her fear of reality not matching expectations? The vast difference between their religious beliefs? Or was it a fear that Bridge had outgrown Alice and her small life? And it was just a matter of time until…

No. She didn't need to go there. Did she?

To be fair, either of the latter scenarios were valid possibilities, but she kept circling back to the tremendous sadness she felt when she thought of a future with Bridge. Being with her had been Alice's desire since she'd first recognized that the love she held for her was beyond any she'd felt before. Yes, even for God. Because her love for God didn't include romance.

So when she thought of Bridge having lost her faith, an enormous sadness infused her. What did it mean for their future together? She had faith enough for both of them. She had to admit, that occasionally, she wondered if Bridge saw her lack of worldliness as an inability to throw off the constraints of a religion that had shunned her, but she tried not to dwell on that. Their love would fortify them as Bridge worked through her issues. Alice believed in resilience.

After getting ready for work, the house seemed quiet. Usually, she'd just go into work early, but hyperaware of Bridge's absence, she was feeling unsettled, her thoughts and emotions swinging widely. Alice wandered into her exercise room, the place that gave her the most peace.

She hadn't felt like her usual self for a while now. Not since Bridge had come back into her life. In a sense, she felt more comfortable in her skin than she had at any other time in her life, as if the various aspects of herself fit more closely together than they ever had. She was just aware of them now, and that made her uneasy.

Contemplative, she stood in front of the tank. The jellies floated serenely. In a way, she'd been a lot like a jellyfish among other jellyfish before Bridge: floating along in the world, drifting, somewhat aware of others but mostly just doing her own thing, not too concerned about anything. Letting go and letting God. It was different now. She had something to lose.

No. She couldn't compare her life prior to Bridge's reappearance to that of a jellyfish, no hopes and dreams, no connection to her family, just a brainless organism spawned from a polyp. She was more than that on her own.

Wasn't she?

Her thoughts turned back to relocating to Santa Barbara. Maybe it wasn't such a bad idea.

She shook herself out of her rapidly spiraling thoughts and headed for work.

❖

Alice's office was chilly. The mission's interior was always a little cooler than it was outside, and the heat wave they'd had earlier in the week had broken. She pulled on a sweater. It was only in the low sixties, but with the humidity, she could feel the chill in her bones.

After her sobering thoughts, Alice wasn't in the mood for a video call, but she had her weekly one-on-one with her boss. If it hadn't been for that, Alice would have stayed home. Her boss was supposed to have been in town for it, but as soon as she'd opened her email, she'd discovered that Dr. Chandra Kapoor had flown back home to Mumbai to be with her sister, who'd given birth to her twins over a month early.

After a few minutes of greetings, an update about the babies, and a conversation about the time difference, they started their meeting, all fairly informal since they'd worked together for almost four years. "I'm surprised you still wanted to meet. It's so late there," Alice said after they'd finished covering the week's schedule.

"We eat dinner late here and stay up later. Melanie is having a hard time adjusting, but I usually fall into the habit quickly."

Alice had met Chandra's roommate Melanie a few times when she'd come down to San Diego with Chandra. She'd said that she liked to tag along when Chandra had some available time off from her work. Alice had once taken her to the Birch Aquarium. "Your roommate went with you? How does she like Mumbai?"

Chandra cleared her throat. "Melanie is my wife, Alice." Chandra shifted on her end of the video feed, indicating her discomfort.

Alice felt awful. She'd never known Chandra to be anything but confident. On top of that, how had she not known this? She searched her memory. Had she or Melanie ever said anything? Or had she just assumed? Chandra had no doubt thought she was like most of the world, wired to assume heteronormativity. "I'm sorry. I…I didn't know. I…" She was trying to figure out a way to say that she wasn't a homophobe, that they were alike in this way, but Chandra saved her from making a buffoon of herself.

"It's okay. I've always introduced her as my roommate." She paused. "I've been meaning to clear it up with you, especially since we'll be working more closely together, and Melanie travels with me so much." She paused again. "I'm going to have to clear it up with everyone soon, anyway. Melanie's pregnant."

"Really? That's great. Better than great. It's amazing and wonderful and…and phenomenal. Congratulations." She was making too much of it in her discomfort.

Thankfully, Chandra's insecurity seemed to dissipate. The excitement Alice felt for her was authentic. She was already thinking about all the baby sweaters and blankets she was going to make. Chandra was beaming now, although shyly, which just added to her charm. "We're only three months along, but I'm planning to take leave when the baby comes."

"Of course. It's a special time."

"It's been on my mind since we talked about additional opportunities for you."

The very mention made Alice's stomach flutter. Mostly in a good way, but change always made her a little anxious. "I guess you need to make plans to make sure things keep running while you take the time off."

"It was good timing when you said you were interested in new things. I know you're hesitant to relocate. But I want to know what it would take to make you reconsider. I'd really like you to take my old position. You're perfect for it."

Anxiety replaced the flutter in Alice's stomach. "I don't know. I mean, thank you. I appreciate your faith in me. But I have a house here and friends."

"I'm not asking you to make a decision today. It's just that I don't think I'll be spending as much time traveling once the baby is here. It will be harder with a family. I'm planning on training you to take over much of that part of my job. It's a lot of traveling, but there will be additional compensation. We can talk about that more when I get back."

It didn't get past Alice that Chandra had no doubt assumed that traveling would be easier for Alice because she was single. It made her feel slightly better about her own assumption but not much.

That was nothing compared to the apprehension that now roiled in her abdomen.

They closed the video call with a few other pieces of business and Alice saying that she would think about the relocation. The knot had formed a stone in her stomach. She'd already settled on accepting a raise and maybe taking on a few new responsibilities. But now a whole new set of expectations was being handed to her. She was happy in Oceana. Not only had she lived there for twenty-five years, but she had friends there. She loved her life exactly where she was. Oceana was her home.

But Chandra needed her.

And there was Bridge.

They'd only been together a couple of months, but Alice was happier than she'd ever been. Even when they'd first been together. Despite some of the inevitable reevaluation of her life, she felt like she was finally living as her real self. Did she want to move two hundred miles up the coast? How often would they get to see each other then?

Or was this what their relationship needed? What if they couldn't overcome their religious differences? Bridge had spoken about slowing down her own traveling. Would it be good for their relationship if Alice started doing some of the traveling to keep everything fresh?

By the time she was done working for the day, her head was a mess, and her heart was in even worse shape.

Chapter Twenty-four

A pause came in the rain that had been falling in Montreal almost all week. The sun had finally made an appearance, peeping through the scattered clouds. With some time to kill, Bridge was inspired to take a walk around the picturesque old downtown.

She'd always loved the cobbled streets and architecture but rarely had a chance to explore much during her hectic business trips. However, the deal that she'd come to close had gone faster than anticipated, and she found an entire morning to herself before she had to leave. Eager to get home early to see Alice, she'd tried to get an earlier flight, but she'd been out of luck.

She had a bounce in her step as she passed shops and cafés, and the smell of fresh bread and various food set her stomach to growling. When she entered the small café she'd eaten in every morning since she'd arrived, she took a seat on the patio. Despite wanting to order poutine that she'd already had twice that week, she settled for a breakfast sandwich and a cinnamon latte, wondering if Alice would like Montreal. She thought about what sights she'd show her, the first being the romantic hotel she'd stayed in a few trips ago on the shore of the St. Louis River. The gardens alone would make Alice swoon. Bridge smiled as she envisioned them holding hands under the limbs of old trees. She would have a picnic, and they could eat it near the little pond. She thought about kissing her and saying that she loved her.

She sighed out loud. What a sap. Smiling and only a little embarrassed, she looked around to see if anyone had heard. No one looked at her oddly, but she didn't care if someone had. She was happy, and she had Alice to blame.

She'd just set her empty cup on its small plate when the church bells began to ring. Most likely Notre-Dame Basilica just down the street. The sound reverberated along the stone, making her feel as if it was ringing right next to her. Something about it reminded her of the many churches she'd seen in Europe. She wouldn't claim to be unaffected by the grandeur and the sense of prominence, but there was an air of aversion within her, too.

She could rarely see a church, especially an opulent one, and not be reminded of the betrayal and abandonment all those years ago. This time—and because she was in a city that felt a little different on that day—there was something else. Something that compelled her. She paid her bill, picked up her backpack, and made her way toward the Place d'Armes, the large square where the ornate church stood.

Flanked by two tall turrets, the front of the solid stone building faced the square where a large fountain gurgled. Several people with cameras, strollers, and shopping bags sat around the fountain, enjoying the respite from the rain. The church stood as if a sentinel watching over the area. Three great arches were evenly spaced along the front of the building, and the middle one displayed a set of open wooden doors with chunky, black iron hinges and evenly spaced rivets.

The doors beckoned to Bridge. No church had called to her since before her time in the convent, not even the mission. Unable to deny it, she walked across the square and through the old doors. Before her feet crossed the threshold, familiar scents assailed her. It never failed to surprise her how all churches seemed to smell the same. Wood polish, incense, and burning candles overlaying a ubiquitous scent of ancient surfaces.

Heavy silence descended now that the bells had stopped ringing. Even with the doors open, the sounds of the square seemed to stop at the vestibule. Her footsteps were almost silent. Although she'd expected a certain ornate splendor, the magnificence of the place stole her breath away. Every surface was covered in museum-quality artwork and decorative details, all of it designed to bring the eyes to the altar that featured life-size statues of Jesus, Mary, and the apostles standing in gilded recessed naves along the wall behind it, four stories high, under a massive arched ceiling.

Opulent gold and white cloth covered the ceremonial surfaces; the altar made her feel small and plain. A richly painted ceiling hung over gleaming lines of pews with velvet kneelers. Above and behind her was the choir balcony, featuring a huge pipe organ and painted alcoves, stained glass, and all the splendor of religious detail. Along one side stood wooden confessionals and an alcove containing a votive candle station. The other side was replete with gorgeous stained glass featuring the stations of the cross and other religious events.

With a tight chest making it hard to breathe, Bridge slid onto a pew near the back, fighting the reflexive instinct to genuflect and cross herself. And the ingrained guilt when she didn't. Breathing deeply, she sat, the tightness in her chest easing slowly with every deep breath she took.

Finally, she was able to relax her shoulders. Swallowing hard felt like there was something in her throat. A sob. With effort, she relaxed her neck, prepared to let the sob go, but nothing came out. Instead, a lightness she hadn't felt in years descended upon her.

She heard a door quietly open somewhere behind her and the soft sound of footsteps and cloth moving came close, moved past. Two figures glided by, nuns in full habit with bowed heads over steepled fingers. She assumed they were in the middle of silent prayer. Her eyes were glued to them, taking in the familiar postures, the robes, the air of sacrifice and devout sanctity.

They genuflected and crossed themselves as they slid into a pew near the front of the altar and knelt, leaning over their hands clasped in front of them. Bridge could almost feel the slick beads of their rosaries sliding through their fingers as they recited the prayers she knew from memory. She knew their expectations of answered prayers, patiently awaited, certainty that their closeness to the divine would bring them what was asked even if it wasn't exactly what they requested. God always knew best.

Bridge wished Alice was there to experience this moment with her. She wanted someone to talk to, and Alice was the only person she knew who might understand the complex mix of emotions welling within her. It was disorienting, watching these women who had given up everything going through the motions of devotion, recognizing the meditative quality of their actions down to the smallest gesture. Even from behind, she knew they had matched their breathing, their lips moving silently over the same words, their fingers passing along the rosaries, minds blind to everything around them. They were like long-distance runners, operating by routine, settled into a cadence that overrode all other ambient sensations, the high of every system working together in harmony-releasing endorphins when everything aligned.

Bridge longed for another moment of it, the life of devotion, the absolute certainty of doing exactly what was needed and expected. Fulfilling her need, too. The need to…what? Give the ultimate sacrifice? Devote her life to God? Not really. It was more about hope. She wanted to give people hope.

But didn't she do that in her profession? She gave people who'd lost limbs the hope of independence and self-confidence.

Something filled her then. A dawning, the beginning of the reconciliation of her past and her present. With it came a sort of anticipation that she was on a good path. It wasn't that she wanted religion back, but she wanted that sense of knowing that she mattered. Not just through her actions but also in a spiritual sense. She craved purpose.

Again, she wished Alice was there. But at the same time, she wasn't sure she'd be able to explain the myriad of emotions this experience had brought up in her.

CHAPTER TWENTY-FIVE

In her entire forty-seven years of life, Alice had never had to drive to an airport, yet in the last six weeks, she'd been to the San Diego one twice. Bridge had tried to say she'd take a Lyft home, but there was something deeply romantic about picking up the woman Alice loved outside the doors. In fact, something sad welled inside her thinking that she would never get the chance to meet Bridge at the gate like people used to do years ago, back when the epitome of romance was awaiting a loved one's return right outside a jetway with a bouquet of flowers.

Still, she couldn't help smiling in anticipation as she made the Sassafras exit off the I-5, then south to West Laurel and onto North Harbor Drive where the sunlight reflecting off the water in the bay served as a backdrop to the picturesque display of boats floating next to the docks. It had to be one of the loveliest airport drives, with the stunning views of downtown, the harbor, and the Coronado Bridge in the distance. No wonder people clamored to visit San Diego.

With the help of texts and automated updates from the airline app, she timed it perfectly. Bridge was striding through the automatic doors just as Alice pulled up to the curb. The bubbling excitement in her stomach intensified. Bridge was impeccably dressed, even in casual cotton shorts and an untucked pastel pink button-up, and a huge smile lit up her face. Alice almost forgot to turn off Ethyl's ignition in her excitement to get out and greet her.

Alice rounded the back of the truck and nearly leaped on her, wrapping her arms around her neck, and squeezing for nearly a full minute before she leaned her head away to say, "Hi," and pressed a kiss firmly on her lips for all the world to see. After a week of separation, Alice couldn't say how excited she was any better than that.

"Wow. That's what I call a warm welcome," Bridge said, squeezing her tightly.

"I missed you."

"I missed you, too."

Alice saw the truth in her gentle eyes and kissed her again. This time with a little more care to take in the softness of her lips. When she pulled away, she saw amusement in Bridge's face. "What?" she asked.

"I like making out with you at the airport. It feels naughty."

"Do you want me to stop?" Alice didn't loosen her embrace, although the conversation gave her a glimpse back to the other night, when she wondered how Bridge saw her. Repressed? Or was that a holdover from the days of hiding their feelings for each other?

Bridge pulled her in tighter. "Not at all. I like it very much."

"Good." Alice looked around, happy. "And it's not like they haven't seen people kissing before. No one's even looking. Plus, I kind of like claiming you. You're a very beautiful human, and I like thinking that people are jealous that I have you, and they don't. Does that sound gross and possessive?"

"It sounds like someone who owns who they are. I like possessive Alice. I mean, I'd have to reassess my answer if you kidnapped me, but even that has its allure." Bridge laughed, and Alice couldn't recall feeling lighter and happier than she did in that minute.

Until she realized that an undercurrent of waiting for a balloon to pop was swirling beneath it all. Like what they had was too good to be true. She tried to ignore it. "Toss your suitcase in, and let's get this show on the road," she said. "I might be okay with kissing you in public, but don't tempt me with your slick words and make me forget my manners."

"Sounds like a challenge," Bridge said after dropping her bag in the bed of the truck and getting into the passenger seat.

Alice squinted at her after she stuck the key into the ignition. "I like to think of it as a warning. You make me do things I never thought I would, despite my good intentions."

Bridge's expression turned serious. "I hope in good ways."

"In very good ways. But I'd rather be alone when clothing starts to get in the way of my good intentions."

Bridge's serious expression changed to one of mischievousness that drove away the remains of Alice's weird sense of wariness. "We couldn't have that."

"Most definitely can't have that." Alice started the truck and merged into the flowing airport traffic. "How was your trip?"

"We closed the deal, and they'll be contacting me for some new research collaboration that always leads to additional orders."

"I was a little disappointed that you couldn't get the earlier flight. What did you do to kill the time?"

"Have you ever heard of the Notre-Dame Basilica?"

"The one in France?"

"Many churches around the world have been named Notre Dame or Our Lady." Alice must have shown her surprise because Bridge chuckled. "I know. I was surprised, too. The one in France is a cathedral, a bishop's seat. The one in Montreal is a basilica."

"I have to admit that religious history, architecture, or whatever that falls under, wasn't my strongest path of study in college."

"Yet your career is historical preservation of the missions."

"I know. Amazes me sometimes, too."

"I had to look it up, too. Anyway, it was just down the street from my hotel."

"Was it glorious?"

Bridge was quiet, seeming to consider the question, and it was a minute before she answered. "It was."

"You seem, I don't know, surprised."

"I haven't been in a church, except for the mission, since we were in convent." Something contemplative tinged her voice.

"What made you go?"

"The bells began to ring, and I just followed them to the square. I probably would have just admired it from outside, but the door was open, so I went in."

"An open door is like an invitation, especially at a church since they're usually kept closed. Maybe because opening the door could be a way of instilling a sense of moving from the secular world into the religious one."

"Does your new church have all the pomp and circumstance, too?"

"Not even close. Far more casual."

"Do you miss it?"

"I do." Alice wondered if visiting the church had brought up old memories and feelings. Of course it had. "Do you miss it?"

"I guess there's a sense of comfort in doing familiar things and not having to come up with new things to do all the time. Going to church? Put on church clothes. Taking communion? Go to confession. Time to sing? Go to Psalm 63." Bridge adjusted the air vent. "I honestly think I could fall asleep and still go through the steps of Mass."

Alice laughed. "I slept through a few, and no one was the wiser."

"I like to think of myself as more of an intellectual than someone who needs a script to perform my spiritual absolutions. You don't even have to think to get through Mass."

"I suppose so." Alice was surprised by how defensive she felt. At the same time, this was the most specific discussion they'd had about their past faith. She didn't want to respond in a way that would shut the discussion down.

It was that intellectual approach to religion that Alice missed, when they would discuss the meaning behind passages of the Bible, trying to unlock the secrets of salvation. Bridge had never failed to raise Alice's level of understanding. It had been a rich and heady time for her.

Her heart beat an excited tempo to think they could do that again. "I guess that's a good business tactic. Lowering the barriers of entrance and then introducing the more intricate details as comfort and knowledge are raised."

Bridge raised an eyebrow. "Did you just make a correlation between business and religion?"

Alice snickered. "I guess I did."

"Clever lady."

Alice beamed.

They were quiet for a moment, and Bridge shifted toward her as much as the seat belt would allow. "Do you think they brainwashed us?"

Dang. That went in a weird direction really fast. Her defenses pinged again. "What do you mean?"

"You know. Indoctrinated. Coerced. Inculcated. Programmed."

"You make it seem like a cult."

"Isn't it?"

Alice bristled. She couldn't help it. She wasn't a member of the Catholic Church because they wouldn't have her, but if they changed their stance on her kind of love, and perhaps on a little of the misogyny, she'd go back. To her, there was no stronger, more elegant, more intelligent religion. And while religion came with its bad players, what institution didn't? "I don't think it's a cult."

"It conforms to all the attributes of one. You have a charismatic leader, a controlled membership, and a requirement to blind devotion."

"How is that different than a bowling league or a sorority? Everything is a cult, then."

"I suppose the difference is malicious intent toward gaining power."

"Again, what corporation doesn't do that exact thing? Even brand names fall within that definition to appeal to a specific demographic in attempts to win loyalty." There were lots of examples, but she needed Bridge to know that she had a few limits. "My current church."

Bridge put a hand on her thigh, helping to quell some of the irritation. Not just irritation, anger. And not a little bit of fear. Were they growing apart already? Was her life too small to keep Bridge interested? "I'm sorry. I didn't mean to infer that your church is a cult. You're right. My own company could be considered a cult under the conditions I named. I guess I do have a few issues to work out. That's where the brainwashing question came from. I doubt your church requires the same kind of blind devotion and unfair rule following from its membership."

Part of Alice accepted the apology. But a small part still wondered if Bridge saw every religion as a cult. What did she think of the people who followed them? What did she think of Alice? "It's understandable to want to figure out what you want and need from religion, given the circumstances."

"You're the kindest, gentlest, most understanding person I think I've ever known." Bridge rubbed her thigh, and Alice couldn't deny the effect it had on her. And it wasn't spiritual. It was hard to regain her focus on the conversation. "Do you think I was too harsh in rejecting religion? I mean, after I was removed from it?"

The question reminded Alice that Bridge had been hurt, just like she had. But Bridge had gone one way with it, and she had gone another. It could have just as easily been Bridge who'd looked for solace elsewhere and Alice who might have eschewed religion had their experiences been different. "It's hard to say. Reality seldom lets us redo things. I think you did what your circumstances led you to do."

"Do you think I should reconsider?"

"Again, I couldn't say." She could, but that didn't mean she should. This was Bridge's journey. "Only you know what's best for you. Anything I suggest would be a guess."

"But you know me best in this respect."

"That also means I don't have an unbiased opinion."

"Fair enough." Bridge looked out the window. "Part of me wishes you weren't such a fair person. It would be easier if you just told me what to do."

Alice pulled into her driveway, turned off the ignition, and faced her. "You? The person who said at the beginning of this conversation that you don't need a script to follow?"

Bridge stared. Alice could almost feel the heat from her hand increase to the point where it felt like a tingle. "Script?" She might have felt it, too because she seemed to have lost the thread of the conversation.

"You know, I shaved my legs before I went to pick you up."

Bridge arched her eyebrow again. "You did, huh?"

"Yep." Alice winked to underscore the hint.

"Your legs are fantastic either way."

"I like how it feels when you touch them shaved."

"Well, then. Is there a reason we're still sitting in the driveway?"

"I can't think of a single one."

"I can either race you or carry you into the house."

Alice let out a small screech. "Last one in…"

She didn't even finish because she was dead set on winning. Lucky for her, she'd sneakily unfastened her seat belt and knew the passenger one had a tendency to stick. Even so, Bridge was only a microsecond behind her when she flung herself on the bed.

Chapter Twenty-six

For a minute, Bridge imagined she was on a boat floating on a gentle sea. She woke on her back, completely relaxed, expecting to see stars above her when she opened her eyes. Instead, a ceiling fan rotated lazily. Not a boat. Better. She was in bed, staring up at the ceiling of Alice's bedroom.

In near darkness, with the window open and the gauzy curtains blowing slightly in the breeze, the sound of waves crashing on the jetty and the scent of briny salt air soothed her. No wonder she'd thought she was on a boat.

Firmly oriented, she reached for Alice, but the other side of the bed was empty and cool. Bridge stretched, remembering how they'd made love when they'd gotten there.

Bridge had chased her into the room, but as soon as she'd had her shirt off, Alice had taken almost all the initiative, surprising Bridge, turning her on, driving her need into the stratosphere. But Alice had teased her, holding back on giving her what she needed until she'd felt like she would combust. She'd hated it and loved it at the same time.

Her climax had exploded within her like an earthquake releasing pressure on a fault line after millennia. She hadn't recognized the sounds coming from her own mouth. And she'd been surprised to hear Alice cry out in ecstasy, too, her hot wet center pressed against Bridge's thigh, her hand producing the erotic sensations that had resulted in Bridge's explosive orgasm.

Sweat had dripped as their skin slid against each other when Alice had lowered herself onto Bridge, arms shaking, kissing her.

Floating on heightened emotions, she'd almost breathed *I love you* into Alice's mouth. But she hadn't wanted the words to be attributed to the dopamine and serotonin rush of her orgasm. She'd wanted Alice to know the truth of her heart. The first time she said it again had to be as pure and authentic as the first time.

She wanted to tell her now.

She got up, ripples of desire still dancing low within her, a side effect of remembering Alice's body on top of her. The bathroom was empty, so she wandered down the hall. A glance into the exercise room revealed Alice sitting on a giant beanbag in front of the jellyfish tank, the blue light bathing her naked body. As Bridge clutched the door frame, enthralled by the sight, Alice caught sight of her.

"How do you do that?"

Alice tipped her head to the side with a little smile. "Do what?"

"Turn yourself into a painting made by moonlight fairies."

"Are you sleepwalking?"

"Maybe. Because you look like a dream."

"Stop. Your smooth lines are making me tremble."

Bridge chuckled and dropped onto the beanbag next to her. Their sides melded against each other, and Bridge snuggled up to her. "I'm sorry I conked out so fast after you had your way with me. I wanted to do mind-blowing things to you, but when you did that magical fingertip thing along my arms, the next thing I knew, I woke up, and you were nowhere to be found."

"It looks like you found me." Alice ran her fingers through Bridge's hair.

Bridge tried to hide a yawn. "We smell like sex."

"Like smelling like onions, fine as long as you both do."

"You are correct." Bridge yawned again.

"Why aren't you still in bed?"

"I missed you."

"Montreal is three hours ahead of here, so it's much later to you than it is to me. You've had a long day."

"But it's only nine."

"I'm okay with you falling asleep. It's not like you left me hanging. We were both quite…satiated, as far as I was aware."

Bridge snuggled more tightly against her. She loved that Alice was comfortable wandering around naked after they'd made love. The press of their skin was the most exquisite feeling Bridge could imagine. "Why did you get up?" she asked, kissing Alice's smooth shoulder.

"I was tossing and turning. I didn't want to wake you. So I came to my thinking place."

"Something on your mind?" Bridge trailed her fingers up Alice's arm.

"Chandra asked me to consider relocating to Santa Barbara so I can be closer to our headquarters. She and her wife are having a baby, and she doesn't want to travel as much."

Bridge's stomach clenched. They'd just found each other again. She quickly did the math. Was the sales saturation of the Santa Barbara region enough to justify her own relocation? It would be a major upset to the distribution of the sales team, but a couple of the senior sales members would scoop up San Diego in a heartbeat if she decided to move. But Santa Barbara was out of the way from the research hospitals and robotics manufacturers she worked with. She couldn't convince the company that it was a good place for her to make her home base.

An overwhelming sense of anxiety fell over her. "Wasn't she going to give you alternatives to the promotion?" She worked hard to not let it sound like a whine. There was no way Bridge was going to try to influence Alice in this decision, even if she wanted to say she couldn't leave. She wasn't going to risk having Alice tell her the same thing Jackie had. She wasn't going to make Alice think her life and goals weren't important.

"They did. And it still isn't a requirement. I can stay in San Diego and travel to Santa Barbara as needed."

Bridge's panic subsided, replaced by an uneasy feeling that there was something Alice wasn't saying. "That's a relief, right? Hopefully, it won't all be windshield time, and they'll let you fly when you need to. That's a long drive."

Alice gnawed on her thumbnail and nodded.

"Is there more?"

Alice looked at her as if she wanted to say more but decided against it and shook her head.

Bridge took her hand and kissed it. "I'm sorry. I just jumped in. Do you want me to leave you to your thinking? Or do you want to talk about it?" She wanted to talk, but she didn't want to rush her.

Alice slid her other hand under her thighs. "You know jellyfish have no brains, right?" The one jellyfish moved up and down in its corner. Most of the others floated in a circle as if a current was guiding them. There was a beautiful near symmetry to the way the jellies occupied the tank. They didn't clump up. "They don't have the same organs many animals do, but they do have a few that relate to what we see as organs, like a digestive system, reproductive organs, eyes, and a nervous system."

"They have eyes?" And why were they talking about jellyfish now?

"Sixteen. At least, the moon jellies do. Each species is a little different. They don't see in pictures but more in contrasts. So without a brain, they aren't conscious. They simply are. They don't worry or plan. They just exist, eating and protecting themselves. They have no sense of time or fear. Yet, they serve a purpose through the products of their existence, whether it's to be food, eat food, or excrete nitrogen into the water."

"Or act as living artwork," Bridge suggested, and Alice smiled. Bridge relaxed a little. "How does this help you think?"

"They stop me from thinking, really. I come in here, and everything slows down. The noise is reduced, and my brain can simplify problems and solutions. Ideas have room to bloom with less effort and more clarity. Did you know a group of jellyfish is called a bloom? It fits, doesn't it?" She took a deep breath and slowly let it out again. "For a long time, I felt like I was the lone jellyfish. I had no bloom. I related to the one who likes to float by itself. I'm good either way, I suppose, but I prefer swimming in the bloom." She looked meaningfully at Bridge. "Sitting in their presence makes me feel part of the greater existence."

It made Bridge think about their conversation earlier. "Does this feeling bring you closer to God? Or further away?" She didn't know why she asked. She didn't want to talk about God. She wanted to talk about them. God had abandoned her a long time ago, and Alice might have been on the verge of disappearing, too. Unless Bridge gave up her own life to follow her. But she hadn't asked. A knot of churning confusion whirled inside her. She tried Alice's trick of taking a deep breath and letting it out slowly.

Alice was quiet for a moment. "I think it *is* God."

Bridge didn't know why, but she had an overwhelming urge to cry. She couldn't remember the last time she'd cried. But an enormous thing inside her seemed to rise, expand, and flow from her. As she released it, it pulled something from her. She wasn't sure if it was something she needed or something she needed to get rid of. But It was something elemental that, at first, she was afraid to let go of. But as it detached from her very essence, she felt an almost physical sense of it separating from her body, like a film of diaphanous skin being peeled away.

She became aware of a freedom she'd never experienced. A wonderful, terrifying freedom. Whatever it was continued to flow, becoming part of everything around her: Alice, the jellies, the dark, the light, the trailer park, the city, and everything beyond that, yet still a part of her and always would be. She wondered if this freedom was the sense of peace some people felt when they meditated.

It wasn't God, though.

The sensation of freedom fell away. Just like that, the flow, the feelings it was causing, the connection to everything, just ceased. It didn't leave a void or any sort of residue. It had come, and it had left. That was it.

The more she pushed away what she considered religion and God, the more entrenched in them she became. She felt like she had to continually explain why she didn't believe anymore. Was she trying to convince herself or everyone else?

That flowing feeling she'd just experienced was a lot like how it had felt to surrender herself to her calling. When she'd simply closed her eyes to everything else and had given herself to her faith. She wished she'd never been forced to open her eyes. But she'd had to open them to open her heart.

It wasn't fair.

She hadn't even been thinking about God. Or had she? She'd asked Alice about whether her feelings brought her closer to God or further away. It was a revelation. She wanted to ask if Alice had a similar experience, but while she understood what it was, she didn't have the words for it. She didn't know how to express the fathomless despair that swept over her, how she felt about the last twenty-five years. How maybe she'd been battling an enemy that wasn't really there. Or if it was, was it the same thing that she'd been battling *for*? Maybe eschewing her religion had been the drastic response of a young woman who had been deserted by the thing she'd given up her life for. Maybe she'd only served to punish herself.

"You're quiet over there." Alice's voice seeped into her musings, and she was able to return to the moment.

Don't mind me. I'm just having an existential crisis brought on by my desperate love for you. "I'm sorry. I guess the idea that you could calm your mind to let the important stuff become clearer resonated with me." She felt like she was at a distance, watching herself and Alice sitting naked on pillows in a mostly empty room. It was a little unnerving. Like coming back from anesthesia. She squeezed Alice's hand to try to bring herself completely back. It helped.

I love her.

The words moved through her brain like the jellyfish undulated through the water. *I love her. I love her. I love her.* Like a bloom of jellyfish, the phrase drifted as symmetrically floating entities through the space inside her mind. *I love you. Please don't move away. I just found you again.*

But she couldn't say any of it. *I love you. Stay here. I want you to be happy, and your job is part of that, but I don't want your job to be more important than me, and I know that's selfish, but it's how I feel, so choose me. Stay for me.* She could only find words for things that weren't as important. "What are you going to do? About your job?"

Alice stared at the tank, then dropped her eyes to their intertwined hands. "I appreciate Chandra giving me a choice, but it's obvious she'd prefer that I move to Santa Barbara to make things easier. She's going to cut her own travel so she can spend more time with her family. If I don't relocate, she won't be able to do that." Alice squeezed her hand, and she squeezed back. "But you just moved here. I just found you again."

A small spark of hope lit in Bridge. "Well, I travel a lot already. I can travel there, too. We can make it work." Her lips felt numb, having trouble wrapping around the hollow words.

Hadn't she had enough disappointment and heartache already? It felt unfair that she'd spent so much of her life getting over the pain of losing Alice, coming to terms with never seeing her again, reconciling herself to the fact that her religion had been both the conduit for her meeting the love of her life and the thing that had taken her away. She was mature enough to know that very few things in life were purely good or bad, but this one time, she wished that her happiness didn't have to come with sacrifice.

Alice needed time to work through her choices. What Bridge did was press closer. She wrapped her body around her, and they cuddled in the soft cushion in the blue light.

CHAPTER TWENTY-SEVEN

Desolation stabbed at Alice's heart as she sat on her front deck and watched the sea on the horizon. The day had been beautiful, but as the evening came, scattered clouds had accumulated over the water. The forecast had not predicted rain, but they might get a little in the next few hours. Normally, she looked forward to a little weather, just to mix up the consistency the people of San Diego were used to. But today, the uncertain weather seemed like a projection of her emotions.

The weekend had been peaceful. It felt like they had talked about the pending move and would work through it together. However, after Bridge's Lyft had taken her away on Sunday night, Alice's emotions had taken a nosedive, and she was now struggling with making the decision. The thing that kept gnawing at her was that Bridge hadn't even suggested she stay in San Diego. She'd gone straight to making it work long-distance. That told Alice that they were not on the same page at all.

It seemed impossible to make a long-distance relationship work. They were too different now. Religion had united them before tearing them apart. Now it stood between them. Added to that was the abyss that separated Bridge's glamorous life and Alice's small one. Maybe long-distance might draw out the spicy aspect, but they both had to be realistic. It was ultimately doomed. And it made Alice's heart ache just as painfully as it had that day when she'd sat in the bus terminal after losing everything, realizing her real home was on her way back to San Francisco.

Already, things had changed. Bridge had decided to spend Sunday evening at her own place, getting ready for her trip instead of leaving early Monday morning to run home and get her things together. Alice loved her house in Oceana, and she was happy that Bridge liked it, too. This and so much more was going to make a move to Santa Barbara difficult. Alice had already decided that no matter what her decision was, she wasn't going to sell her house here. She'd keep it even if it was financially difficult. Oceana would always be her safe place. She needed it.

As she watched the horizon, marooned in her gloomy contemplations, a familiar figure walked along the glass front wall of Oceana. Taylor. She was carrying a cardboard cup of coffee and a notebook. She must have just come from the Seaside Café, probably from a writing meetup. A pang of disappointment shot through Alice at the knowledge that she'd missed the last several because she'd been with Bridge. She missed hanging out with Taylor. There was so much she'd put on hold when Bridge had come back into her life. She wouldn't have done it differently, but it still made her sad.

She shot a text to Taylor, asking if she wanted to come over for a little bit, and she was delighted when she showed up a few minutes later.

"Hey, you," Taylor called out from the sidewalk as she strode toward the house. "Perfect timing. I was just around the corner."

"I saw you walking from downtown. How was the writing meetup?"

Taylor plopped into a chair at the patio table. "It was cool. There are a couple of newbies. I'm no longer the only person under thirty-five. Everyone misses you. I told them you were shacking up right now, so it might be a while before you came to group again."

Alice raised her eyebrows. "You did not."

Taylor took a sip of coffee, grinning with a mischievous glint in her beautiful eyes. "I didn't. But I wanted to. I told them you've been hammered at work."

"You didn't need to lie for me."

"Oh, I should have told them you were shacking up?"

Alice flapped her hand and smiled. "You're a troublemaker."

"*So* how has the shacking up been? I've been giving you your space, but I miss hanging out with you."

Alice wasn't one to discuss things she hadn't already figured out, but Taylor always made her feel like she could if she wanted to. Taylor was real and honest and had a way of seeing things just as they were without adding layers of complexity or assumption.

"You not answering makes me feel like there might be a little something going on?" Taylor said.

Alice shrugged. "I don't have a lot of experience with relationships, so maybe I'm just worrying about things to worry about." She knew that was definitely not the case, but she found it hard to just say what was going on when she really didn't know herself.

"You meet things head on. Maybe you wait a little bit to get the lay of the land, but you don't just let things sit."

Alice liked that. She'd always tried to be up front. "Thank you for saying that."

"I mean it. Also, you do have a lot of experience with relationships. You're friends with everybody. Friendships are just as much relationships as romantic entanglements are. You're good at them. You might hold back a little, but you're not shady about it. It's just who you are. You reveal what you want to, and that's just fine."

"Hold myself back?"

"Well, you surprised everyone when you told them you were a nun."

"It just never came up."

"Would you have asked me if I was trans if I'd never brought it up?"

"That's not the same thing."

"Nothing is ever the same thing as anything else. They're just varying degrees of different. But would you have?"

"No."

"Why?"

"First, it wasn't something that occurred to me. Your gender isn't something I think about."

"Sure it is. We never discussed pronouns, but you automatically called me she."

A pang of shame hit Alice. "Oh no. I'm so sorry. Do you prefer something else?"

"No. But that's not the point. We all use contextual clues to orient us in our surroundings. But not everything is what it appears to be, and sometimes, we've created a false illusion even when they are what they appear to be. We are always shifting, learning, relearning. You're amazing at it. It's impossible to always guess correctly using the context, and you're good about finding clarity, whether it's asking about it or figuring it out. You're also good about not being nosey. You're curious, aware, and you care about things."

"I guess I'm just not into making conversations all about me."

"It makes sense. A person who was once a nun is probably more concerned about taking care of others."

It was true. "I see what you're saying. Maybe I should try to be a little more giving of who I am to others."

"Only if you want. I'm not saying that you're doing anything wrong. People can ask more about you, too. But as far as the nun thing goes, that's not something someone guesses."

"True." The idea hit a chord in Alice despite Bridge telling her the same thing. Maybe she'd needed an outside opinion.

"It sort of feels like we went on a tangent because we were talking about you and Bridge."

Alice was about to say they were figuring things out, but while that was the truth, it wasn't quite on point. "We're working through some things."

"Like what?"

"Well…" And she found herself talking about what was going on. How her job was asking her to relocate, how she didn't want to, but at the same time, Bridge might get bored. Her life was small compared to Bridge's, and Bridge was put off by her religious life.

And in the past, Bridge had preferred a long-distance relationship when she'd gotten bored. Now, Alice felt like she needed to accept the relocation to give their relationship a chance.

"Whoa. Whoa. Whoa. That's a lot," Taylor said when she finished. "First, you better not go anywhere unless you're absolutely sure it's what you want. Because, news flash, I don't want you to leave. Second, did Bridge tell you that she wanted to do this long-distance?"

Alice was touched by Taylor's declaration. It reminded her that she had more to think about than Bridge. It also made her wish Bridge had said it just like Taylor had. "Not in those exact words. But she hasn't said she doesn't want me to move, either. She's already planning trips to come see me. She sounds excited."

"That's kind of weird. I can see how you'd be sad." She contemplated the situation. "She probably has her own feelings about you moving after just finding you again. Do you think she's simply being supportive?"

"Supportive by encouraging me to move?"

"Well, yeah. Does she know you love your job and are excited by the promotion?"

"I enjoy my job, but I can't say that I love it. I only asked for the promotion because she suggested it."

"Last time you and I talked about it, you said you were bored with your job. I'd think the promotion was a good thing."

"I would have been happy with getting a few new things to do. The promotion is actually more than what I wanted."

"Oh, wow. So you're considering it to make Bridge happy?"

Alice shook her head, and then stopped. Something dawned on her. "Maybe it's to make Bridge think I'm more interesting than I am."

"What? You're one of the most interesting people I know. I think I know what's going on here, and it has nothing to do with Bridge. Alice, you don't see what a fascinating and wonderful person you are, do you?"

She sat back in her chair. How could such a simple question throw her for such a loop?

Chapter Twenty-eight

B ridge should have known the trip to Denver was going to be a rough one when the plane never took off the fasten seat belts sign. The plane was tossed about like a kite in a storm. She was used to the ride being a bit bumpy flying in and out of Denver, but this was the worst she'd experienced.

Five years ago, when Denver had been her home base, the office had been one of the best run offices in the company. It's location, central in the North American region, made it a hub for many divisions, especially the sales team. With Bridge's leadership, the office had become the standard that each other office aspired to. Aside from Bridge's ability to land the biggest clients and nurture research partnerships, she considered the success of the Denver office to be her crowning achievement at AthletaHealth. However, when she arrived, the entire office was in disarray. The replacement manager she'd helped select had had a health emergency six months after taking over, and a series of managers had worked to turn the office into the worst in the company.

"Sage, you weren't kidding. This place is a mess." Alone after a long day, Bridge walked around the conference table, peering at Denver from the twenty-sixth floor of the downtown AthletaHealth building. A light, late autumn snow was falling, but it hadn't started to stick. City lights glittered in the melt that covered the sidewalks, streets, and highways.

"How bad is it?" Sage asked.

Bridge could almost see her pursing her lips, the one sign that she was angry. Her tone never changed. Her body language remained neutral, but the deeper the indents in her cheeks went, the angrier she was. Bridge expected she'd look like she'd bitten into a lemon by the end of the conversation.

"I'm not going to sugarcoat it. It's worse than expected. The team knew I was coming in today, and about ten percent of them showed up."

"Out on calls?"

"Working from 'home,'" she said, using air quotes she knew Sage couldn't see. "I'd put calendar holds for all of them to ensure attendance. When it was time for the meeting, I received a flood of texts asking for the link. When I told them there was no link, they began to panic. It only went downhill from there. I asked Tara how things were going."

"Tara? From administration?"

Bridge smiled. She'd had to really work with Sage not to call the administrative assistants secretaries. "If you want to know the good stuff, administration has all the dish. The majority of the sales team is dialing it in, both figuratively and literally. Most don't come into the office. Many don't even visit the clients."

"No wonder the numbers are so dismal. They're not bringing in anything new?"

"A few are working hard, but a good number are working the numbers. And Adam is inflating his." Bridge sighed. "The good news is this can turn around. Except for Adam. Lying to get bigger commissions is stealing."

"Fuck."

"Yeah. I'll get it all straightened out."

"I blame you."

Bridge huffed. "What? Me?"

"You set them up too well. They really don't need to make their quotas on new sales with the legacy accounts you handed over."

Bridge grimaced. "I'm glad you can joke about this." Sage had warned her that transferring the accounts to the local team would be almost a disincentive, and she was right. Bridge had intended the transfer to show them the potential. Kind of a windfall for them, but she didn't need the money or responsibility hanging over her. Also, it would have been selfish for her to continue making money on accounts she wasn't actively working on. "You were right."

"I can joke because I know you can fix it. But say it again. I like to know I'm needed around here."

"You were right. I was wrong."

"I'll never get tired of hearing that." Sage tittered out her signature giggle-laugh. "Keep me posted on how it goes. Do what you need to do."

Bridge got off the phone and started putting a plan together. She hated to admit it, but it felt good to be seen as a hero of sorts, sweeping in and cleaning up a mess before it got out of hand. It was a little discouraging to know that she'd left the office poised for success just five years earlier. On the other hand, it had taken five years for Adam to screw things up. That said something about the quality of the work she did.

A few hours later, after drafting a plan of action, Bridge spun her chair around and looked out over Denver again. She'd missed it. The snow had started to stick, and the city was bathed in a peaceful blanket of white. Only a handful of cars were navigating the slick streets. It was a huge change from the constant hustle and bustle of San Diego.

She picked up her phone, noting the late hour, amazed at how quickly time had raced by. Would Alice still be awake? There was a voice mail from her from a couple of hours earlier, checking in and asking Bridge to call if she got a chance. It was a simple message, not much to it, but just having someone checking in on her felt good.

It was late, but she needed to hear Alice's voice. When she'd left, something had been off between them. Probably because they had some major decisions to make. She'd hated to leave without discussing it, but she hadn't known how to bring it up.

The call was answered before the first ring ended. "Hi."

"Hi, yourself," Bridge said with a smile.

"How's your trip going? The weather app says it's snowing there."

"It's beautiful. I wish you could see it. Oh wait." Bridge snapped a picture and sent it to her.

"Look at that. I forgot what snow looks like. Are you in a high-rise hotel?"

"I'm still at the office on the twenty-sixth floor."

"Why are you still working? Are things worse than you'd hoped?"

"Quite a bit worse. I'm going to have to extend my trip for a few days."

"I guess that's what happens when you make yourself indispensable." Alice seemed to think her job was more glamorous than it was.

"I guess so. What are your plans for the week?"

"Without you here, I guess I'll be doing a lot of sitting around and staring into space."

Bridge laughed. "I seriously doubt that."

"I think I'll go to the church to see if they're ready for the holidays. I haven't been helping as much as I like."

"I hope it isn't because of me."

"It's definitely because of you. I like spending time with you."

Bridge should have felt good about the comment. Instead, she felt a flare of irritation. So many of her relationships had ended because women had accused her of being inaccessible, of working too much, letting her career get in the way. The worst thing was when Jackie had said that Bridge had sabotaged her identity. That Jackie didn't know who she was anymore because she'd tried so hard to be what Bridge wanted. Had tried so hard to be the perfect woman. The thing was, Bridge had never asked her for those things. Jackie had accused her of all the things she'd confessed to being afraid of. But as much as Bridge hated it, it was exactly what she had done. No woman could be the perfect woman in her head.

They weren't Alice.

She didn't want the real Alice to feel like that. "You should spend time doing what you like. I don't want to get in the way of that. Especially not your spiritual life. Just because I don't have one doesn't mean you shouldn't." To her dismay, she still heard some of that irritation in her voice and wished she'd tried harder to hide it.

"It sounds like you might be under some pressure. Would you like to go back to work?" Alice sounded level and upbeat, but Bridge was pretty sure she wasn't feeling that way. Not after suggesting hanging up before things got too intense. Alice never let her tone reveal her displeasure. Bridge had forgotten about that. She wondered how many other things Alice hid behind her even voice.

"I'm just tired."

"I'm sorry."

"You have nothing to be sorry about. I'm feeling better just talking to you. I have a feeling they'll ask me to come back a few more times to get this office back on its feet."

"That bad?"

"Worse. But nothing that can't be fixed." She just didn't want to be the one to fix it.

"Can you say no?"

"If I was anyone else, it would be an assignment. If I was anyone else, it would take twice as long to fix, too."

"Does it matter that you just settled in San Diego?" It sounded like Alice wanted her to turn it down.

Bridge appreciated that. "They'd make it worth my while. But I'm not going to take it. I'll get the ball rolling with a plan this week, but they'll have to find someone else to do the work of overseeing it."

"I like to hear you talk all bossy businesslike."

"Well, I like to hear you talk all historical preservation-like."

"Oh, come on. That's not even the same thing." Did Alice think she was making fun of her?

"It's not, but it's still a turn-on."

"I'll take your word for it."

There was something in her voice that made Bridge think that she was a little frustrated by the conversation, but she wasn't sure how to redirect it. "Well, I'm going to extend my trip to Friday instead of Wednesday. That will give you a little more time to miss me."

"I already miss you."

This time, Bridge was sure she heard something in Alice's voice, even though her tone was just as level as it always was.

Chapter Twenty-nine

With Bridge in Denver, Alice and Tripp had a date for a cutthroat game of Hearts. It had been weeks since Alice had spent any time with him. It used to be their thing to play cards once or twice a week. He kept her informed about all the goings-on around Oceana.

But ever since Bridge, they hadn't spent much time together. Aside from the bonfire, they'd only crossed paths a few times lately, mostly exchanging smiles and waves. She missed sitting with him over a game of cards. There was something about it that brought out their competitive sides, and the tension over who would win was always palpable. She'd been on a winning streak for almost a year, considering Tripp's health concerns. But he was almost back to his old self now, and the games had become competitive again.

A sparkle of anticipation lit inside her as she carried a carafe of hazelnut coffee, a container of fresh cookies, and the scorebook over to his house.

"What do we have here?" he asked as she entered his garden. He stood from the patio table and came to greet her, taking the tin and carafe before giving her a kiss on the cheek.

"One of the priests at the mission went up to Solvang and brought me a pound of hazelnut coffee and some Danish tea cookies."

"The ones in the blue tin? I love those cookies."

"Don't get excited. I already ate them, but I brought snickerdoodles."

He lowered the container with an eager smile. "I love your snickerdoodles more."

"That's the right answer," she said with a wink.

He sat, shaking the cards from the box. "I think I might need a refresher. It's been a little while since we've played."

She eyed him. "Not so long that you'd forget the rules."

He settled in his seat as he shuffled. "Swiss cheese. That's what my memory is. It's tragic, really. All that knowledge gone just like that." He snapped his fingers.

He'd suffered a series of strokes, and his memory had been affected. They'd all been happy to see him recover. Alice had prayed harder than she ever had, and his recovery had been remarkable. Part of her wanted to be gentle with him because it had been a horrible thing to watch. Another part of her wouldn't put it past him to capitalize on her kindness to finagle a win. Health issues aside, she wasn't about to throw him a win out of pity.

She filled their mugs with coffee, even knowing they'd be picking out the falling leaves from a nearby jacaranda tree. "I can't believe how fast this year has flown by."

"You and me both. Of course, I don't remember chunks of it," he said, shuffling again. "What's it gonna be? Unless it's Crazy Eights or Go Fish, I'm at a disadvantage. On account of my poor brain, you know."

"Uh-huh." Yep. He was milking it "We're playing Hearts. I'm sure it will come back to your poor brain. But if you have trouble, just let me know, and I'll help you out."

"This old man is so lucky to have you as his friend."

"And I you, young man," she said. It didn't matter that he was teasing her, a swell of love filled her heart.

He dealt the cards. "So how's it going with Bridge and you?"

She was a little surprised that he jumped right into it. He used to be a little more circumspect. But then again, she'd never been in a relationship around him before. "Good," she said. Bridge was coming home from Denver the next day. Little sparks danced in her stomach, mixed with some worry. They needed to talk, but she wasn't sure how to bring it up, even after Taylor had suggested being direct.

"She seems intelligent. She makes robotic body parts?"

"She sells them, but she is beyond intelligent." Alice sorted her cards. "Her clients are research hospitals who work with military personal who lost a hand during service."

His eyes lit up. She knew he'd like that last detail because of his own service in the Army. He'd initially opened Oceana specifically to help service members find a place to live after discharge. "I knew she was good people. As soon as I saw you two at the bonfire, I could see her shine."

She liked that he had picked up something from Bridge, but she wondered what he meant. "You mean figuratively, right? Or can you see auras with your gift, too?"

"I guess you could call it her aura."

She looked up. "You always describe your gift as something you sense. Not something you see."

"It's not a one-dimensional thing. But you're right. Normally, it's something I sense. There have been times when someone just stands out. Before I ever talk to them. Before I know anything about them, I see the shine. I saw it with my sergeant in the Army in Vietnam. I saw it in Lupe, the love of my life. I see it in all my family to a certain extent, which makes it feel like a connection type of thing. But who am I to question it? It is what it is." He pointed at her. "I saw it in you in that bus station."

"Me?" This was the first she'd heard that.

He looked at his cards. "Your light was bright. It dimmed for a while. But over time, it shined again. Especially when Bridge came. You've been like a lighthouse."

Alice was pretty sure Tripp was talking about how her spirit had been depleted for the few years after her release from the convent. Before she'd lost hope of ever seeing Bridge again. Before she'd found her new church. "You said Bridge has a light, too?"

He nodded as he selected something to discard. She'd lost track of how many hearts had been thrown. "Her light is like yours. Almost as strong. But when you're together, it's so bright, even people who can't see it know it's there. I think you feel it, too. I think it would be impossible not to."

Alice looked at her cards without seeing them. She did feel it.

"You're thinking really hard over there, my friend," he said.

She lowered her cards, no longer trying to play. She felt it. In her heart, she knew Bridge felt it, too. "Is it there when we're apart? I mean, is mine shining now?"

"You always shine, Alice. I don't know Bridge that well, but I think she's the same."

"Me too."

"If you don't mind me bringing it up. I know you're struggling."

She wasn't surprised. "I am."

"You don't need to tell me about it, but what I sense is that you are trying to fix for other people what you need to fix in yourself."

She was slightly confused. She'd been thinking about her conversation with Taylor that had confirmed her old habit of not giving voice to difficult things was alive and well. But she hadn't been aware that she was ignoring her own issues.

"I might not have said that right," Tripp said after a moment, as if he'd picked up on her confusion, and of course he had. "You are a helper, Alice. It gives you joy. You rely on this nature to keep the balance between making others happy and keeping yourself happy. The world needs more of you." He waved a finger in the air. "But it isn't the only thing that makes you happy. And when something comes up that could make you happy but it isn't in line with making others happy, you lean toward the others. Your focus should be on you. You came to Oceana for a reason, Alice."

"You invited me."

"I was led to invite you as much as you were guided to live here."

She'd never thought of it like that. Here, she'd helped Gem grieve her mother's death and seen how her gift really was a gift. She'd also been there when Shia had been struggling to find her place in the world. Even Joe the bulldog had encouraged her to volunteer at the shelter. More recently, she had a feeling that Taylor was part of it but hadn't figured out quite how yet. Oceana had been keeping her in place to help those who came in and out but maybe also to make sure she'd be here when Bridge came back. And now, what did Oceana have in mind for her besides just being a safe place to live all these years?

"The two of you are like two puzzle pieces." Tripp continued to mull over the point he'd been trying to make. "You make more sense together than apart. Her presence brings your light out more fully. But there's something else there, too. It's a positive thing, but I can't quite put my finger on it. You challenge each other, but the thing that most challenges the two of you is also the thing that makes you both stronger."

"I'm not sure what that means." Alice had long since given up the game. Her cards were lying facedown on the table.

His expression was contemplative, giving her the impression that he was trying to figure out how to express what he was picking up. He'd once told her that his gift was a lot like the expression, "A picture is worth a thousand words."

"There's a connection between you. It's strong. Greater together than it is individually. But there's a…thin barrier that prevents it from truly joining. It very much wants to merge. No. That's not the right word. Combine? No. Unite. That's it. I only saw you together at the bonfire. You fit when it's right, but that barrier is very strong."

Alice knew what it was. It had been dancing on the edge of her mind for days. Ever since Bridge had asked her about her religious beliefs. Bridge's life had grown outside of the convent, and Alice's had shrunk. Bridge had an exciting career that included making people's lives better, traveling around the world. And here Alice was, a blind sheep following a religion that she loved that had forsaken her many years ago. She'd never set foot out of California since she'd arrived. She'd never even flown on a plane. For God's sake, a move that was little more than two hundred miles away had her terrified. Not only because it left Bridge behind but because it wasn't home. How could Bridge remain interested in a woman with such a simple life that her pets were brainless jellyfish?

Still, she knew there was a reason they had been brought back together. She just didn't know why.

CHAPTER THIRTY

After a morning of meetings and making progress on getting the office together, Bridge had gone for a walk. Most of the snow had melted quickly after her first day, and it was nice to get out in the fresh air. She was tired of sandwiches in the office. The sign of an Irish pub and restaurant, the Draught House, caught her eye, and she went in. It was a little past the noon rush, so the place was slow.

Bridge took a seat at the bar and ordered a plate of shepherd's pie and a glass of water. The variety of whiskey on offer was impressive, but not only did she have meetings later, the altitude in Denver also made her a lightweight of epic proportions.

She'd nearly finished her lunch when a handsome man dressed in black sat on a stool one down from hers. He glanced at her, nodded a smile, and perused the menu.

"Aw, come on, Father Patrick. You know you'll order the bangers," the bartender said, slapping a beer coaster in front of him and pouring a Guinness from the tap.

"I have to check to see if the menu has miraculously changed. Which it hasn't. So, yes. I will indeed have the bangers, Stewart." He slid the menu back into the holder.

They laughed as Stewart walked down the bar and entered the kitchen at the other end of the bar.

"He thinks he knows me, but I am a man of mystery," Patrick said as he shrugged out of his long wool coat. A leather wallet fell out of his pocket, and a stack of business cards fell out. Bridge slid off her chair to help him pick them up.

"Thank you," he said with an easy smile as she handed him the cards. He had beautiful eyes. "I don't know why I even carry them. I never give them to anyone."

"Same. I still have most of the box I ordered over a year ago. Welcome to the digital age." She noticed his collar. "I thought the bartender was joking when he called you Father."

"I know. How odd that a Catholic priest would take lunch at the Irish pub." They both laughed, and he shrugged and slid one of the cards toward her.

She looked at it. "St. Germain's. That's the church on the corner, right?"

He nodded. "Going on ten years. I do the ten o'clock Mass on Sunday. Traditional. Come check it out."

She shook her head. "I'm just here on business. Before about six weeks ago, I hadn't set foot into a Catholic church in twenty-five years. Since then, I've been in two, and here I am talking to a priest." Why had she said all of that?

"Sounds like you have a history with the Church."

"You could say that." She took a sip of water. *May as well go all in.* "I used to be a nun."

Stewart placed the order in front of him and moved down the bar to another patron before Father Patrick responded. "I can't say that I've heard that one before. I'm guessing you willingly stepped away from your calling?"

"I was asked to leave." She looked at him. "*We* were asked to leave," she repeated, emphasizing *we*.

His brows furrowed, and in that moment, he looked familiar. But the feeling went away as his brows smoothed. He nodded. "It's not unusual for romance to blossom between nuns and priests."

"Close," she said. "We were both nuns." She wasn't surprised that she felt like she was giving confession. A sense of relief washed over her. Strange.

"Ah. Thus, twenty-five years since you've been in a church."

"For me. She still practices with a Unitarian congregation."

He smiled. "You're still together."

She picked at the corner of her napkin. "We lost touch the day they asked us to leave. Interestingly enough, we recently found each other again."

He lifted his brows and smiled. "That's amazing. I won't guess at what this means to you, but the Lord works in mysterious ways."

Despite the reference, Bridge liked him, and she found herself telling him their story: the good, the not so good, and the interesting. As she did, she felt a weight lift from her. "It's funny."

He held up a hand. "Let me guess. You feel like you're in confession again."

She tossed her head back and laughed. "There is no way I would have confessed any of that to a priest when I was a postulate."

"Yet, here you are."

"Yes." She chuckled. "Here I am. I left the church all those years ago, and since we've reunited, I find myself visiting churches, talking to priests, discussing religion more than I have in years. It feels like something is trying to tell me something."

"Or maybe you're simply working through some unresolved shit." He put a hand to his mouth. "Sorry about that. When I have a beer, I get a bit of a potty mouth."

"I'm the last person to be offended by a few choice words," she said. "So yeah. I guess I have unresolved shit." She picked at the corner of the napkin again. "You know, I don't think I hate the Church so much as I hate myself for failing, not recognizing who I was before I entered the convent. I would have never become a nun if I'd had time to figure myself out beforehand. But then again, I would never have met her."

"I think you need to examine what you just said. The number one rule in any religion, or any social group, for that matter, is love one another. That begins with yourself. How can you love others if you don't know how to love yourself?" He looked puzzled. "I don't think we exchanged names."

Feeling even lighter, she held out her hand. "Bridge Moore." He shook it. "And you're Father Patrick…" She looked at his card. "Father Patrick Johns." She glanced at her watch to find that she had ten minutes left until a meeting. "Thanks for the chat. You're a good one."

"I appreciate you saying so, Bridge. I've had my ups and downs, but it's been a fulfilling career. I also have a soft spot for nuns. My sister being one."

"I'll bet she's just as good as you." She meant it, wishing she could continue their chat but relieved they couldn't. "I'm sorry to have to run, but I have a meeting in nine minutes. Have a great day!"

Bridge's flight from Denver landed almost twenty minutes early in San Diego on Friday afternoon, continuing what had been a perfect day of travel, with everything on time or early. She'd been waved through security, and her request for an upgrade had been approved. The one and only thing she'd change about the day was that Alice wasn't there to pick her up. She'd come to look forward to seeing Alice waiting at the curb. But Alice had her own business trip that week, and her plane didn't arrive until much later.

When Bridge arrived home, her house seemed quiet and hollow. She'd never noticed how sounds echoed against the tiled floors and unadorned walls. She'd always believed it was the austerity of living in a convent that had stuck with her. She'd never liked clutter, even before, but once she'd settled into her cell at the convent, the sparse décor had been a comfort. She'd kept up the habit, finding it interesting that it had a name when minimalism had become a fad.

When her friends had talked to her about the, "Does it give you pleasure?" phenomenon, she'd been amused. She could have written the book herself. Aside from clothes and a selection of favorite books, she had no collections. Not art, not hobbies, not even a ring of random keys she'd saved just in case a lock turned up that belonged to one of them. She'd liked it that way. With her frequent moves for work, it made things easy.

The one thing she'd clung to that wasn't useful was the box she'd taken from the convent. For a second, something lurked in the recesses of her mind, something that questioned whether her sparse existence was as much a penance as it was convenience, but it was gone before she could catch it.

Tossing her keys on the table beside the door, she parked her carry-on next to the sofa. Looking around her living room, she missed the plants, pieces of artwork, and shelves of books that decorated Alice's space. Her house wasn't cluttered, but it reflected her personality. All aspects of it. Religious tokens were interspersed with bright sculptures of sea creatures. The books were organized haphazardly, with religion next to romance and science next to science fiction. Alice's house was an extension of herself, unlike hers. Or was it?

Enough.

She wanted to change her clothes and go see Alice. But with her not due back from Santa Barbara until later, Bridge poured a glass of wine and wandered onto the balcony: the specific feature she'd bought the townhouse for. It overlooked the ocean, and she could see for miles up and down the coast. She didn't have any patio furniture yet, but the minute she'd looked at the photos of the place online, she'd pictured herself sitting on the balcony with a book and a drink, taking in the sunset. In the steady breeze off the ocean, she felt herself begin to wind down from the day of travel. Normally, she loved this time, but her heart was missing Alice, not just in the moment, but in the past and quite possibly, the future. Her mind wandered into the scary realm of the meaning of her life. Was she destined to always want what she couldn't have?

That put her on the edge of the downward spiral, and if she allowed herself to go there, she might not make it back up. She focused on the good work she'd done in Denver.

The whole experience had led her to see that she'd expended her growth opportunities at AthletaHealth. It would have been easy to relax and coast, just like the Denver team had done. Hell, she'd been busting her ass for years for the company. She believed in it. The work they did mattered. And she was proud of her contribution. But had she peaked?

She'd moved to San Diego in anticipation of this. She'd known her career was winding down, and her hopes of finding Alice had been long gone. With nothing left, she'd planned a slow exit from work, transitioning from meetings to trips on her boat, until…what? She couldn't see that far.

But she'd found Alice. And her unknown future had become full of hope and visions of adventures alongside the woman she'd always loved. She'd been happier than she'd ever been.

Yet, here she was again, faced with a life without Alice except for stolen moments, their lives moving in different directions while Bridge took solace on solo boat trips, until…she couldn't see that far.

And here she was again.

Two things had become clear to her: Alice's religion wasn't a real issue for her, and she didn't want another long-distance relationship. As the minutes ticked by and the sun slid lower on the horizon, Bridge knew what she had to do.

If Alice decided to move to Santa Barbara, there was only one thing Bridge could do. But first, she had to talk to a few people.

CHAPTER THIRTY-ONE

Apprehension settled over Alice as she climbed the steep steps from the parking lot to the front door of Bridge's townhouse. She'd only been there twice before, once for Bridge to show her around, and a second time to check an alarm sensor that was causing the remote application on Bridge's phone to go off when she'd been out of town. The alarm had turned out to be a bird that had built a nest right next to the motion detector near her front door. Alice had called a friend from the Wild Bird Sanctuary to come relocate it.

This time, she wasn't there by invitation, and she was reminded of all the romance novels she'd read where one of the protagonists snuck into the other's space only to find something that they didn't want to know. Shaking her head at her ridiculous imagination, she keyed in the entrance code and strode into the house with a sack of groceries, a bundle of flowers, and a pitcher of red wine pomegranate punch made from fruit she'd picked at the mission.

Bridge would be home any minute now, and she wanted to greet her with the scent of dinner cooking. Denver had been a challenge for Bridge, who had seemed distracted and saddened by the state of the office. Alice wanted to help lift her spirits. However, when she went to the alarm, she found it already disarmed. The sound of shuffling and a grunt came from down the hall.

"Hello?" she called.

"Alice?" Bridge's voice was a blessing. Still, Alice hoped the secrets-revealed trope wouldn't be the next revelation. Just as fast as the idea materialized, she shooed it away. Bridge wasn't like that.

Bridge came from down the hall with a box in her hands. *Penance* was written across its side. Alice knew exactly what it was. Aside from the label, she'd once had one just like it.

"I didn't expect to see you until later," Bridge said, smiling widely and dropping the box on the sofa.

Alice found herself relieved of the items in her hands and swept into an embrace she'd been longing for all week. Her arms slid quickly around Bridge's neck, and the kiss that followed was everything she needed to set her world to rights. There was nothing like the feeling of safety and desire she felt in Bridge's embrace.

Bridge pulled back and kissed her again, this time more slowly, ratcheting up the desire.

"Didn't your plane land just minutes ago?" Alice said breathlessly when they paused to take a breath. She wanted to unbutton Bridge's soft cotton shirt, but she settled for sneaking her fingers under the hem and placing slow caresses on the soft warm skin she discovered there.

"It landed early, and there was almost no traffic on the 5." Bridge kissed her again. This time, more deeply. When she leaned back, Alice saw her own desire reflected in Bridge's eyes. "What about your flight? It's not supposed to take off from Santa Barbara until later."

Alice gently extracted herself from Bridge's arms before her willpower gave way. The news she'd brought home from her trip had her emotions dialed up to turbo, which was amplifying everything she felt. "I finished early. With nowhere to go, I went to the airport. But when I checked in, they asked if I would be interested in changing to an earlier flight."

"I can't tell you how happy I am to see you." Bridge gestured toward the things she'd set on the counter. "What's in the bag? And flowers? What's the occasion?"

Alice picked up the flowers and looked for a vase to put them in. "I brought fresh chicken cordon bleu and asparagus to cook for dinner. You crave home-cooked meals when you come home from a trip. I planned to surprise you when you walked in."

Bridge handed her a decorative glass cylinder. "We should be celebrating your official promotion."

Alice's heart tugged uncomfortably as she filled the cylinder with water. She wished Bridge was just a little sad about how the promotion meant them being apart. "My priority right now is feeding you."

"How did I get so lucky?" Bridge teased. "I'll have to get all your recipes before you leave. And maybe take some cooking lessons." She sounded distracted, and Alice turned from her flower arranging to see her absently picking at the tape on the box. "You made it to Santa Barbara and home in one piece, so I imagine you now have confidence for all the trips to come?"

"You did a great job talking me through getting there. Coming home was a breeze."

"Eventually, you'll be able to navigate the whole thing in your sleep."

Alice didn't want to keep talking about how she would get used to traveling back and forth. "I made some wine punch," she said, pulling a couple of wineglasses from a rack under a cabinet and dusting them off. She pointed to the box Bridge was picking at. "Is that what I think it is?"

Bridge looked at it for a few seconds before she answered. "If you're thinking it's a box of regret and recrimination, it is." She must have seen the pain that swept through Alice at her words. "Habits and whatnot."

Alice turned away, knowing Bridge didn't see her as a regret, but she felt like she might be in the splash zone. "I'm surprised you still have it."

"That's why I brought it out. I think it's time to get rid of it."

Alice poured them each a glass. "What are you going to do with it?"

"I didn't know until today. But just now, I was thinking about tossing it into the fireplace."

"Like an offering?"

Bridge turned to her with a half-smile. "More like a cleansing."

"Like when people in movies burn the stuff their exes gave them?"

"Exactly."

Sadness gripped Alice. She wondered if her trip to Santa Barbara had been a mistake. Did Bridge want to cleanse more than just the ancient part of her past? Was she preparing herself for their separation? Alice suddenly felt like she'd intruded. "I shouldn't have just shown up. Do you want privacy?"

"I think it's only fitting that you be here for it." Bridge picked up the box and dropped it on the small hearth in front of the fireplace before turning on the gas to ignite the fire. The fireplace lit with a whoosh. With a sense of foreboding, Alice brought over their glasses and a pair of scissors she'd pulled from the knife block.

Bridge took a sip and licked her lips. Alice felt a pleasant slow roll in her lower abdomen at the sight, but it quickly disappeared as worry about having made a mistake took a stronger hold of her emotions.

"That's so good." Bridge's voice was husky. The slow roll returned to Alice's stomach. After slicing through the layers of tape that had yellowed around the top of the box, Bridge rested her arms on it before opening it. "I haven't looked in here since it was packed."

"Maybe you should just toss the whole box in." At the sound of her own words, a weird feeling enveloped Alice, as if burning the contents of the box was a desecration. It was almost as strong as the feeling she'd had when thinking about getting rid of her own convent things. It had taken months before she'd taken it down from its spot in her bedroom closet and looked through the contents: her habits, nightclothes and underthings, along with the simple wooden cross she'd worn around her neck, a Bible, and the crucifix wall hanging that had been the only decoration in her cell at the convent.

She'd hung the crucifix in what had become her exercise room, and the Bible had gone on her bedside table, but the rest had been put on the table near her front door with the intention of throwing it away. She'd walked by the folded pile every day, unable to bring herself to toss it in the kitchen garbage or take it to the community bins. Finally, one day, on her way to work at the school, she scooped it up with the intent to toss it. But she'd driven right past the dumpsters with the garments in her lap as she'd wrestled with the voices of recrimination in her mind. When she'd gotten to work, she'd parked next to the school dumpsters and tossed it all in as she walked past. She hadn't even slowed. And that was that. A strange sense of peace had descended over her almost as soon as the cloth had left her hands; the voices had stopped, the tightness in her chest had released, and she could finally draw deeper breaths.

She knew exactly why Bridge needed to do this. Burning was a bit much, but she'd carried this weight for so long. It deserved a grand gesture if that was what she needed. The idea that it was desecration left Alice's mind. It was closure.

Bridge rubbed her chin. "The box won't fit in the fireplace."

"Can you throw each piece in individually?" Alice examined the glass enclosure for the first time. "Does it even open?"

"It doesn't look like it." Bridge sighed and ran her fingers around the edges. "I had plans to cook s'mores here, too. I've been bamboozled." She sounded relieved.

"You sound like you might be happy that it isn't going to work out."

Bridge's expression grew serious again. She ran a hand down the back of her neck. "I'm feeling a lot of emotions right now."

Not talking about things didn't stop bad things from happening. Bridge's words from weeks ago hung in the air between them. "I have something to tell you," Alice said.

Bridge's expression grew even more serious. "Has good news ever followed that sentence?"

"I don't know. It's just that, I'm not...well, I turned down the promotion." There. She'd said it. If Bridge was truly intent on doing things long-distance, the distance would have to be the five miles between her townhouse and Oceana.

"What?"

Alice felt exposed and vulnerable under the scrutiny. "You probably think I'm being foolish or unambitious. But I don't want to leave." She was being a coward. "This is my home, and it's even more my home now that you're here."

Bridge wore an unreadable expression, as if she didn't know how to feel. "What about your job?"

Alice was disappointed "I can keep the one I have. I can also find a new job. They have a non-volunteer job at the Humane Society that sounds fun. There's also the wild bird sanctuary. Heck, I can do a lot of things. If there was such a thing as a cookie maker, I'd do that." She wasn't going to pretend that her job mattered to her as much as it seemed to matter to Bridge.

"There is. It's called a baker. I know one. She's the best." Bridge's voice trembled as she smiled. She also looked...happy. Maybe a little relieved.

Alice felt her shoulders relax. Relief tentatively replaced what had been deepening disappointment. "I knew that. I was testing you."

Bridge's eyes twinkled. Or was it the reflection of unshed tears? "Uh-huh."

The light banter was a relief, but Alice had more to say, things she should have said earlier. "The thing is, a job is just a job for me. I need one to pay my bills, and I'd like to enjoy it and hope that it would benefit other people, but I honestly don't care what I do as long as I'm happy. And…" She paused for a few seconds. "I'm happiest when I'm with you."

Bridge stepped closer. "I'm happy when I'm with you, too."

Alice blew out a breath. "I don't want you to feel trapped or anything, but I don't want to do a long-distance thing with you."

Bridge's brow furrowed. "Trapped? Where is that coming from?"

"You said that long-distance brought back the spice for you and Jackie."

"We still broke up."

"You liked the spice."

"The spice was fun in a failing relationship. We, you and me, we have spice now, and I want to keep it that way. Together. Not apart."

"But you encouraged me to move to Santa Barbara."

"Only for the promotion I believed you wanted. I hated that you were going to leave."

A flare of hope was pulsing inside Alice, but she was afraid to believe it. "Why didn't you tell me?"

"When we talked about the promotion, you got excited. I didn't want to turn around and say never mind just because I didn't like the terms."

"I only got excited because you were."

"And I was because *you* were," Bridge said.

Alice couldn't believe that they'd fallen for one of the oldest tropes in the book: the old *I only want my beloved to be happy* one. She hated that one almost as much as she hated the *trying to read the other main character's mind* trope. "I should have just talked to you. I should have asked how you were feeling instead of just assuming you were happy and then justifying my conclusion by hearing what I wanted to hear."

"You wanted to hear me say that I wanted to have a long-distance relationship because I was into some sort of long-distance kink?"

"Well, not now that you say it like that…"

"But before?"

"I just wanted to make you happy."

"I am happy."

"I mean, you've had a lot more experience with relationships than me. I've only ever known love with you. I wanted to follow your lead, and it seemed like you were happiest, at least for a little while, when you were in that long-distance relationship."

"Which, again, did not last." Bridge took her hands. "Look. I might have had a few more romantic partners than you. But honestly, it really hasn't been that many. I've buried myself in work over the years. I've only ever known love with you."

Alice felt like the air had been sucked from the room. Her breath was hard to catch, and her head was dizzy.

"Are you okay?" Bridge peered at her with concern. "You look dazed."

"I'm sorry. I thought I just heard you say..." She stopped because it was stupid. There was no way.

"That I've only ever known love with you?"

Alice stared, knowing she probably looked confused.

Bridge laughed. "I've told you that."

Alice shook her head. "You most certainly have not." She would have remembered.

"I've made it clear in other ways."

"For someone who's always telling me that not saying it out loud doesn't mean it won't happen, I need to tell you that not saying it out loud can and does make it not a thing, too."

"What?"

Alice waved her hand. "Exactly what I said. I almost took a promotion and moved away because you didn't tell me you'd rather I stay." Alice saw the look of confusion on Bridge's face. "Okay. That's not a great example. I just mean that we both have some work to do on talking things through, and maybe we need to understand that everything isn't always going to be binary. One thing or another. Yes or no. Good or bad."

"About that."

Alice waited. When Bridge appeared to be thinking hard but not saying anything, she prompted her. "About what?"

Bridge studied her face. "We've been avoiding something else." She tapped the box. "It's the religion thing."

Alice sucked in a breath. "I knew it."

"Knew what?"

"I wave it in your face too much. Talk about it too much."

Bridge took her hand. "Just the opposite. I'm afraid you're holding back. It's a huge part of your life, but you don't talk about it very much. You only ever go to church when I'm out of town. I get the feeling you try to avoid it."

"I don't want to bring up bad memories, and I know you aren't religious. You get tense when it comes up."

"You're not a sales executive, and I talk about my job."

"It's what you do."

"Your religion is what you do, too."

Alice examined what she'd said. "I guess you're right. But religion is a sore subject for you."

"Being kicked out of the convent is a sore subject for me. Religion is fascinating. Just because I don't practice and don't subscribe to the teachings doesn't mean I don't want to talk about it. Don't get me wrong, I don't want to become religious. At least, not right now. But who knows? I used to love talking about scripture. It's always been more of a philosophy to me. I don't want you to hide your religion."

"That's easier said than done."

Bridge squeezed her hands. "Have I made you uncomfortable about it?"

"It's a touchy subject. For everyone."

"I don't think it has to be. It can be as simple as you and me agreeing that it's okay that you like walnuts in your chocolate chip cookies, and I don't."

Alice couldn't believe what she'd just heard. "Wait right there. You don't like nuts in your chocolate chip cookies?"

"I don't."

Stricken, Alice shook her head. "I can't believe…"

"I'll still eat them. But there's a simple solution, right?"

At first, Alice couldn't see it, but it hit her. "I can make some with and some without."

"Exactly. I think our ideas around religion can be as simple."

Alice tipped her head to the side. "Maybe."

"You're the kindest person I know. That makes it easier."

Alice usually liked when people described her as kind. It was important to her. But this time, she had mixed feelings. "I wonder if your memory of me is better than the real me. You saw a very narrow part of me twenty-five years ago. We were young. In love for the first time. We were high on being good people, building ourselves to be nuns. We weren't perfect, but we were as close as we could be. That's enough to put a halo around anyone."

Bridge paused as if considering. "Is that how you see me? As a gilded memory?"

"Not at all."

"Then, why would you think that's the only way I see you? You are the kindest person I have ever known."

"Maybe that's just another way of saying I'm boring." She hadn't meant to say it.

Bridge looked confused. "What?"

"My God. I just took my first trip on an airplane. I am the epitome of boring."

"Having flown or not isn't an accurate litmus test of boring. I have colleagues who've flown around the world several times that could put me to sleep just by looking at them."

"But you have a fascinating job. You make million-dollar deals. You are so far out of my league, it's not even funny." It felt good to say. "I am nowhere near as interesting as you are."

"I'm a good salesperson, sure. I sell bionic hands. But once you've seen one, you've seen a million. Yes, it improves lives. But you improve lives, too, just being around people. You are loved by everyone who is blessed by your presence."

A warm glow filled Alice. She wanted to be that person more than anything else in the world. "I'm in awe of who you are."

"What if I told you I've decided to retire? Now who's more interesting?"

Alice laughed. "Right."

Bridge's face remained serious. "I'm ready for a quieter life. I want to spend more time with you. I was ready to move to Santa Barbara with you."

"Are you serious?" Alice couldn't believe what she was hearing.

"More serious than I've ever been. I love you. I've lost too much time already. There is no way I want to live apart from you."

Alice felt warm tears rolling down her cheeks. "I love you, too, Bridge. I've loved you since I met you."

Bridge touched her cheek, and she could feel the truth in the warmth and pressure. In that moment, she felt like she deserved the love she'd spent her entire adult life longing for.

CHAPTER THIRTY-TWO

The pop and hiss of burning pine and eucalyptus took Bridge back to her childhood as she piled more logs and planks onto the growing bonfire. It reminded her of the large fireplace in her grandparents' house in Noe Valley, sold when they were no longer able to climb the multiple flights of stairs. Bridge had lay in front of their fireplace, soaking in the warmth, playing with her toys, more times than she could count.

She looked up to see Shia approaching, and the whole essence of Oceana's community swept over her. Goose bumps pebbled her skin, and a shiver ran through her. The feeling of being right where she was meant to be filled her heart. "Hey, Shia."

"Hey, Bridge." Shia turned to a woman who looked like Shia might in fifteen years. "This is Sharon. My mom. We're just coming back from coffee."

"I knew you were related as soon as I saw you. I wish I lived close to my mom."

Shia glanced at her mother through her eyelashes, almost shyly, and Bridge wondered if there was a story there. Then, Shia's face lit up with a smile. "That's a great fire you got going there."

"Thanks. Coming from the resident fire-maker, I take that as a high compliment. I appreciate you letting me have the privilege tonight."

"Are you kidding? When Alice called to ask if you two could use some firewood for some sort of ritual, I couldn't help but invite myself. I'm up for a righteous bonfire any time. As you can see, I'm not the only one."

Alice, Rose, Mikayla, Taylor, and several of the residents of Oceana gathered around the picnic table, and the collection of snacks and beverages kept getting bigger by the minute. "Alice told me that bonfires are not taken lightly here. Something about moths and flames and friendships forged in fire."

Shia snorted. "If I'm the resident fire-maker, she's the resident friendship blacksmith."

"I'm beginning to see that," Bridge said, watching Alice commune with her people. Bridge couldn't imagine how she could have considered leaving Oceana. Alice would have done it for her, though, and the love in her heart swelled to fill her soul. Thank God they'd figured things out before Alice had given up such an elemental part of herself.

Alice came up behind her, wrapping an arm around her waist. Bridge felt the comfort throughout her body.

Taylor stood next to her. "There's something so California about a roaring bonfire near the ocean. It's almost magical."

"Especially in Oceana," Alice said, snuggling into Bridge's shoulder. "It seems to channel a special energy, whether it's magical, the universe, or God. It's hard to describe. But it's there."

Taylor nodded with a contemplative look. "I vibe with that. Does it have to have a name? Why can't it be all of those and just be what it is? You know, like love?"

Alice squeezed Bridge with one arm and rubbed Taylor's back with the other. "I like that."

"Me too," said Shia, taking Rose's hand as she drew near.

"Are you ready for the big event?" Alice asked.

"I think I'll have another glass of your delicious pomegranate wine first." Bridge drank the last of what she had in her cup.

"What's the big cleansing event about anyway?" Shia asked. "And will there be naked dancing as part of this ritual?"

Alice looked at Bridge, who shrugged back. She felt a little goofy making such a big deal of getting rid of the artifacts of her biggest failure. Alice patted the center of her chest and turned to Shia. "She's cleansing her life of old baggage. We're going to burn the stuff she saved from the convent."

Rose did a little bounce, and her eyes gleamed. "Naked dancing is not compulsory, but if anyone is moved to do so, please mind the sparks from the fire. One of my friends did that on what would have been her first anniversary with the ex who broke their engagement a week before their wedding. Not the naked dancing, but the ritual burning. He was a total douche. Met an exotic dancer on his bachelor trip to Las Vegas. She said it freed her of all the negative feelings she'd been holding on to."

"I love that idea," Mikayla said. "Would it be okay if I burned something, too?"

Bridge was all for it. She was uncomfortable making this a big deal, but she loved having the support of her new friends while she relieved herself of old regrets. "The more the merrier."

Mikayla kissed Gem and ran to her house. Bridge laughed when she saw Gem watch her leave and then follow her, too.

Rose clapped her hands against her thighs and stood. "I'm not gonna let this opportunity go to waste."

Alice raised an eyebrow. "It seems you aren't alone in needing a clean break from your past. I think I'm going to get the other pitcher of punch. Be right back."

Before she knew it, Bridge was alone at the fire with Sharon. They shared an easy silence as Sharon stared into the fire with a small smile. Bridge enjoyed the quiet for the moment, aware of the box sitting at her feet. She considered how easy it had been to move that box from city to city, never opening it, simply pushing it into the dark corner, only pulling it down to move it to the next place, remembering her "sins." The only real sin had been how long she'd kept it.

The others returned. Most of them had left with a certain amount of energy, some of them laughing, but they returned quietly, holding their retrieved items. Even Tripp had come back with Rose and Gem.

Alice refilled their glasses. "How do you want to do this, love?"

"I'd like all of you to go first if that's okay. Just so I can get my thoughts together."

Gem stepped closer to the fire. She held a black composition notebook in her hands. "These are the notes I used to keep track of my dad's medications and his physical and mental condition over the last four years. Every time I wrote something, a little piece of me crumbled as I saw him slipping away. I don't need it anymore." She looked up at Tripp. "I'm so glad to have you back, Dad. Every day with you in it is a gift," she said as she tossed the book into the fire. Tears shone in both her and her father's eyes.

Mikayla stepped closer to Gem and stroked her cheek before lifting a folded piece of paper that she started to flatten out. "I drew this picture of my mom with some of her friends when I was a kid. It won an award at the Del Mar Fair. My mom told me it was terrible and hid it away. I stopped drawing after that. I recently discovered she hated it because she was the subject, not because I was a bad artist. I've decided to start drawing again. I might not be as good as my sister, but art isn't about that. This picture isn't terrible, but it is a reminder of how easily I gave up a piece of myself once. Good-bye, *Ladies Playing Bridge*. I've got other things to draw now."

Gem gave Mikayla a kiss and whispered something in her ear that made her smile. Bridge wondered if she'd just offered to be her first model.

Shia raised a thick manila envelope, shrugged, and tossed it in the fire. "See ya later, social services file." She glanced at her mother like she was seeking approval and then sat between her mother and Rose on the picnic table. "Take my word for it. They don't put good memories in envelopes like that."

Rose ran her hand up and down Shia's leg before she stood. "I tried keeping a journal after my ex cheated on me, and I had to move back to my parents' house. I'd just dropped out of college for the second time, and I was working at the café, thinking I'd let everyone down. This depressing thing is full of bad poems, self-pity, and the idea that everyone in my family thought I was a loser." She looked at Shia, who rested a hand on the skin below the back of her crop top. "That person doesn't exist anymore...except the bad poetry. I still excel at that." She tossed the flower-covered journal into the fire. "Good riddance, sad Rose."

Taylor looked pensively at a photo in her hand. "I've kept this picture tucked deep inside my wallet. I don't know why. The person in the photo doesn't exist anymore. Never really did." She tossed it into the fire and burst into a beautiful smile. "Fuck. That feels good!"

Alice let go of Bridge to clap, which made everyone else clap, and a few more happy tears were shed among the gathering.

"I think I misunderstood the assignment," Tripp said when the applause stopped. He pulled a garden wagon full of yard waste up to the pit and flapped his hand. "I'm just happy to be here."

Gem gave him a big bear hug. "I'm happy you are too, old man."

"I guess it's my turn." Alice stepped forward, and Bridge was surprised because she'd seen her bring out the fresh pitcher of punch but nothing else. "I don't need these anymore," she said pulling something out of her pocket. "I'm not sure how many of you have noticed, but Mikayla helped me upgrade my wardrobe recently." Shia wolf whistled, and the group giggled. "I'm a new fashionista from my head to my toes now. I even upgraded my knicker game." She waved a large white piece of fabric. "This is the last bit of my dumpy clothes. A pair of granny panties I found tucked into the corner of my underwear drawer. Unless anyone wants to claim them, I'm tossing them into the flames. One. Two. Two and a half?" She looked around. "Everybody sure they don't need a car cover? No? Okay. Good-bye, my trusty granny panties. You won't be missed." She tossed them onto the flames, and everyone clapped.

Bridge pulled her close and dipped her backward. "I'd love you in a potato sack."

Alice winked. "I know."

Bridge drew her in for a passionate kiss, and her whole soul sang. When she finally stood Alice up and released her, she realized everyone was watching them with sappy looks, and they all broke into applause. She shook her head, glad that her blush probably couldn't be seen in the warm firelight falling over everyone. She cleared her throat. "I want to raise my glass to all of you for keeping Alice safe and happy until I found her again. Her good friends and family of choice are now my good friends and family of choice. To new beginnings."

"To new beginnings," everyone repeated, raising their own cups.

Bridge took a long drink, handed her cup to Alice, and turned to the box at her feet. She lifted the top. The faint smell of dusty lavender tickled her nose. A picture of small bundles of fresh lavender blossoms tied with string sitting next to her Bible on the bedside table in her room at the convent filled her mind. Alice had replaced the bundles weekly, and the ones that had been on her table on the day they'd left were sitting, dried but intact, on top of the yellowed tissue paper wrapping the rest of the contents. Bridge lifted the two delicate bundles and handed them to Alice, who sniffed them and promptly sneezed.

"Bless you," Tripp said with a chuckle.

Alice handed the dried flowers back to her and motioned for her to toss them. They were the first to fall into the fire. The faint scent of lavender mingled with the smoke. Shia and Rose whooped and pumped their fists in the air. It made it easier for Bridge to part the tissue paper and look at the other items. Black fabric filled her hands. Below it was white. Her old nightclothes and underthings. A pair of chunky leather shoes lay beneath that, along with a few pairs of black nylon leggings. At the bottom was the Bible her parents had given her as a going away present when she'd left for the convent, the necklace of polished wooden beads with the chunky wooden cross pendant she'd worn over her habit, and the one decoration from her room: the brass and wood crucifix.

With slightly shaking hands, she lifted the habit, holding it from the shoulders, letting the full length of it hang from her fingers. Someone cleared their throat, but other than that, the group remained silent. She could feel their eyes as she tried to analyze how she felt. It was just a pile of fabric, but it represented such a fraught period of her life: anticipation, religious fervor, joy, love, comfort, satisfaction, gratitude, sexual awakening, embarrassment, anger. The list of emotions went on. Interestingly enough, the prominent ones she felt now were nostalgia and a surprising sense of pride. She'd once embarked on a life she thought she'd been called to, giving up everything to answer it. She'd served with humility, renouncing everything outside of her religious duties. While performing them, she'd found the love of her life, who'd become inextricably woven into the passion she gave to her church. For reasons beyond her control, all of that had been taken from her, but she'd survived. Not only survived, she'd excelled at the new life she'd found after it, even finding her one true love again. The habit was a uniform from her past, yet it represented a life she'd left.

She'd anticipated anger or vindication, but it felt more like she was about to burn a flag that had served its purpose and was now being disposed of. Not so much with reverence but with respect. When the garment landed on the flames, she didn't remember making that decision, but she was glad it was done. The rest of the garments, including the shoes, followed, and she watched as it all burned. When none of it was recognizable, she looked at the box. The contents remaining were a different story. They were meant to be more enduring symbols and tools of a life that had once been devoted to an organization that no longer supported her.

In a shocking discovery, she didn't feel any of the old anger, hurt, or hostility. The pride at having offered everything up in the name of religion was what she felt. The betrayal no longer haunted her. It simply didn't matter. She had what she needed now. Her life had still mattered to all those who she'd helped become whole. She stood next to the woman she loved, among people who'd accepted her without hesitation. The tools of her old life were just that, tools. She put the top back on the box and picked it up. She looked at the people she'd come to love and who'd become her safe harbor. She smiled before she dropped the box onto the fire.

"Ashes to ashes and dust to dust," she said.

A loud chorus of cheers rose as the sparks from the fire rose to meet the night sky, and a huge weight lifted from Bridge's shoulders as Alice wrapped her arms around her and watched the fire dance, casting a warm glow over all she held dear.

EPILOGUE

Eighteen months later

From a handwritten notice posted on the locked door of a quaint, bungalow-style house next door to Seaside Café:

Dearest Friends and Family,
Wonderland Cookies will be closed for two months while my lovely wife Bridge and I celebrate our honeymoon.
Many thanks to all who attended our beach wedding and boogied the night away around the bonfire reception. We couldn't have dreamed of a better way to celebrate our ceremony. Thank-you notes are in the mail, and we adore all the jellyfish-themed gifts. The donations you gave to North County Coastal Cleanup and the Oceanside Humane Society were greatly appreciated, too, and you'll be happy to know every one of the animal guests that were invited have been adopted into loving homes.
You can accompany us virtually on our travels by subscribing to our TikTok channel @NunsontheRun, where we will upload videos of our travels through Italy, Greece, and aboard our boat to destinations unknown. Our final stop will be to watch Shia take the trophy at the Australian Surf Championship. Please keep us company by leaving comments and pictures of your pets.
All of our love,
Alice and Bridge

About the Author

Kimberly Cooper Griffin is a software engineer by day and a romance novelist by night. Born in San Diego, California, Kimberly joined the Air Force, traveled the world, and eventually settled down in Denver, Colorado, where she lives with her wife, the youngest of her three daughters, and a menagerie of dogs and cats. When Kimberly isn't working or writing, she enjoys a variety of interests, but at the core of it all she has an insatiable desire to connect with people and experience life to its fullest. Every moment is collected and archived into memory, a candidate for being woven into the fabric of the tales she tells. Her novels explore the complexities of building relationships and finding balance when life has a tendency of getting in the way.

Books Available from Bold Strokes Books

Blood Rage by Illeandra Young. A stolen artifact, a family in the dark, an entire city on edge. Can SPEAR agent Danika Karson juggle all three over a weekend with the "in-laws," while an unknown, malevolent entity lies in wait upon her very skin? (978-1-63679-539-3)

Ghost Town by R.E. Ward. Blair Wyndon and Leif Henderson are set to prove ghosts exist when the mystery suddenly turns deadly. Someone or something else is in Masonville, and if they don't find a way to escape, they might never leave. (978-1-63679-523-2)

Good Christian Girls by Elizabeth Bradshaw. In this heartfelt coming of age lesbian romance, Lacey and Jo help each other untangle who they are from who everyone says they're supposed to be. (978-1-63679-555-3)

Guide Us Home by CF Frizzell and Jesse J. Thoma. When acquisition of an abandoned lighthouse pits ambitious competitors Nancy and Sam against each other, it takes a WWII tale of two brave women to make them see the light. (978-1-63679-533-1)

Lost Harbor by Kimberly Cooper Griffin. For Alice and Bridget's love to survive, they must find a way to reconcile the most important passions in their lives—devotion to the church and each other. (978-1-63679-463-1)

Never a Bridesmaid by Spencer Greene. As her sister's wedding gets closer, Jessica finds that her hatred for the maid of honor is a bit more complicated than she thought. Could it be something more than hatred? (978-1-63679-559-1)

The Rewind by Nicole Stiling. For police detective Cami Lyons and crime reporter Alicia Flynn, some choices break hearts. Others leave a body count. (978-1-63679-572-0)

Turning Point by Cathy Dunnell. When Asha and her former high school bully Jody struggle to deny their growing attraction, can they move forward without going back? (978-1-63679-549-2)

When Tomorrow Comes by D. Jackson Leigh. Teague Maxwell, convinced she will die before she turns 41, hires animal rescue owner Baye Cobb to rehome her extensive menagerie. (978-1-63679-557-7)

You Had Me at Merlot by Melissa Brayden. Leighton and Jamie have all the ingredients to turn their attraction into love, but it's a recipe for disaster. (978-1-63679-543-0)

All Things Beautiful by Alaina Erdell. Casey Norford only planned to learn to paint like her mentor, Leighton Vaughn, not sleep with her. (978-1-63679-479-2)

Appalachian Awakening by Nance Sparks. The more Amber's and Leslie's paths cross, the more this hike of a lifetime begins to look like a love of a lifetime. (978-1-63679-527-0)

Dreamer by Kris Bryant. When life seems to be too good to be true and love is within reach, Sawyer and Macey discover the truth about the town of Ladybug Junction, and the cold light of reality tests the hearts of these dreamers. (978-1-63679-378-8)

Eyes on Her by Eden Darry. When increasingly violent acts of sabotage threaten to derail the opening of her glamping business, Callie Pope is sure her ex, Jules, has something to do with it. But Jules is dead…isn't she? (978-1-63679-214-9)

Head Over Heelflip by Sander Santiago. To secure the biggest prizes at the Colorado Amateur Street Sports Tour, Thomas Jefferson will do almost anything, even marrying his best friend and crush—Arturo "Uno" Ortiz. (978-1-63679-489-1)

Letters from Sarah by Joy Argento. A simple mistake brought them together, but Sarah must release past love to create a future with Lindsey she never dreamed possible. (978-1-63679-509-6)

Lost in the Wild by Kadyan. When their plane crash-lands, Allison and Mike face hunger, cold, a terrifying encounter with a bear, and feelings for each other neither expects. (978-1-63679-545-4)

Not Just Friends by Jordan Meadows. A tragedy leaves Jen struggling to figure out who she is and what is important to her. (978-1-63679-517-1)

Of Auras and Shadows by Jennifer Karter. Eryn and Rina's unexpected love may be exactly what the Community needs to heal the rot that comes not from the fetid Dark Lands that surround the Community but from within. (978-1-63679-541-6)

The Secret Duchess by Jane Walsh. A determined widow defies a duke and falls in love with a fashionable spinster in a fight for her rightful home. (978-1-63679-519-5)

Winter's Spell by Ursula Klein. When former college roommates reunite at a wedding in Provincetown, sparks fly, but can they find true love when evil sirens and trickster mermaids get in the way? (978-1-63679-503-4)

Coasting and Crashing by Ana Hartnett Reichardt. Life comes easy to Emma Wilson until Lake Palmer shows up at Alder University and derails her every plan. (978-1-63679-511-9)

Every Beat of Her Heart by KC Richardson. Piper and Gillian have their own fears about falling in love, but will they be able to overcome those feelings once they learn each other's secrets? (978-1-63679-515-7)

Grave Consequences by Sandra Barret. A decade after necromancy became licensed and legalized, can Tamar and Maddy overcome the lingering prejudice against their kind and their growing attraction to each other to uncover a plot that threatens both their lives? (978-1-63679-467-9)

Haunted by Myth by Barbara Ann Wright. When ghost-hunter Chloe seeks an answer to the current spectral epidemic, all clues point to one very famous face: Helen of Troy, whose motives are more complicated than history suggests and whose charms few can resist. (978-1-63679-461-7)

Invisible by Anna Larner. When medical school dropout Phoebe Frink falls for the shy costume shop assistant Violet Unwin, everything about their love feels certain, but can the same be said about their future? (978-1-63679-469-3)

Like They Do in the Movies by Nan Campbell. Celebrity gossip writer Fran Underhill becomes Chelsea Cartwright's personal assistant with the aim of taking the popular actress down, but neither of them anticipates the clash of their attraction. (978-1-63679-525-6)

Limelight by Gun Brooke. Liberty Bell and Palmer Elliston loathe each other. They clash every week on the hottest new TV show, until Liberty starts to sing and the impossible happens. (978-1-63679-192-0)

Playing with Matches by Georgia Beers. To help save Cori's store and help Liz survive her ex's wedding they strike a deal: a fake relationship, but just for one week. There's no way this will turn into the real deal. (978-1-63679-507-2)

The Memories of Marlie Rose by Morgan Lee Miller. Broadway legend Marlie Rose undergoes a procedure to erase all of her unwanted memories, but as she starts regretting her decision, she discovers that the only person who could help is the love she's trying to forget. (978-1-63679-347-4)

The Murders at Sugar Mill Farm by Ronica Black. A serial killer is on the loose in southern Louisiana and it's up to three women to solve the case while carefully dancing around feelings for each other. (978-1-63679-455-6)

Fire in the Sky by Radclyffe and Julie Cannon. Two women from different worlds have nothing in common and every reason to wish they'd never met—except for the attraction neither can deny. (978-1-63679-573-7)

A Talent Ignited by Suzanne Lenoir. When Evelyne is abducted and Annika believes she has been abandoned, they must risk everything to find each other again. (978-1-63679-483-9)

An Atlas to Forever by Krystina Rivers. Can Atlas, a difficult dog Ellie inherits after the death of her best friend, help the busy hopeless romantic find forever love with commitment-phobic animal behaviorist Hayden Brandt? (978-1-63679-451-8)

Bait and Witch by Clifford Mae Henderson. When Zeddi gets an unexpected inheritance from her client Mags, she discovers that Mags served as high priestess to a dwindling coven of old witches—who are positive that Mags was murdered. Zeddi owes it to her to uncover the truth. (978-1-63679-535-5)

Buried Secrets by Sheri Lewis Wohl. Tuesday and Addie, along with Tuesday's dog, Tripper, struggle to solve a twenty-five-year-old mystery while searching for love and redemption along the way. (978-1-63679-396-2)

Come Find Me in the Midnight Sun by Bailey Bridgewater. In Alaska, disappearing is the easy part. When two men go missing, state trooper Louisa Linebach must solve the case, and when she thinks she's coming close, she's wrong. (978-1-63679-566-9)

Death on the Water by CJ Birch. The Ocean Summit's authorities have ruled a death on board its inaugural cruise as a suicide, but Claire suspects murder and with the help of Assistant Cruise Director Moira, Claire conducts her own investigation. (978-1-63679-497-6)

Living For You by Jenny Frame. Can Sera Debrek face real and personal demons to help save the world from darkness and open her heart to love? (978-1-63679-491-4)

Mississippi River Mischief by Greg Herren. When a politician turns up dead and Scotty's client is the most obvious suspect, Scotty and his friends set out to prove his client's innocence. (978-1-63679-353-5)

Ride with Me by Jenna Jarvis. When Lucy's vacation to find herself becomes Emma's chance to remember herself, they realize that everything they're looking for might already be sitting right next to them—if they're willing to reach for it. (978-1-63679-499-0)

Whiskey and Wine by Kelly and Tana Fireside. Winemaker Tessa Williams and sex toy shop owner Lace Reynolds are both used to taking risks, but will they be willing to put their friendship on the line if it gives them a shot at finding forever love? (978-1-63679-531-7)